W9-BZO-844

# DIAGNOSIS MURDER

# THE SHOOTING SCRIPT

## Lee Goldberg

BASED ON THE TELEVISION SERIES CREATED BY

## Joyce Burditt

A SIGNET BOOK

SIGNET
Published by New American Library, a division of
Penguin Group (USA) Inc., 375 Hudson Street,
New York, New York 10014, U.S.A.
Penguin Books Ltd, 80 Strand,
London WC2R 0RL, England
Penguin Books Australia Ltd, 250 Camberwell Road,
Camberwell, Victoria 3124, Australia
Penguin Books Canada Ltd, 10 Alcorn Avenue,
Toronto, Ontario, Canada M4V 3B2
Penguin Books (NZ), cnr Airborne and Rosedale Roads,
Albany, Auckland 1310, New Zealand

Penguin Books Ltd, Registered Offices:
80 Strand, London WC2R 0RL, England

First published by Signet, an imprint of New American Library,
a division of Penguin Group (USA) Inc.

First Printing, August 2004
10 9 8 7 6 5 4 3 2 1

Ⓓ REGISTERED TRADEMARK—MARCA REGISTRADA

Printed in the United States of America

PUBLISHER'S NOTE
This is a work of fiction. Names, characters, places, and incidents either are the product of the author's imagination or are used fictitiously, and any resemblance to actual
persons, living or dead, business establishments, events, or locales is entirely coinci-
dental.

BOOKS ARE AVAILABLE AT QUANTITY DISCOUNTS WHEN USED TO PROMOTE PRODUCTS OR
SERVICES. FOR INFORMATION PLEASE WRITE TO PREMIUM MARKETING DIVISION, PENGUIN
GROUP (USA) INC., 375 HUDSON STREET, NEW YORK, NEW YORK 10014.

# Praise for the
## *Diagnosis Murder* novels

### The Death Merchant

"Dr. Mark Sloan returns in a crime story that seamlessly interweaves two radically different story lines while taking the reader on a roller-coaster ride through the delights—and dangers—of Hawaii. If you liked the broadcast episodes, you'll love *The Death Merchant*."

—Jeremiah Healy, author of the John Cuddy mysteries

"This novel begins with tension and ends with surprise. Throughout, it is filled with gentle humor and a sure hand. *Diagnosis Murder*, the television series, could always be counted on for originality and a strong sense of humor, particularly when Lee Goldberg's name was on the scripts. This is not just a novel for fans of the television series."

—Stuart M. Kaminsky, Edgar Award–winning author of
*A Cold Sunrise*

### The Silent Partner

"A whodunit thrill ride that captures all the charm, mystery, and fun of the TV series . . . and then some. . . . Goldberg wrote the very best *Diagnosis Murder* episodes, so it's no surprise that this book delivers everything you'd expect from the show . . . a clever, high-octane mystery that moves like a bullet train. Dr. Mark Sloan, the deceptively eccentric deductive genius, is destined to join the pantheon of great literary sleuths. . . . You'll finish this book breathless. Don't blink or you'll miss a clue. A brilliant debut for a brilliant detective. Long live Dr. Mark Sloan!" —Janet Evanovich, *New York Times* bestselling author

"An exciting and completely satisfying read for all *Diagnosis Murder* fans. We were hooked. . . . Goldberg's skill in bringing our favorite characters to the printed page left us begging for more."

—Aimée and David Thurlo, authors of the Ella Clah,
Sister Agatha, and Lee Nez Mysteries

"For those who have, as I do, an addiction to Mark Sloan, Lee Goldberg provides a terrific fix. . . . Will cure any *Diagnosis Murder* withdrawal symptoms you might have had."

—S. J. Rozan, author of *Winter and Night*

To Madison, author of "The Adventures of Kitty Wonder," who has promised to support me one day with her writing

# ACKNOWLEDGMENTS

Once again, Dr. Doug P. Lyle was an invaluable asset, available day and night for my insane medical questions. Any errors are entirely my fault and I am already deeply embarrassed about them.

I couldn't have written this book without technical assistance in matters of law, technology, ballistics, accounting, and computer science from Robert Bruce Thompson, Stuart Dumas, Paul Bishop, Jason Stoffmacher, Jacquelyn Blain, Gerald Elkins, and Gary G. Mehalik.

And finally, special thanks to Tod Goldberg, William Rabkin, Gina Maccoby, Dan Slater, and most of all my wife, Valerie, for their continued enthusiasm and support.

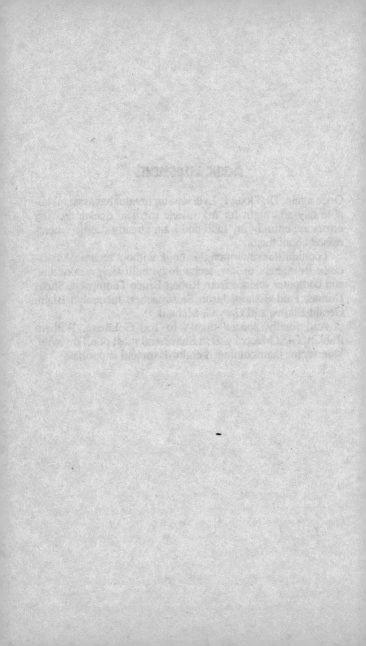

# PROLOGUE

Over the years, dozens of hospital administrators have tried to force Dr. Mark Sloan, Community General's eccentric chief of internal medicine, to follow some simple rules of conduct.

All they asked was that he maintain a professional demeanor, attend regular administrative meetings, operate his department within a strict budget, and not indulge his inexplicable interest in homicide investigation on hospital time.

By and large they were an impressive bunch of administrators. Smart, capable, often fearsome, but Dr. Sloan had conquered them all.

That wasn't going to happen with Noah Dent. Community General's new chief administrator was fresh from the Hollyworld International corporate office in Ft. Lauderdale, where the thirty-one-year-old had been a rising star in the acquisitions department. Although primarily known for its amusement parks, Hollyworld had diversified into cruise lines, fast-food franchises, office buildings, and hospital ownership.

Dent's aggressive, take-no-prisoners approach to the hostile takeover and absorption of businesses into the Hollyworld corporate family impressed his superiors, who felt he was just the right person to wring a wider margin of profitability from Community General.

Before Dent was transferred to his new post in Los Angeles, he put together a detailed file on Mark Sloan and the administrators the doctor had defeated. Now, in advance of Dent's first meeting with Dr. Sloan, the administrator once again studied the case histories of his immediate predecessors to see what lessons he could learn from their embarrassing failures.

Kate Hamilton came to Community General after steering two mismanaged hospitals from the brink of bankruptcy to profitability. But within a year, Dr. Sloan defanged her, convincing her to quit her job, sell her home, and use the proceeds to establish a nonprofit food bank in the inner city.

Norman Briggs, her successor, showed great promise as a hard-line bottom-liner, having spearheaded the hostile takeover of the hospital by Mediverse Corporation. But somehow Dr. Sloan managed to compromise Briggs completely. Not only did Briggs let Dr. Sloan use hospital resources and staff as he pleased in his murder investigations, but the administrator became his eager flunky.

When Community General was sold to Healthcorp International, they brought in General Harold Lomax, who'd spent ten years running battlefield medical operations for the United States Marine Corps before being lured into the private sector. Healthcorp was certain that Lomax could bring Dr. Sloan, and the Community General budget, under control. But eight months later, Lomax resigned with an extreme case of irritable bowel syndrome and left behind a hospital literally in ruins, decimated by a serial bomber stalking Dr. Sloan.

From what Dent could tell, it wasn't that Dr. Sloan possessed any Machiavellian political skills. In fact, it was quite the opposite. He wore his administrative adversaries down with his utter affability, gentle humor, and relentless goodwill.

Those days were about to end.

Noah Dent was immune to humor and goodwill, especially where business was concerned. Mark Sloan would find himself powerless against him.

Mark showed up promptly at the appointed hour, which was at the end of a long shift on a weekday afternoon. Dent had chosen that time purposely to catch Mark at his lowest ebb, when he was tired and off his game. Even so, Mark entered flashing a warm smile and extending his hand.

"Welcome to Community General," Mark said. "I'm Dr. Mark Sloan, but I hope you'll call me Mark."

Dent offered the tightest of polite smiles in return as he shook Mark's hand. "It's a pleasure to finally meet you, Dr. Sloan. Please, take a seat."

He motioned Mark into his spartan office and tried to hide his disappointment. In the flesh, Mark Sloan just didn't live up to Dent's expectations.

Although Dent knew Mark's weapons were his charm and good-natured humor, he still expected the doctor to be an overpowering force of nature, to fill a room with his indomitable personality. But compared to the corporate executives Dent had symbolically beheaded in the past—men who commanded a room and exuded hurricane-strength charisma—Dr. Sloan seemed decidedly weak. He was just a white-haired old doctor in a wrinkled lab coat.

Mark took the seat that was offered to him and smiled as warmly as he could, considering the chilly temperature of both the room and the man who inhabited it.

"I'm sorry we haven't had a chance to get together until today," Mark said. "My life has been kind of chaotic lately and is only just settling down again."

"Indeed." Dent settled into his chair behind his desk and opened the file in front of him. "You've been traveling a lot over the past few weeks. Hawaii, Colorado, New Mexico, Palm Springs. Quite an itinerary."

"I wish I could say it was for pleasure, but I was helping the authorities pursue a killer," Mark said, well aware that Dent already knew that. The details had been widely reported by the media, mostly because the case involved the kidnapping and murder of a Las Vegas casino owner's teenage daughter.

"I'm sure the FBI and the LAPD appreciated having an internist on the case," Dent said. "I just wish you put as much effort into your duties at this hospital as you do playing amateur sleuth."

Mark was prepared to defend himself to Dent; it was something of a ritual for each new administrator to try to exert some control over him. But he didn't expect such a direct attack.

"I've been on the staff of this hospital longer than any other doctor here," Mark said. "I've treated generations of families and trained countless physicians over the past forty years."

"I don't doubt your qualifications, Dr. Sloan, or your skills as a physician. You're a respected member of your profession," Dent said. "What I question is your commitment to this hospital and your blatant abuse of the privileges you've been granted here."

"I haven't been *granted* anything, Mr. Dent. Whatever I have, I've earned." Mark was surprised how quickly Dent had managed to get under his skin.

Dent sighed wearily. "An inflated, and misplaced, sense of entitlement. That's usually the excuse employees use to justify to themselves stealing office supplies, padding the expense account, and making long-distance calls on office phones."

"I admit sometimes I forget to take my pen out of my pocket before I go home," Mark said. "If you like, you can deduct the cost from my paycheck."

Dent referred to the file in front of him. "Your son, Steve, is a homicide detective with the Los Angeles Police Department. Frequently over the years you've assisted in his investigations."

"I'm a consultant to the police," Mark said.

"Really?" Dent said. "Do they pay you?"

"No, I volunteer my time."

"That's not all you volunteer," Dent said. "You also freely offer the resources of this hospital and the services of its employees. Who do you think pays for the overtime when Dr. Bentley pulls an all-nighter dissecting a corpse for you?"

"Amanda is the adjunct county medical examiner," Mark said. "The county compensates her for her work."

"Yes, they do, for the work *they* order, not the work *you* ask her to do," Dent said. "Let's be honest, Dr. Sloan. The medical examiner's satellite office is here for your amusement and convenience—a personal playground cleverly paid for by our shareholders and Los Angeles taxpayers."

"The medical examiner's office is here because they

desperately needed additional manpower and more morgue space," Mark said. "We're providing a service to the community."

"But it was you who suggested they open their morgue here at Community General and staff it with one of our pathologists."

"Because it was a fast, simple, and inexpensive way to solve a serious problem facing the county and help shore up the hospital's finances at the same time."

"And it brought you a constant supply of fresh corpses to play with," Dent said, shaking his head with disgust. "I don't know how you managed to pull it off, Dr. Sloan."

"As I recall, the board voted unanimously for the project," Mark said stiffly, trying to keep his rising anger in check.

"The same board that drove Healthcorp International into bankruptcy," Dent said. "Which is why they no longer own this hospital and we do."

"I can't tell you how thrilled we all are about that, too," Mark said. "I've always wanted to work for a division of an amusement park company."

"Hollyworld International has diversified into many areas," Dent said. "But we treat each of them as if they were our core business."

"Which is to make as much money as possible," Mark said.

"Of course," Dent said. "You say that like it's a bad thing. Making money is the whole point of operating a business, Dr. Sloan."

"I don't look at medicine as a business."

"That is abundantly clear," Dent said. "You look at it as a way to subsidize your detective work."

"It's unfortunate that you see things that way." Mark glanced at his watch and rose from his seat. "As much as I've enjoyed our chat, I'm coming to the end of a long shift. I should be getting home."

"Well, that's one thing we agree on, Dr. Sloan," Dent said. "In more ways than one."

\*    \*    \*

Cleve Kershaw was irresistible and he knew it. He had the complete package: money, charm, and power. Looks had nothing to do with it, though by his estimation he was no slouch in that department, either.

Part of his undeniable allure, he knew, was his casual self-confidence, which came from having an accurate sense of who he was and where he stood in the Hollywood universe. He was a player. Certified, bona fide, and blow-dried. Somebody who made things happen. Somebody that nobodies aspired to be. A producer, with a capital "P."

"God, it's beautiful," Amy Butler said, standing on the wide deck of Cleve's Malibu beach house, the gentle breeze rippling the thin fabric of her sheer, untucked blouse as she admired the view. "Just awesome."

Cleve was also admiring an awesome view—at least what he could see of it when the wind hit her shirt just right.

Amy was irresistible and probably knew it, too. She had it all: beauty, youth, and innocence, though the fact she was with him now put that last quality in doubt. Not that he cared. Amy's ability to project innocence she didn't have revealed a natural talent for acting, which was more valuable than innocence, anyway.

Amy was in a great shape, but not in the surgically enhanced sense—also a plus. She was a one hundred percent natural beauty with a lean, strong, supple body. There didn't seem to be a molecule of body fat on her. She exuded so much youthful vitality, she made Cleve feel elderly at forty—but not so elderly that he doubted for one second that he'd have her in bed before the afternoon was over.

They were two irresistible people who wouldn't be resisting each other much longer.

"Do you live here?" she asked.

Cleve shook his head. "This is just where I go to get away from it all."

"Get away from what?"

He shrugged. "The hustle and bustle."

"I thought you liked the hustle and bustle," she said with a sly grin.

"It depends with whom," said Cleve, so smooth his

words could be poured. He saw himself as Dean Martin in his prime, only without the singing voice.

"So where do you live?" she asked.

"I got a place in Mandeville Canyon."

It was a loaded and carefully premeditated reply. By calling his house a *place,* he made it seem unremarkable, which made him come across as relaxed, easy-going and self-deprecating—the very definition of charm.

By slipping in that his *place* was in secluded Mandeville Canyon, he was actually saying he lived in a mind-blowing estate and that he could afford the ridiculous extravagance of owning two magnificent homes, each worth a high seven figures, that were barely twenty miles apart.

If all the subtext in that deceptively simple remark didn't make her swoon, she wasn't a woman.

"The movie business has been very good to you," Amy said.

It was a good thing she was holding on to the rail, Cleve thought, or she might swoon right into the surf.

"It's going to be very good for you, too."

"Starting when?" Amy said, her eyes sparkling with mischief and possibility.

"Starting now," he said.

The formal seduction had begun at lunch at Granita. The informal seduction began six months ago when he saw her picture in an *LA Times* ad for Macy's fall clearance sale. What most people saw, if they noticed her at all, was a fresh faced girl modeling a discounted sports bra. What Cleve saw was a potential action superstar. He tracked her down, talked her into dumping her agent, and immediately began remaking her.

Of course, she knew Cleve was married, and who he was married to. Everybody did. That was half the attraction for her. Maybe two-thirds. She knew exactly what he was bringing to the party. But so far, she'd been doing all the partying. There hadn't been any festivities for Cleve yet.

That was about to change.

After lunch, Cleve invited her to see his "little beach place" just down the road. Amy said sure, left her Volkswagen Bug in the lot, and let him drive.

She'd ceded control of the afternoon to him the moment she'd slid into the hand-stitched leather interior of his Mercedes SL. Of course, she'd ceded control of so much more six months ago.

And now here they were at his beach house on an exclusive stretch of sand on a bright, sunny, perfect California afternoon. What was going to happen next was as inevitable as the setting of the sun, the dawn of a new day, and the thousand-dollar minimum he spent every time he took his Mercedes in for service.

Cleve went inside and uncorked a bottle of champagne.

"I hope you like Dom Perignon," he said, filling their glasses.

"What are we celebrating?" she asked as she joined him.

"The future," Cleve said.

They clinked their glasses together, unaware that they were sharing a toast to their last two hours alive.

# CHAPTER ONE

Mark Sloan was many things: A doctor, a detective, and an amateur magician. But he wasn't a great painter, or even a mediocre one. The seascape he was trying to paint certainly proved that to him.

He was sitting outside at an easel on the second-floor deck of his Malibu beach house, trying his best to capture on canvas the inspirational beauty of the frothy surf, the rolling dunes, and the seagulls floating gently on the breeze.

But there was something missing from the painting and Mark had a pretty good idea what it was.

Talent.

What he'd painted looked like a lopsided blue cake being attacked by a swarm of huge, feathered mosquitoes.

Mark wasn't surprised. He'd never been able to draw, much less paint, but the art supplies were a birthday gift last year from his son. Steve thought his father might enjoy painting in his free time as a way to relieve the stress of being chief of internal medicine at Community General Hospital.

At least that's what Steve said. What his son really wanted was for Mark to occasionally find something else to do besides poke into whatever homicides Steve was investigating for the LAPD.

It wasn't that Steve didn't appreciate Mark's uncanny deductive skills. If he didn't, he would have moved to another city and another police department years ago, far from his father's considerable shadow. Steve genuinely admired and respected his father's innate ability to solve crimes and was grateful to have him to turn to. Even so, Steve had few real opportunities to prove his own abilities within the department, and as much as he admired his father, he still wanted to establish his own reputation apart from him.

So every year, Steve presented his father with a new potential distraction in the guise of a birthday present. A set of golf clubs. Elaborate model airplanes to assemble. A fishing pole and two dozen colorful lures.

With his next birthday fast approaching, Mark felt obligated to finally give last year's present a try. At least with this present, he wouldn't break any windows, glue his hand to any tables, or catch his own buttock with a three-hooked galactic spinner. So when Mark got back home from his shift at the hospital late that afternoon, he finally lugged out the easel, the canvas, and the paint onto the deck, faced the ocean, and began work on his masterpiece.

Mark regarded his seascape for a moment and had a great idea. He'd give the painting to Steve as a gift. Better yet, he'd surprise Steve by hanging it in his son's place. Maybe that way he'd get a good present from Steve this year.

There were many advantages to sharing a house with his son and the opportunity to play a joke like this on Steve was one of them.

He wondered how long Steve would keep the feathered mosquitoes on the wall before the painting was destroyed in a freak accident.

The idea amused Mark so much, he was seriously considering the idea of painting an entire series of awful paintings for his son. But he quickly forgot about all that when he heard the two gunshots.

He instinctively turned in the direction of the shots, the sharp cracks still reverberating in the air. It sounded close—maybe only a few houses away. Almost immediately there was another shot, then one more.

Mark bolted from his seat and rushed into the house, snatching up his medical bag and cell phone on the move, dialing 911 as he hurried out the front door.

He identified himself to the operator, reported the shooting, then told her he was a doctor and that he was going to see if anybody was hurt. Mark hung up on her before she could object.

The right thing to do, Mark knew, was to wait for the police to arrive and secure the scene. But it was rush hour on the Pacific Coast Highway and if there were gunshot victims in the house, they might die before paramedics could arrive to treat them.

Mark wasn't going to let that happen.

The houses were aligned along a narrow, private road just below the highway and led to a dead end. No cars were speeding past him. Nobody was running away. No one was screaming. Either the shooter was still in the house or had fled onto the beach.

The front door was ajar at a house midway down the street. He'd walked past the place many times before over the years, but he'd never met whoever lived there. Unlike Mark, most of the residents along this exclusive stretch of beach were notoriously private people, many of them celebrities or high-powered executives. They kept to themselves and never left their front doors open.

Mark knocked on the door, pushing it wide open as he did so and examining it carefully. There were no obvious signs of forced entry. The lock and the door seemed intact. He supposed the lock could have been picked, but if the door had been pried open, there would have been some splintered wood.

"Hello?" Mark shouted. "Anybody home?"

There was no reply. He could see clear across the living room to the back deck and the ocean beyond. The sliding doors were open. The breeze off the water wafted through the room. Except for the rhythmic sound of the crashing surf outside, it was eerily quiet.

"I'm Dr. Mark Sloan, your neighbor. I heard the shots." Mark put on a pair of rubber gloves and took a tentative step into the house. "I just stopped by to make sure nobody was hurt."

When no one immediately responded, he marched right in, making sure he was loud and obvious about it.

"I'm alone, but the police and paramedics are on their way," Mark said.

He didn't see any signs of a struggle, but plenty of evidence of a romantic interlude. There was an empty champagne bottle in a bucket full of melted ice. Two empty glasses, one smudged with lipstick, were on the coffee table. The entertainment center was on, but whatever CD had been playing was long over. A woman's high-heeled shoes were flung on the floor. A man's tie was shed on the arm of the couch like a snake's skin.

There had been lovers here. But where were they now?

"There's no reason to hide," Mark said. "I only want to help you."

He glanced out the French doors that opened onto the deck. It was late on a weekday afternoon on a beach lined with private homes. The nearest public access was two miles away. If the shooter had run onto the beach, Mark would have seen him. But there was no one on the sand in either direction for at least a hundred yards.

Was the shooter still in the house?

If he was, Mark would find out soon enough.

He followed a short hallway to what he assumed was the master bedroom, listening intently for any sounds of life and peering into each room he passed. His entire body was tense. It was exactly the way he felt watching a horror movie, his muscles coiled in anticipation of a scare at any moment.

Only this time, the horror was all too real.

Mark pushed open the bedroom door and found the lovers. They were lying naked on the blood-splattered bed. The man appeared to be in his early forties, the woman in her late twenties. They had both been shot once in the head and once in the chest. They were beyond his help now, but he knelt beside them and checked their pulses anyway.

Neither one of the victims was holding a weapon, which ruled out a murder-suicide.

This was an execution.

There was nothing more Mark could do here.

He started back towards the hallway when he felt that familiar tingle in his neck, a shiver from his subconscious telling him there was something wrong with what he'd seen—some telling detail he saw but didn't consciously register.

It was a feeling he'd learned to respect and never ignore, so he reluctantly turned and surveyed the crime scene again. He studied the bodies and the blood spatter that covered the clock radio, bottled water, and lip balm on the nightstand.

What happened here was clear.

The victims had been in bed, making love, when the killer came in. The shooter stopped at the corner of the bed closest to the door and fired four shots. It was over in less than a minute, neither victim having any chance to react. Their killer was cold and remorseless, strengthened by the resolve that comes either from experience, certainty of purpose, or blind rage.

Mark was sure of all those things.

The story was written in the blood and he'd learned long ago that blood never lied.

*The blood.*

He knelt beside the bodies and studied the pools of blood, which were thick and mottled with clots that looked like dark red slugs.

Now he knew what he'd seen that bothered him. It wasn't one little, obscure detail. It was everywhere and unavoidable.

*The blood.*

Mark glanced at his watch, then back at the bodies again. It was 4:36 P.M. Only five minutes at most had passed since he heard the gunshots. What he saw didn't make any sense; not if he believed his own eyes and ears. So how was it possible? The bodies in front of him held the answer, and he knew if he acted quickly, he could find it.

Mark took a scalpel and a thermometer from his bag and made an incision in the upper-right portion of the woman's abdomen, just beneath the ribs, exposing the liver. He made a small cut in the liver and inserted the thermometer into the organ. After a moment, he pulled the thermometer out and examined the reading, solving one riddle and opening up another, just as two police officers burst into the room, guns drawn and leveled at him.

"Don't move," one of the young officers said. "Or we will shoot."

"It's okay," Mark said. "I'm Dr. Mark Sloan, I'm the one who called this in. I'm also a consultant with the LAPD."

The officer didn't blink, pinning him with a deadly gaze. "Drop the knife *now*."

That's when Mark realized how bad things must look to them. They saw a man in surgical gloves kneeling over two dead bodies with a thermometer and a bloody scalpel in his hands.

Mark dropped the blade on the bed and flashed his most avuncular smile. "Perhaps you know my son, Lt. Steve Sloan? He's a homicide detective."

If the officer heard him, he didn't acknowledge it. "Step back slowly from the bed, lock your hands behind your head and face the wall."

Mark did as he was told.

The officer shoved him flat against the wall, expertly patted him down for weapons, then pulled his arms behind his back and handcuffed him.

"You're under arrest," the officer said and began to read Mark his rights.

# CHAPTER TWO

Mark sat handcuffed on the floor in a corner of the living room, watched warily by one of the cops, as more uniformed officers arrived, followed by the paramedics and then, finally, by a homicide detective.

Lt. Steve Sloan didn't acknowledge his father at first, preferring to enjoy Mark's discomfort for a few minutes.

Steve sought out Officers Blake and Jackson, the first cops at the scene, and got their report. They said they showed up about six minutes after Mark's 911 call. When they arrived, the door was wide open and they found the suspect cutting one of the victims with a scalpel. The officers detained the suspect and read him his rights.

Steve glanced at Mark. Judging by the embarrassed expression on his father's face, Mark knew exactly what his son was hearing.

Officer Blake handed Steve his father's driver's license. "His name is Dr. Mark Sloan. Any relation?"

"I'm afraid so," Steve said.

The officers shared a worried look.

"Don't sweat it, guys," Steve said. "You did the right thing."

"Would you like us to uncuff him?" Officer Blake asked.

Steve shook his head. "There's no hurry. Tell me about the victims."

"The male is Cleve Kershaw," Officer Blake said, handing over the evidence Baggies containing the victim's driver's licenses. "According to the registration, the SL out front belongs to him. We're on a private road and he's got a resident parking sticker on the windshield, so this is probably his place, too. The car is registered to a Mandeville Canyon address. The female is Amy Butler. She lives in Hollywood—at least according to her driver's license."

Steve knew who Kershaw was, but had never heard of the girl. She'd be famous now, though.

"She's got to be at least ten years younger than the guy," Officer Jackson said. "He sure knew how to live."

"When I go," Officer Blake said, "I hope it's in bed with some young naked hottie beside me."

"I'll be sure to tell that to your wife next time I see her." Steve handed the Baggies back to Officer Blake. "Have you recovered a weapon?"

"Just this." Officer Jackson held up an evidence bag containing Mark's scalpel.

"We're looking for a gun." Steve took the Baggie from Officer Jackson. "Assemble two teams, one to canvas the street and the beach for the murder weapon. Get some divers out in the water, too. I want the other team going door-to-door, to see if anyone besides my father saw or heard anything."

"Cool," Officer Blake said. "I hear Steven Spielberg lives around here."

"Isn't that Drew Barrymore's place at the end of the street?" Officer Jackson asked.

"No, it isn't, so you can keep your great, unproduced screenplay in your patrol car," Steve said. "And the first officer who asks anyone for an autograph is gonna get mine—on a suspension order. Is that clear?"

The officers nodded glumly and started to go, but Steve stopped them.

"One more thing. The press is going to mob us as soon as they figure out who this house belongs to. Corral them in the Trancas Market parking lot on the other side of PCH. This is a private road and I don't want to see any reporters on it."

The officers nodded again and headed off on their assignments.

Steve went straight to the bedroom, intentionally avoiding his father's imploring gaze. He wanted to see the crime scene for himself and develop his own interpretation of events before hearing his father's—something that usually wasn't possible if Mark was there, too.

There wasn't much to interpret. Steve could read the blood, too, and it told him a story of revenge by a jealous lover or spouse. He'd seen a thousand crime scenes just like it. What made this one different was Cleve Kershaw and who he was married to.

This was no longer simply a murder. It was a media event.

Within hours, news of what happened in this bedroom would be broadcast all over the world. Every move Steve made from this moment on would be put under intense scrutiny, from the department and the media.

And the first question they'd all be asking was why his father was dissecting the bodies before they were even cold.

Steve took a deep breath and let it out slowly. His work had only just begun, but he already knew one thing with absolute certainty: This investigation was going to be a living hell.

The crime scene mice, as the techies in the department's Scientific Investigation Division were called, scurried into the room and, with a nod of permission from Steve, began taking pictures, lifting prints, and collecting forensic evidence.

Steve left them to their work, returning to the living room, where he finally approached his father. Mark got to his feet to greet him.

"Am I glad to see you," Mark said, turning his back towards his son and lifting his cuffed wrists. "Could you get these off? They're very uncomfortable."

"Really? I didn't know that." Steve stuck his hands in his pockets. "I'll notify the department right away and see to it we get those padded or something."

Mark turned back to his son. "Having a rough day?"

"I wasn't until now," Steve said, glancing at one of the SID techs, who was using a camcorder to document the crime scene. "What are you doing here, Dad?"

"My civic duty," Mark said.

"Is that so?"

"I was out on the deck, painting a seascape, when I heard

gunshots," Mark said. "Did I ever mention just how much I enjoy that wonderful birthday gift?"

Steve ignored the question. "Your civic duty ended when you called 911 and reported the shooting."

"But it was rush hour, and I knew how long it could take the paramedics to get here," Mark said. "What if those two in the bedroom were still alive? I might have been able to save them."

"What if the shooter was still in the house?" Steve said. "I might have been looking at three corpses now instead of two."

"There was no chance of that happening."

"How do you know?"

"Because the shooter was gone a half-hour before I got here," Mark said.

"You were here two minutes after you heard the shots."

"But the shots I heard weren't the shots that killed them."

"What?"

"I'd explain, but I can't think clearly with all the circulation cut off to my hands." Mark turned his back again to Steve and lifted his wrists again.

Steve just stood there, hands in his pockets. "What are you talking about?"

"Those fleshy things with five fingers at the ends of my arms," Mark said. "Some people use them to grasp keys and unlock stuff."

That's when Mark saw Dr. Amanda Bentley, the Community General staff pathologist, striding towards him in her blue MEDICAL EXAMINER windbreaker. Her path lab did double duty as an extension of the county morgue and so did she as the adjunct county medical examiner.

"I knew you'd be here as soon as I heard where the crime scene was," Amanda said, flashing a knowing smile. "I'm surprised you haven't already done the autopsy."

"He started to," Steve said.

Amanda glanced at Steve and saw from the expression on his face that he wasn't joking. She gave Mark an incredulous look.

"I didn't do much," Mark shrugged sheepishly. "I took a liver temp from one of the victims."

She raised an eyebrow. "You cut into one of the victims?"

"I wouldn't put it quite like that," Mark said. "I made a precise, surgical incision."

"Why did you do that?" she asked.

"Because I wanted to establish a definite time of death."

"That's what I'm here for," Amanda said.

"I couldn't wait," Mark said, turning his back to Amanda, showing her his cuffed wrists. "You think you could pick the lock on these for me?"

"Tampering with the evidence at a murder scene is a crime," Amanda said. "Especially when it's my evidence."

Mark glanced over his shoulder at her, then back at Steve, then sighed wearily. "Maybe I should explain."

"That would be nice," Steve said.

"I heard the gunshots at four thirty," Mark said. "I grabbed my medical bag and was here within five minutes. But when I discovered the bodies, the blood was completely clotted."

"That's not possible," Amanda said.

"Why not?" Steve asked.

"A gunshot victim will continue to bleed out for a few minutes as death actually occurs," Mark said. "It takes five minutes for the blood to even start clotting, another ten or twenty before it's completely clotted."

"There wasn't enough time between the sound of the gunshots and Mark's discovery of the bodies for that to happen," Amanda said.

"If they were killed when I heard the gunshots," Mark said. "That's why I checked the body temperature of the female victim. Her temperature was 97 degrees."

Amanda was puzzled, but not as much as Steve.

"What does that mean?" he asked her.

"The body loses roughly 1.5 degrees per hour after death," Amanda said, then turned to Mark. "They were killed at least thirty minutes before you heard the shots. If you hadn't shown up when you did, we never would have known."

"Why not?" Steve said.

"Look at your watch, Steve. I didn't get here until an hour and a half after the bodies were discovered," Amanda said. "I wouldn't have noticed anything unusual about the blood."

"But that doesn't change how long it takes for the bodies to lose heat," Steve said. "You're very good at what you do. You would have discovered the time of death didn't jibe with when the gunshots were reported."

"I'm good, but I'm not perfect," she said. "In the absence of irrefutable evidence, like a video or eyewitnesses, determining the time of death is, at best, an educated guess. A lot of factors go into it and one of the big ones would have been when the gunshots were reported to the police. Honestly, Steve, I probably would have been fooled if Mark hadn't caught it."

Amanda tipped her head towards Mark. "You should thank him."

Mark gave his son a big smile. Steve dug a key out of his pocket and unlocked the cuffs.

"So who fired the shots and why?" Steve asked.

"I can't tell you the *who*," Mark said, massaging his wrists. "But I can guess at the *why*. He wanted to fudge the time of death and, perhaps, use the extra half-hour to establish his alibi. The murderer was counting on rush-hour traffic to delay the arrival of the police and paramedics so the clotting of the blood wouldn't be noticed. I don't think the killer knew a doctor lived only a few doors down and would arrive immediately at the scene."

"Talk about bad luck," Amanda said.

"Even if the shooter did know," Steve said, "I doubt he expected anyone to start dissecting the bodies on the spot."

"If the killer didn't stick around to fire the shots that Mark heard," Amanda said, "that means he had an accomplice."

"Who did an amazing disappearing act," Mark added. "I didn't see anyone on the street or the sand. Of course, he could have been hiding and slipped away while I was examining the bodies."

"Speaking of which, that's what I'm supposed to be doing," Amanda said.

"When can you have an autopsy report for us?" Mark asked.

*"Us?"* Steve said. "What makes you think you're going to be involved in this investigation?"

"I'm already involved," Mark said.

"That doesn't mean you have to *stay* involved," Steve replied.

Amanda gave Steve a look. "And I hear two plus two equals five now, and that the laws of gravity have been suspended, too."

"Thanks for the support," Steve said.

"Stop by the path lab in the morning," Amanda said. "I'll have a report ready for you both."

She trudged into the bedroom to start her work. Mark rubbed his hands together, though Steve wasn't sure whether it was to get the blood flowing or signal that he was anxious to get to work.

"So," Mark said. "Where to now?"

# CHAPTER THREE

Steve withstood the temptation to use his siren as he drove himself and his father south along the traffic-choked Pacific Coast Highway to Sunset Boulevard, which they followed east as it snaked around the Santa Monica Mountains towards Mandeville Canyon.

"Who are the victims?" Mark asked.

"Cleve Kershaw and Amy Butler, an actress."

"How do you know she's an actress?"

"She was a great-looking woman in her twenties who lived in LA," Steve said. "It would be unusual if she *wasn't* an actress. But she was also in bed with Cleve Kershaw, and if that wasn't enough, she had a Screen Actors Guild card in her wallet."

"All you had to say was that she had a SAG card," Mark replied.

"The explanation was more fun," Steve said. "And I wanted to see if you had any idea who Cleve Kershaw is, and you don't."

"Should I?"

"Only if you paid the slightest bit of attention to what's happening in popular culture."

"I have a basic working knowledge," Mark said, "as I do of many things."

"Okay, name the friends on *Friends,*" Steve said.

"He was on *Friends*?" Mark replied.

"No," Steve said. "I'm making a point."

"Not very well," Mark replied.

Steve sighed with frustration. Mark turned to glance at the view so his son wouldn't see his smile.

"Cleve Kershaw is a movie producer," Steve replied wearily. "And he's married to Lacey McClure."

"The actress?"

"At least you've heard of her," Steve said.

"Actually, I haven't. I was just guessing."

"She's one of the top female action stars in the world," Steve said. "How could you not know that?"

"Do you know who Dr. Paul Quarrington is?"

"No."

"He's one of the most gifted heart transplant surgeons in the world," Mark said. "How could you not know that?"

Steve glared at his father. "She's been in the news a lot."

"So has Dr. Quarrington."

"Do you want to hear about who we're going to see or not?"

Ordinarily, Steve wouldn't have minded Mark's gentle teasing, especially considering that he'd kept his dad in handcuffs for so long at the crime scene. But the fact his father didn't realize just how big this case was, and what a media feeding frenzy it would create, taxed what little patience Steve had left.

"Of course," Mark said. "Please continue."

"They've done three movies together, Lacey starring, Cleve producing," Steve said. "They've all been modest hits, but not nearly as big as her home video was last year. That's why she's been in the news so much."

"What was so special about the video?"

"It's Lacey starring, Cleve producing, only this time in the privacy of their bedroom. Or so they thought. The XXX-rated tape was stolen by somebody on the construction crew remodeling her house who went off and sold a million copies of it over the Internet. Lacey and her husband immediately sued to stop the distribution."

"Did she win?"

"Depends on how you look at it. The judge ruled in her favor, but the tape has already been duplicated countless times all over the world. It's still available in streaming video on hundreds of adult websites, and frame-captures have been posted all over the Net. And you can get pirated CD-ROM, DVD, and video copies on just about any street corner," Steve said. "But she got a tremendous amount of free international publicity. She's come out of it looking like a sympathetic victim to some and a sex symbol to everybody else. As long as she's not truly mortified by the whole thing, it's a no-lose situation for her. Kind of makes you wonder if the tape was actually stolen."

"The tape must have made someone millions of dollars," Mark said. "Has anyone followed the money?"

"The gossip magazines tried but the website that sold the tapes is hidden behind a bunch of shadow companies and operates out of someplace in Eastern Europe."

"How is her marriage?"

"Judging by what we've seen today," Steve said, "not good."

They turned off busy Sunset Boulevard into Mandeville Canyon, driving under a canopy of old oaks and sycamores. On either side of the street, vast residential compounds were hidden behind imposing gates and tall, vine-shrouded walls.

Steve drove deep into the canyon before turning off into a short driveway that faced a thick, polished wood gate. A security camera on the tall adobe wall, aimed down at them, affording whoever was watching a clear view of the driver.

Steve rolled down the window and leaned out to press the buzzer, then waited for someone to answer on the speaker. A moment later a woman's voice, raspy in a worldly, provocative kind of way, offered a suspicious and not the least bit welcoming hello.

"I'm Lt. Steve Sloan, LAPD." Steve held his badge out the window so the camera had a clear shot of it. "I need to speak to Lacey McClure."

"Regarding what?" the voice asked.

"That's between me and Ms. McClure."

"How do I know you're really a police officer?" the voice asked.

"Call 911, tell them a man identifying himself as Lt. Steve Sloan is outside your door," Steve said. "Have them call me and confirm my location."

Steve sat back in his seat and waited.

"She's cautious," Mark said.

"She's smart," Steve said. "Stalkers have become as clever as they are insane. They'll use just about any ruse to get past a star's gates."

A moment later, the LAPD dispatcher called on Steve's radio to confirm his location. He responded with Lacey McClure's address. He'd barely returned the microphone to its cradle on the dash when the gates yawned open like the doors of Oz.

What lay beyond the gates was decidedly less grandiose than the Emerald City, but no less impressive, at least as far as real estate value was concerned. The driveway curved through a lush garden and over a burbling stream to a rambling, low-lying ranch-style house bathed in the dappled light of overgrown eucalyptus and redwood trees. In the San Fernando Valley, the same house on the same acre would have cost under a million dollars. But here, nestled between Pacific Palisades and Brentwood, it was easily worth five times as much.

Mark emerged from the car and glanced over at the corral behind the house. There were no horses, but there was plenty of horsepower. A perfectly restored '64 Mustang was parked in the center of the corral beside a vintage '70s Chevy Nova and a bright yellow Hummer. The barn doors were ajar, just enough to reveal it had been converted into a gym and work-out room.

Steve was approaching the front door of the house when Lacey McClure stepped out to meet them. She had the easy, catlike gait of someone acutely aware of her own physicality. She wore a tight black tank top and loose-fitting, gray shorts, her hair slicked back and wet. It struck Mark as a calculatedly casual look designed to accent her muscular shoulders, slender neck, and long limbs. Her facial features were sharply defined, her gaze intense enough to boil water. The energy she exuded was palpable. On camera, Mark assumed it translated as simmering sexuality. But in person, it was like being in the presence of a lion ready to pounce on a zebra. Mark was glad he wasn't wearing stripes.

Steve started to badge her again, out of habit, but Lacey waved it away dismissively.

"I've seen it," she said in her distinctive, throaty voice. "They told me on the phone that you're a homicide detective."

"That's right," Steve said, stumbling over his words a bit.

He liked to think of himself as incapable of being starstruck, of being completely immune to the powers of celebrity. But it wasn't being in the presence of someone famous that affected him, it was her beauty. She was even more striking in person than on-screen.

Lacey glanced at Mark who, having never seen her before, wondered if the camera diminished the intensity of her gaze or magnified it.

"Who's he?" she asked.

"I'm Dr. Mark Sloan," Mark said. "I'm his father and a consultant to the police."

She turned back to Steve, appraising him. "The news must be pretty bad if you thought you had to bring a doctor along. Is he here for you or me?"

"Maybe we should go inside," Steve said.

"You can tell me what you have to say right here," she said, almost defiantly.

People usually needed to sit after receiving the news he was about to deliver, to absorb the impact and gather their wits again. But if she wanted it now, he'd give it to her.

"Your husband was shot to death at your beach house this afternoon."

She blinked once, hard, but otherwise her gaze and her stance didn't waver. "Was Cleve alone?"

"No," Steve said.

"Was he with a woman?"

"Amy Butler, an actress. She was killed, too," Steve said. "Did you know her?"

"No, but I'm sure she was young and beautiful," she said in an offhand way, simply commenting on the obvious, without any bitterness creeping into her voice or expression.

Lacey glanced past them both to the stream, not that there was anything to see happening there. Mark figured she just needed a place to rest her gaze while she considered the news. She didn't appear to be trying to cope with what she'd heard; instead the expression on her face was more analytical and detached. There wasn't any hint he could see of any emotional distress or shock in her demeanor.

In his years as a doctor, Mark frequently had the sad task of delivering tragic news to people about their loved ones. He'd never seen a reaction quite like this.

"You don't seem very upset," Mark said.

Lacey looked at Mark as if acknowledging his presence for the first time. "Maybe I'm just a very good actress."

"I'm sure you are."

She kept her gaze fixed on him, a hint of amusement in her eyes. "Did you expect me to collapse when I heard the news? Is that why you're here?"

"I'm here because I discovered the bodies," Mark said. "I live a few doors down from your beach house."

"It's my husband's beach house now," Lacey said. "He's been living there for a while. It's not public knowledge, but we're separated. We were planning on getting a divorce in a few months."

"Why were you waiting?" Steve asked.

"*Thrill Kill* is coming out next week," she said. "We didn't want news of our marital problems to eclipse the promotion of the movie. The first weekend of release can make or break a film. We both agreed, for the good of the movie, that it was best to keep our separation a secret."

"What were your marital problems?" Steve asked.

"I don't see how that's relevant," she said.

Steve looked at her incredulously. "Your husband was murdered in bed with another woman and you don't see how your marriage is relevant?"

"You don't think that I killed him, do you?"

Steve shrugged. "Where were you this afternoon around four o'clock?"

"I'm in production on a new movie, *Kill Storm*. It involves a lot of night shooting. I didn't get home until late this morning. I've been here all afternoon, sleeping."

"Alone?"

"Yes, alone," Lacey said indignantly. "I didn't kill my husband or his lover, Detective. But I know who did."

# CHAPTER FOUR

The interior of Lacey McClure's house was what LA designers like to call "upscale ranch," with plenty of rich leather furniture, dark wood beams and cabinets, and large, reddish-brown terracotta tiles on the floor.

Lacey sat in the center of a couch that could easily have accommodated a dozen people and sipped from a large bottle of Glacier Peaks mineral water.

Mark and Steve sat in two matching, sloped-back leather easy chairs inspired by Adirondack outdoor furniture. The Sloans faced Lacey across a huge, hand-hewn wooden coffee table with legs thicker than railroad ties and a surface area equivalent to a king-sized bed.

The setting made it clear to Mark that Lacey McClure was a woman who didn't welcome intimacy, who liked to put more than a little distance between herself and others. It made her detached reaction to her husband's brutal murder a bit easier for him to understand.

"Cleve owned a dry-cleaning business in New Jersey and was one of the investors in my first movie, *Bloodbath Day Camp for Girls,* a low-budget slasher pic," she said. "I was just one of the horny kids who got killed by the ax-murderer, but Cleve was sure I was going to be a star. The amazing thing was, he wasn't just trying to get me into bed. He really believed it."

"What does this have to do with who killed him?" Steve asked.

"I'm getting to that, Detective," she said with an edge to her voice. "Cleve fell in love with the movie business. After

*Bloodbath Day Camp* he couldn't go back to dry cleaning. He took out a loan against his business to finance another film for me to star in. I played a sweet preschool teacher who's actually an ex-CIA assassin with amnesia. When her enemies find her, she rediscovers her forgotten skills and kicks some ass."

"*Good Morning, Miss Killer,*" Steve said, for Mark's benefit.

Lacey allowed herself a tiny smile of pride. "The movie was a huge hit. After that, Cleve sold his business and convinced me we should move out here. He became my manager, my producer, and my husband."

"In that order?" Mark asked.

"Not in my mind, maybe in his," Lacey said. "I truly loved him. But he became more interested in me as a business than as a wife. He was away or on the phone all the time, lining up financing, meeting with distributors. The business, *that* was his mistress. So, like any wife, I got real interested in what was distracting him from me. I hired a private detective to follow him and an accountant to go over the books. And I didn't like what I found."

She nervously picked at the label on her water bottle, flicking the shreds onto the table. After a long moment, she looked up, her face tight with anger, which made Mark wonder whether she'd needed the time to get her feelings in check or to get into character for a performance.

"I discovered that Cleve was using my movies to launder money for the Mob," she said. "They were the ones who loaned him the money to make *Good Morning, Miss Killer.* They were the ones who bought his dry-cleaning business so we'd have the cash to get started out here. On my next two films, they put up money for foreign distribution and, in addition to getting a percentage of the box-office gross, he paid them an up-front 'convenience fee' of $300,000 in cash for the opportunity to do business with them."

"You didn't know anything about the arrangement before?" Mark asked.

"Of course not. I concentrated my attention on staying in shape, learning my lines and hitting my marks. I left all the business to him," Lacey said. "When I found out what he was doing, I confronted him with it. He didn't deny a thing, said it was how business is done. It made me sick. So I walked out on him. Personally and professionally. I refused to do the next movie he'd set up. I'm doing *Kill Storm* for Pinnacle Studios, which is financing the whole thing themselves. Cleve is a producer on it in name only."

Steve sighed with impatience. "I don't see what this has to do with your husband and a young actress getting murdered in your beach house."

"A month ago, Cleve came to me. He was desperate. He said his friends in New Jersey were outraged. I had to do the movie and pay the convenience fee, or they'd make things very unpleasant for us. I told him that was his problem, not mine." She paused for a moment, picking at the last remnants of the label on her water bottle. "I guess he was right."

"You think the Mob killed your husband?" Steve asked.

"Isn't it obvious?" she said. "They were making a lot of money from my films. Now they aren't. Who else are they going to blame for that?"

"They could blame you," Mark said.

Steve glanced at his dad and got up from his seat. "Excuse me for a moment, I need to make a call."

Lacey watched Steve go outside, then she turned to Mark. "Do you really think I could be in danger?"

"If your theory is true," Mark said, "I suppose it's possible. If you're worried about hit men coming after you, you might want to hire some bodyguards for a while."

"You say that as if you don't believe me."

"I'm not the one you have to convince," Mark said.

"I've got the accountant's report," she said. "It's all there."

"If you were really concerned about your films being used to launder money for organized crime, why didn't you go to the police or the FBI with your evidence?"

"I play an action hero on film, Dr. Sloan, I'm not one in real life. I have no desire to take on organized crime," Lacey said. "And I wasn't about to go public with the fact that all my movies were financed by the Mob. Can you imagine what that would do to my career?"

"I guess we'll find out soon enough," Mark said. "It's all going to come out now."

Her eyes widened and, for the first time since he'd met her, Mark saw some emotion in her eyes. It was fear.

Steve came back in, carrying a black bag. "Ms. McClure, I've just been granted a telephone warrant by the court to search this house. A copy of the warrant will be delivered to you in a few hours."

"Why?" Lacey McClure said, rising to her feet, her face reddening in anger. "I told you what happened."

"You gave us one explanation, and it was dandy." Steve set his bag on the coffee table, unzipped it, and took out a pair of rubber gloves, which he put on as he spoke. "The thing is, your husband was killed in bed with another woman. The most likely suspect is you."

"But we were separated," she said. "I don't care who he was sleeping with."

"I've only got your word that you were separated," Steve said, taking some damp, white swabs from a container in the bag.

"It was a secret," Lacey said. "I told you why."

"And even if it's true, it doesn't mean you weren't upset about him sleeping around," Steve said. "I'd like to see your hands."

She kept her arms at her side.

Steve sighed. "I have a warrant. How hard do you want to make this on yourself?"

She reluctantly held out her hands in front of her. Steve ran the swabs over her hands and up her arms.

"What are you doing?" she asked.

Steve glanced at the swabs, then showed them to Mark. The swabs was peppered with tiny black particles.

"Checking for gunshot residue," Steve said, then held up the swabs for her to see. "And you're covered with it."

"Of course I am," Lacey said, irritated.

"Maybe this would be a good time to read you your rights," Steve said.

"I didn't kill my husband or that woman," she said. "I'm starring in an action movie, Detective. We were filming a shoot-out last night. Naturally I'm covered in gunshot residue."

"Then you won't mind if we search your house," Steve said, not that he needed her permission. He slipped the swabs into plastic containers and sealed them with evidence tape. "The crime-lab techs will be here in fifteen minutes."

"Be my guest." Lacey sat back down on the couch. "Just don't drop any bloody gloves on the property while you're at it."

Her pointed allusion to the O. J. Simpson case, and all that it implied, wasn't lost on Steve. The O. J. debacle had been on his mind from the instant he first saw Cleve Kershaw's body. What Steve found interesting was that it was already on her mind, too.

Mark and Steve left Lacey McClure's compound as soon as the crime scene mice and some uniformed officers arrived, which was shortly after nightfall. Steve knew that, at best, he only had an hour or two head start on the media. He wanted to get to Amy Butler's place and find out what he could before the reporters showed up there.

Mark was silent during most of the drive from Mandeville Canyon to Amy Butler's apartment in Hollywood, twenty miles east and several socioeconomic classes away. He was mulling everything he'd seen and heard since he'd discovered the bodies.

"I can see you thinking," Steve said. "I can almost hear it."

"It's a difficult case," Mark said.

"Just the celebrity aspect and all the media attention that comes with it," Steve said. "Otherwise, the murder itself is no mystery."

"It is to me," Mark said.

"That's because it's so mundane," Steve said. "Don't let the celebrity part fool you: This is simple murder, like most of the cases I deal with every day and that you never get involved with. A married man is found murdered in bed with his mistress. Happens daily. Nine times out of ten the killer is going to be the spouse or lover of one of the victims."

"So before we met Lacey McClure, before she even said a word, she was already your prime suspect."

"Even more so after she opened her mouth. If cheating on her wasn't enough reason to kill her husband, his financial misdeeds were," Steve said. "Factor in the gunshot residue on her hands and her lousy alibi, and it's obvious. Lacey McClure killed Cleve Kershaw and his lover, too."

"So why didn't you arrest her?"

"If she wasn't a movie star," Steve said, "I would have."

"You're telling me she gets special treatment just because she's a celebrity?"

"Of course she does. We arrest people every day and nobody cares what happens. But a celebrity's case gets intense public scrutiny," Steve said. "We can't make a single honest mistake. If we arrest a 'normal person,' and a few hours or a day later find out we were wrong, we let him go and we apologize. Nobody hears about it. If we make the same mistake with a star, the next day the media is all over us and everybody is saying the police are incompetent and corrupt."

"So even though you think you have enough circumstantial evidence to bring her in, you're going to wait."

"At least until we know more about Amy Butler. I want to be sure it wasn't somebody out of Amy's life that pulled the trigger," Steve said. "Besides, there is one advantage to dealing with a celebrity."

"What's that?" Mark asked.

"Lacey McClure is recognizable all over the world. She can't skip town and disappear. So I can wait to arrest her until I've covered every detail, which is a fancy way of saying 'until I'm sure I've covered my ass.' "

"Then you have a serious problem," Mark said.

"I do?" Steve asked.

"Even if Lacey McClure is guilty—and I'm inclined to agree with you that she is—there's still a mystery you have to solve."

"Which is?"

"The murder makes absolutely no sense."

"Sure it does. It's about jealousy or money or both,"

Steve said. "Take your pick. They're both right at the top of the short list of reasons why people kill each other."

"I'm not talking about the *why*, I'm talking about the *how*," Mark said. "I heard the gunshots at four thirty, but when I got to the scene five minutes later, I discovered the victims had already been dead for at least thirty minutes. So who fired the shots I heard and for what reason? How did the shooter get away? What really happened this afternoon?"

The next time Mark glanced at his son, he could almost hear him thinking, too.

# CHAPTER FIVE

"Amy was always the lucky one," Elsie Feikema said, taking a deep drag on her cigarette and blowing the smoke out slowly.

"Not today," Steve said, leaning against the kitchen counter, across the room from where Elsie sat on the couch, her legs drawn up to her chest, one arm hugging her pale knees.

"Today was the exception," Elsie said.

"I'll say," Steve replied, trying not to inhale too much of the smoke blown in his direction. He glanced over at his father, who was listening to the conversation while quietly poking around the two-bedroom apartment.

The place was decorated with space-age, '70s furniture and quirky swap-meet finds. Lava lamps of all sizes were scattered throughout the apartment; Mark went around the room, admiring each one of them.

"She was always winning. For example, at McDonald's, whenever they'd hand out those scratch-and-win cards, she always won an entire, free meal," Elsie said. "Me? I got small fries, maybe a small drink."

"It's not quite the same as winning the lottery though, is it?" Steve said.

"But in a way she did, that's the thing," Elsie said. "About two years ago, she started waiting tables at the pizza joint where I worked. Of course, she had other aspirations. Nobody who's a waitress in this town wants to be a waitress, you know?"

"And in other towns waitressing is a career goal?" Steve said.

If the place didn't smell like an ashtray, he'd be enjoying his interview. It was playing out the way he liked it. The person open, maybe too open, letting him just sit back and mostly listen, while another detective, in this case his dad, was free to snoop around unobserved.

In fact Mark was, at that very moment, drifting unnoticed by Elsie into the short hallway leading to the two bedrooms.

"In LA, every waitress is an aspiring actress," Elsie said. "I was taking a different route. I was modeling on the side. When my old roommate moved out to live with her boyfriend, I asked Amy if she wanted to share the rent with me on this place. She did, but it was a little steep for her. So, to help her make a few extra bucks, I showed her how to get into modeling."

Elsie shook her head about something and took another long drag on her cigarette. Steve didn't bother prodding her; he knew she'd keep talking.

"I've modeled merchandise in a hundred throwaway fliers, newspaper ads, and department store catalogs," Elsie said. "Nothing ever came from it for me. Who really notices the woman in the ad, smiling like a lunatic about the discount toilet bowl cleaner she's holding? Amy does one newspaper ad for a crummy sports bra and she's discovered by a big-time movie producer."

"That's what you meant by winning the lottery," Steve said.

"Cleve Kershaw is sitting on the can one morning, leafing through the newspaper, and finds his next star, the next Lacey McClure," Elsie said. "I was in the same ad. I was in a sports bra, too. He looked right past me. I'm good-looking, aren't I?"

"Breathtaking," Steve said.

Elsie studied Steve for a moment. He tried hard to look sincere. She was about the same age as Amy, and wasn't in bad shape, but to Steve it was like comparing the filet mignon at Sizzler to the one at a five-star restaurant. Same fine cut of meat, far different flavor.

Apparently Steve passed the sincerity test, or at least

came close enough, because she exhaled another stream of smoke and decided to continue her story.

"So Kershaw tracks her down, tells her he's gonna make her the next big thing. He gets her to quit her job, then foots the bill for her living expenses, acting lessons, and martial arts training. He even buys her a bunch of new clothes and expensive gifts to reward her for all the effort she was putting in," Elsie said, with more than a little envy in her voice. "Can you believe it?"

Hearing that, it wasn't hard for Mark to pick out which bedroom belonged to Amy. A large, flat-screen television dominated one wall, an elaborate sound system occupied another. Half-melted scented candles were arrayed throughout the room—not so much for romance, he guessed, than to combat the smell of her roommate's cigarettes.

"How did her boyfriend feel about that?" Steve asked.

"Amy didn't have one," Elsie said, "but even if she did, it wouldn't have mattered, because this was strictly business. She wasn't sleeping with Kershaw. I mean, c'mon, you know who he's married to, right?"

Amy Butler certainly did, as Mark discovered. In the drawer of her nightstand he found a stack of lifestyle and movie magazines, each with dog-eared pages marking a Lacey McClure interview or a review of one of her movies. He also found a pair of *nunchaku*—two pipes strung together with a short length of chain. But on this set, the pipes were covered with rubber so they couldn't do any harm. They were for training.

"Maybe Cleve intended to make Amy the next Lacey McClure in more ways than one," Steve said. "They were killed in bed together."

Surprised, Elsie caught her breath for a moment, smoke floating in her half-open mouth like a layer of fog.

"Then things must have changed," Elsie said. "I mean, it's not like Amy wasn't entertaining some fantasies about the guy dumping his wife, but she knew they were fantasies. He was married to Lacey McClure, a rich, beautiful movie star. Why would he toss her out of bed for a waitress who models discount sports bras?"

"Did Amy have any enemies?" Steve asked.

"She wasn't Mary Poppins or anything, there were people who didn't like her," Elsie said. "But nobody hated her or wanted to hurt her, at least not that I know about. Even if somebody did, Amy could have handled it. If I were you, I'd start checking hospitals."

"Why?" Steve asked.

"Because Amy would have gone down fighting," Mark said emerging from the hallway, clumsily twirling Amy's *nunchaku* in his hand. "She'd been studying Tae Kwon Do for some time. I saw her uniform and her brown belt."

He abruptly lost his grip on the *nunchaku*, sending it spinning into a bookshelf, where it narrowly missed shattering one of the lava lamps.

"Sorry about that." Mark picked up the weapon and set it down in front of Elsie. "How long had Amy been training?"

"Off and on for years, when she could afford it," Elsie said. "When Amy was a kid, her mother got assaulted on the street by some mugger. So it was important to Amy to be able to take care of herself."

"Was she any good at it?" Steve asked.

Elsie leaned forward and snubbed her cigarette out in the ashtray as if she were squishing a bug with it. "Good enough to kick the gun out of a guy's hand and make him eat it."

A harsh, unnaturally white light suddenly seeped in through the closed drapes of the window.

"What the hell is that?" Elsie asked.

Steve went to the window, parted the drapes, and peered at the street.

The lights were coming from atop a CNN satellite broadcast truck parked across the street to illuminate the building and create a backdrop for the reporter on the sidewalk, who was facing a cameraman and delivering a live report.

In a moment, more reporters would be showing up, and they'd all want to talk to the Elsie Feikema about her murdered roommate. Within the hour, Elsie's face would be on TVs from LA to Minsk. She was about to become an instant celebrity. All it took was a double murder.

Steve closed the drapes and turned to Elsie. "I think your luck is about to change."

\* \* \*

There were six television sets on the wall in Police Chief John Masters' office at Parker Center, and on every one of them he saw the same image. He saw Lt. Steve Sloan brushing past reporters camped outside murder victim Amy Butler's Hollywood apartment building, mumbling a brusque "I have no comment at this time," before hurrying to his car.

But that wasn't what caught the chief's attention.

One of his TVs was connected to a TiVo, a digital video recorder which allowed him to freeze live footage as if it was already on tape. He aimed his TiVo remote at one of the screens and froze the broadcast, backed up a few frames, and found what he was looking for.

While the cameras were focused on Steve, nobody paid any attention to the man with the grocery bag walking down the sidewalk and around the corner behind him. But Masters recognized the flash of white hair and the merry stride that belonged to only one man.

And now, in the frozen image, he could see the man glancing over his shoulder, a mischievous smile under his white mustache.

Dr. Mark Sloan.

It was obvious to Masters that Steve had timed his dive into the pack of reporters to coincide with Mark discreetly slipping out the back door of the building. Masters assumed Mark waited around the corner, out of sight of the reporters, for Steve to pick him up.

As much as the chief disliked the idea of Mark being involved in the case, he was thankful that Steve was smart enough to keep his father away from the media. If Mark Sloan had been on camera, it would have made it look like the LAPD was incapable of handling a high-profile murder case without the help of a civilian.

It was only a brief reprieve. Masters knew it was inevitable that the press would find out that Mark Sloan discovered the murders and that he was up to his neatly trimmed mustache in the investigation.

Ever since Masters had become chief of police, he'd tried to sever the department's ties to the meddling doctor. It didn't matter to Masters that Mark had an impressive record when it came to solving difficult cases. In the chief's opinion, the more successful the doctor was, the more incompetent it made the LAPD appear.

That opinion didn't change even after Mark Sloan foiled a plot by a corrupt city councilman to implicate the chief in the murder of a police officer. If anything, the experience only strengthened the chief's belief that Mark Sloan undermined public confidence in the LAPD.

His one attempt to co-opt Mark Sloan, by appointing him as a member of a special civilian task force examining cold cases long abandoned by the LAPD, had backfired badly. Mark Sloan discovered there was a killer who'd masked his murders by making them appear to be the work of other serial killers. As a result, scores of convicted serial killers were appealing their convictions, forcing dozens of complex cases to be retried, taxing the already overburdened resources of the LAPD and the district attorney's office.

And now Mark Sloan was inextricably involved in a high-profile celebrity murder case. Even without his involvement, the case was a ticking bomb for the LAPD. There was no question the bomb would explode; the question was how to contain the damage to the department when it did.

He muted the sound on the TVs and turned to look at the city from his window. It's what he always did in times of crisis. It centered him, like a needle in a compass pointing true north.

The ex-football player and former Marine reminded himself he was the chief of police of the city of Los Angeles. This was the city he was sworn to protect. To do that, the people had to respect him and his officers. So it was essential to maintain the authority and prestige of the LAPD.

The last major celebrity case, involving statutory-rape charges against actor Abel Marsh, who played the lovable and wise inner-city priest on the hit TV series *Heaven Sent,* put the LAPD on trial, too. The department was accused of entrapment, sloppy evidence-handling and coercing false statements from witnesses. There was just enough truth to the accusations to topple the previous LAPD regime and bring Masters to power. He didn't relish the idea of history repeating itself, but he knew that to some degree it was unavoidable.

Celebrity murder cases always became scandals.

And, more often than not, he knew that the detectives who got stuck with the case were probably working the last investigation of their careers. The white-hot intensity of the media was too much. Every blemish on their records would be exposed, every personal failing revealed, every weakness exploited. Most cops in that situation retired immediately after the trial, leaving humiliated, disgraced, and disgusted. A few lucky ones got book deals, or ended up being portrayed by Greg Harrison, Greg Evigan, or some other has-been Greg in a low-budget TV movie.

All of a sudden, Mark Sloan's involvement in the Lacey McClure case didn't seem bad at all.

It was fortuitous, in fact.

Masters allowed himself a smile. If he played things right, when all of this was over, it wasn't the department that would face the scrutiny of the press and the wrath of the public.

It would be Dr. Mark Sloan.

Chief Masters wasn't the only man at that moment who, after watching the local evening news, stood at his office window, contemplating the inevitable ramifications of what was already becoming known as "The Lacey McClure Case."

The law firm of Tyrell, Dinino & Barer occupied three floors of a building at the corner of Beverly Drive and Wilshire Boulevard, at the geographical epicenter of wealth and power of Hollywood.

Arthur Tyrell was a large man, affectionately described as "big-boned" by his mother and "double-wide" by his father. He wasn't fat, but he was large, and he liked to live large, too.

When Tyrell looked out the window of his mahogany-paneled corner office, he saw the exclusive stores and restaurants of Rodeo Drive, a street devoted to thriving on the outrageous excesses of the rich and self-absorbed. And he saw the buildings that housed the major talent and management agencies, which swarmed like blood-thirsty mosquitoes over the biggest stars, feeding on their obnoxiously bloated salaries ten percentage points at a time.

It was a far different view than he'd had ten short years ago, when his office was in downtown Los Angeles, the epicenter of urban decay, a short walk away from the Criminal Courts Building. His client list then was a who's who of nobodies. He represented rapists, burglars, hookers, drug dealers, car thieves, and gang members. There was always plenty of work, even if it didn't pay all that well.

But then a couple of hookers Tyrell represented got arrested in a Van Nuys motel room, where they happened to be sharing a bed with Nick Drago, one of the teenage stars of the suburban teen angst drama *Model Homes*.

It was seeing that kid, sitting miserably in a holding cell, that Tyrell had a revelation: Celebrities are afflicted with the same vices, lusts, and stupidity as everybody else. They just have a lot more money to spend on keeping themselves out of jail.

Tyrell offered to represent Drago and, to everybody's shock, convinced the kid to plead guilty. His defense? The kid was researching a role in a movie that would explore the dark, disturbing underbelly of suburbia in America today. All Drago was doing was getting into character. That's how utterly devoted the talented young thespian was to his craft.

There wasn't a movie, of course. There wasn't even a script. But there were two dozen of them waiting for Drago when he walked out of the courtroom, sentenced to probation and a couple hundred hours of community service.

The movie that finally got shot made $70 million at the box office, with critics praising the "startling verisimilitude" that Drago brought to his "searing, unforgettable performance" by virtue of his "daring research" and into the "dark, unplumbed depths of teen despair and sexual depravity."

The arrest, rather than ruining Drago's career, sent it soaring to new heights, and Tyrell's along with it. Within months, Tyrell moved from downtown to Beverly Hills, where he became the lawyer of choice for any celebrity caught with their pants down, a coke spoon up their nose, or a bloody knife in their hand.

Tyrell was doing the same thing he'd always done, only now he was doing it for a higher class of criminal scum. It wasn't just the improved compensation that made his new practice so much better. It was also a simple quality-of-life issue. A junkie actor who dressed in Prada and lived in gated splendor in Bel Air was a lot more pleasant to be around than the average junkie who wore soiled pants and lived under a freeway overpass.

Arthur Tyrell had never met Lacey McClure. But after watching the news, he knew he soon would.

In anticipation of the inevitable, Tyrell summoned one of his assistants to his office and gave the surgically enhanced young woman a list of very important tasks.

He wanted complete personal, professional, and financial histories on Steve Sloan, Cleve Kershaw, Amy Butler, and Lacey McClure.

He wanted detailed background on every homicide case Steve Sloan had investigated during his time with the LAPD and a copy of his confidential personnel file.

And finally, and most importantly, Tyrell wanted the names of the top home-theater designers in the city, reviews of the best projection equipment, and a catalog of leather screening-room furniture. Lacey McClure was going to pay for the private home screening room of Arthur Tyrell's dreams.

She just didn't know it yet.

# CHAPTER SIX

When Mark awoke at six, he put on his bathrobe and padded barefoot into the kitchen, where he found Steve dressed and already at the table, the morning paper open in front of him.

"How did you sleep?" Mark asked.

"I didn't," Steve said. "I had this on my mind."

Steve closed the paper and held it up for Mark to see. The front page was dominated by a huge story on the murders, illustrated with file photos of Lacey McClure, Cleve Kershaw, and Amy Butler. There was also a picture, taken from a distance, of the morgue truck parked amidst the police vehicles in front of the beach house where the killing occurred.

"Did they at least get the facts right?" Mark asked.

"Yeah, probably because there aren't that many yet," Steve said. "Mostly the story is full of movie-industry people talking about how shocked they are by the murders, and the impact they might have on Lacey McClure personally and professionally."

"Anything in it we don't already know?"

"Just this." Steve opened the paper and began to read from somewhere toward the end of the article. " 'McClure hasn't made a statement yet, though a spokesman from Pinnacle Pictures, the studio making her new movie, said that production would continue 'at her request,' and that she would be reporting to the set this evening.' "

Mark went to the coffee maker while he listened, poured himself a cup of coffee, and carried his steaming mug back to the table, glancing out at the beach on his way. What he saw made him stop.

There was an armada of boats just beyond the shore, all filled with photographers, aiming their long lenses at Lacey McClure and Cleve Kershaw's beach house, the sand around it cordoned off with yellow police tape.

" 'It was also reported,' " Steve continued to read, " 'that her most recent film, *Thrill Kill,* will be released this weekend as previously scheduled, again at the actress' request. Her representatives quoted her as saying, 'Cleve would have wanted it that way.' Yeah right, I'm sure his last thoughts were, 'Damn, I hope this doesn't delay the release of my movie.' "

"This being Hollywood," Mark said, "you never know."

When Mark looked back out at the water again, he saw that several of the cameras were now aimed at him. He abruptly stepped back and closed the drapes.

"There's a nice picture of Elsie Feikema here, and an entire sidebar on Amy Butler's short life," Steve said. "They don't mention anything about how lucky she was."

"Do they happen to mention my name anywhere?" Mark asked.

Steve cocked an eyebrow, surprised. "Since when are you interested in attention from the press?"

"I'm not," Mark said, motioning to the closed drapes. "They seem interested in me."

"All it says here is that the bodies were discovered by a neighbor," Steve said, "but I imagine by now they've pulled the property records to find out who lives in each of the houses on this stretch of sand. I'm sure that as soon as your name came up they assumed you were probably involved, especially since your son is the lead detective on the case."

Mark sat down across from his son. "Have you heard anything from the department brass yet?"

"I talked briefly to the captain," Steve said. "He offered me all the resources I needed, ordered me to keep him informed of any developments, and instructed me not to make any statements to the press."

"There are two ways of looking at this," Mark said. "Either they have enormous confidence in your investigative skills or—"

"Or they're saving themselves," Steve interrupted, finishing the thought, "and sacrificing me to the wolves."

"I'm afraid I don't know the first thing about department politics," Mark said. "What can you do to fight back?"

"I can solve the murder," Steve said, rising from his seat. "I don't blame the captain or anybody else for the situation I'm in. There were no political machinations involved, except on my part. I took this case from the detective on duty as soon as I heard it was you who called in the shooting."

Mark grimaced. "I'm sorry, Steve."

"It's not your fault," Steve said. "I blame whoever did the killing."

Unless there was a rush-hour car accident, or some other unforeseen disaster, mornings in the Community General emergency room were generally slow—time the medical and nursing staff used to catch up on paperwork, order supplies, and read the latest medical journals. But for Dr. Jesse Travis and his girlfriend, nurse Susan Hilliard, it was a chance to learn the details of whatever homicide Mark Sloan was currently investigating.

Jesse was always eager to get involved in any of Mark's cases, to learn whatever he could from a man he considered not only a great doctor, but an amazing detective. He didn't aspire to become a detective himself, but he enjoyed the search for clues, the thrill of the hunt, and the excitement of discovery. But most of all, Jesse liked how close it drew him to Steve, Amanda, and especially Mark, who he openly and unabashedly considered a father figure. Remaining close to them was a big reason why he'd partnered with Steve to buy BBQ Bob's restaurant a few years ago. BBQ Bob's had become his second home. Between the hospital and the restaurant, Jesse was rarely at home or at Susan's place.

Susan shared Jesse's respect for Mark, but didn't really have an interest in homicide investigation. Her interest was in Jesse and making sure he didn't risk too much personally or professionally in his desire to be a member of the team and to please Mark Sloan. She didn't need a father figure, nor was she desperate to be a part of the crime-solving group. She knew that because of this, no matter how close she and Jesse remained, she would always be an outsider, and she was fine with that. Although she rarely helped Mark with his homicide inquiries—and even then only when he specifically asked—she gladly helped out at BBQ Bob's because it guaranteed she got to spend time with Jesse.

So now Susan was in the pathology lab with Jesse, standing across from Mark Sloan over the cold, pale, bullet-riddled bodies of Cleve Kershaw and Amy Butler, who were laid out side by side on adjoining autopsy tables.

Susan was very uncomfortable, but not because she was around death. She was used to that. It was because she and Jesse were together, looking down at the naked corpses of two lovers. She couldn't help but feel a connection and it unnerved her.

While Amanda remained at her desk, working on the last details of her autopsy reports, Mark briefed Jesse and Susan on everything that had happened since he heard the gun shots the previous afternoon.

Jesse had worked with Mark long enough to know this briefing wasn't just for their benefit. Repeating the facts gave Mark another chance to sort out all the information, visualize the crime scene, and reconsider everything he'd been told by suspects and witnesses. When Mark finished his account, Susan was, uncharacteristically, the first to speak up, much to everyone's surprise.

"Lacey McClure did it," she declared emphatically.

"You're just saying that because she's hot," Jesse said. "You treat me like I'm cheating on you every time I go to one of her movies, even if you go with me."

"Because you sit there with this dopey look on your face, panting at the screen," Susan said with a grin. "But that's not why I think she's the killer. It just seems so obvious."

"And that's exactly what bugs Mark," Jesse said, turning to Mark for agreement. "Right?"

"No, I think Lacey McClure did it," Mark said.

"You do?" Jesse said. He wasn't used to Mark accepting the simple explanation for anything, especially when it came to murder.

"The evidence against Lacey McClure is solid and quite convincing," Mark said. "She had motive, opportunity, and gunshot residue on her hands. And she'd have a key, which explains why there were no signs of a break-in at the beach house."

"Then what *is* bothering you?" Jesse asked.

"A few little things," Mark said, "I can't figure out why Cleve and Amy didn't hear her come in, or why they didn't even get out of bed when she walked into the room."

"Yeah," Jesse said, "It's almost a reflex to jump out of bed when you're caught doing the nasty."

"How would you know?" Susan asked teasingly. "Personal experience?"

"Of course not," Jesse offered quickly, "I've seen it a lot on TV."

"There's something else I don't get," Mark said. "Amy Butler studied Tae Kwon Do for years. So why didn't she attempt to defend herself? There were no signs of a struggle."

"I can answer that," Amanda said, rising from her desk to join them, the autopsy reports in her hand. "Amy was drugged. I found rohypnol in her system. I doubt she was even conscious when the killer came in."

"You mean this movie producer guy slipped her a date-rape drug?" Susan asked. "What a sleazebag."

"Actually, I found rohypnol in his system, too," Amanda said, handing Mark the autopsy reports. "I doubt they took it knowingly. It's hardly considered a recreational drug, unless your idea of a good time is a deep nap."

"At my age," Mark said, "it can be."

"I called the crime lab and asked them to test the champagne bottle I saw in Kershaw's living room," Amanda said. "I haven't seen the official report yet, but a buddy of mine in the lab gave me a preview. It appears that someone injected the drug through the cork into the champagne bottle."

"Whoever killed them wanted to be sure there wouldn't be any kind of struggle," Mark said, skimming through the autopsy reports.

"If the killer had the opportunity to spike the champagne, why not inject it with a lethal dose and be done with it?" Jesse asked. "Why come back and shoot them? The killer took a huge, unnecessary risk. She was lucky she wasn't caught in the act."

"She should have been," Mark said. "That's the biggest puzzler of all."

"Based on the body temperature readings you took at the scene, I'm estimating the time of death at between three thirty and four p.m.," she said. "Otherwise, based on what I know and what I saw, I'd have pegged it at four thirty, the time you heard the gunshots."

"Which brings up another big question," Mark said. "Who was Lacey's accomplice?"

"Accomplice?" Jesse asked. "What makes you think anyone but Lacey McClure was involved?"

"Someone shot Cleve Kershaw and Amy Butler between three thirty and four o'clock, presumably using a silencer, because no one heard the shots," Mark said. "Then I'm assuming someone else came at four thirty and fired the shots that I heard, strictly for show, to establish the time of death."

"But why?" Jesse asked, genuinely confused.

"To establish an alibi," Mark replied. "To make us all think the murder happened a half-hour to an hour later than it did."

"If Mark hadn't shown up immediately after the gunshots," Amanda said, "we never would have known there was a discrepancy. It was a great plan."

"It could have been Lacey both times," Jesse said.

"That's true," Mark said.

Susan frowned with confusion. "So if it's Lacey McClure and she, alone or with an accomplice, went to the trouble of establishing the time of death at four thirty, wouldn't she have come up with a better alibi than taking a nap?"

"You're right, Susan," Mark said. "And that's the one reservation I have about her guilt, despite the evidence and my gut instinct that she did it."

"Let me see if I've got this straight," Jesse said. "You have every reason to believe that Lacey McClure is the killer, except for one thing. The murder was done in such a way as to give her a perfect alibi and she doesn't have one."

"Exactly," Mark said.

"Maybe that's her cunning plan," Jesse said.

"It seems pretty stupid to me," Amanda said.

"That's what makes it so cunning," Jesse said. "The stupidity is actually genius."

Jesse smiled, quite pleased with himself, oblivious to the withering look Amanda gave him. She didn't bother to comment on Jesse's theory; instead she turned her attention to Mark.

"Maybe it was a Mob hit," Amanda said. "It would explain the execution-style murder."

"But not the drugging," Mark said.

"Maybe what's hanging us up is that we're looking at this all wrong," Jesse said. "What if the drugging and the shooting were totally unrelated?"

"What do you mean?" Mark asked, genuinely curious.

"Maybe whoever spiked the champagne meant to kill them and screwed up," Jesse said. "And whoever it was had no idea some shooter was going to come along in the afternoon and cap them."

"*Cap* them?" Amanda said, giving Jesse a look.

"That's what they call it," Jesse said. "You've got to get out of this lab more often."

"I've got to watch *The Sopranos*," Amanda said.

"If I'm right, the shooter probably didn't know what to think when he found his targets out cold," Jesse said. "But he still had a job to do, so he did it: *bang, bang.*"

"It's a good theory," Mark said. "But it doesn't explain the inconsistency between the actual time of death and when I heard the gunshots."

"Oh," Jesse said, realizing Mark was right. "My theory might need a little work."

"Don't take it too hard, Jesse. All of our theories do," Mark said. "There's a vital piece of the puzzle we're still missing and I'm determined to find it."

"Is there anything I can do to help?" Jesse asked.

"I'd like to know more about Lacey McClure," Mark said. "I borrowed some magazines Amy Butler collected with stories about her, but I haven't seen any of her movies. Can you put together a little Lacey McClure film festival for me?"

"My pleasure," Jesse said with a grin.

"Oh God," Susan said. "You're already getting that dopey look on your face."

"This is my usual, ruggedly handsome look," Jesse said. "There's nothing dopey about this."

Mark met Jesse's eyes. "I'd like you to get me all her movies."

"All?" Jesse said, dragging the word out and letting the implication hang.

Susan swatted Jesse's shoulder, startling him.

"What?" he exclaimed.

"Don't even think about it," she said playfully.

"I don't know what you're talking about," Jesse replied.

"Especially that one," Mark said.

Susan and Amanda looked at Mark in surprise. But he didn't show the slightest trace of embarrassment.

"Why aren't you hitting *him*?" Jesse asked, massaging his shoulder.

"I don't look forward to watching that particular tape," Mark said. "But one of the murder victims and his possible killer are in it. I should see it."

"You got it," Jesse said quickly, earning him another swat from Susan. "Hey, I'm just agreeing to his request."

"A little too enthusiastically, if you ask me," Susan said. "Besides, I thought you didn't know what I was talking about."

"You weren't very clear," Jesse said, scrambling for the door before Susan, grinning, could swat him again.

They stopped cold in the corridor, like two kids caught misbehaving, when they saw Noah Dent, the hospital administrator, leaning against the counter of the nurse's station directly outside of the pathology lab. Dent had a scowl on his face. He merely pointed his index finger sharply at both Jesse and Susan and motioned them to follow him into an empty hospital room.

As soon as they were inside the room, Dent closed the door behind him and confronted the two of them.

"I was under the impression you were both on call down in the emergency room," Dent said.

"We are," Jesse said. "We were conferring on medical matters with Dr. Sloan and Dr. Bentley."

"About a current patient of yours?" Dent said.

"Not exactly," Jesse said. "We confer frequently, to share experience, give advice, that sort of thing."

"I see," Dent said, turning his gaze to Susan. "And what expertise were you contributing to this discussion?"

Susan flushed. "I was hoping to learn something. I'm considering going to medical school, maybe becoming a doctor myself."

"You want to learn something?" Dent asked. "I have a lesson for you. When you're being paid to be a nurse in the emergency room, it's a good idea to actually provide nursing services in the emergency room."

He stared at her. She didn't move.

"Now," Dent said.

Susan shot a glance at Jesse, then hurriedly left the room.

Jesse's face tightened with anger and he took a step toward Dent, who didn't move.

"You had no reason to talk to her that way," Jesse said. "She isn't your dog or your servant."

"And she won't be a nurse at this hospital either if she continues neglecting her duties. She's been coasting on her relationship with Dr. Sloan and enjoying preferential treatment for too long," Dent said. "The same goes for you, Dr. Travis. I know full well what was going on in that pathology lab. You were participating in Dr. Sloan's personal investigation into the killings in Malibu yesterday. And you were doing so on the hospital's time."

"Dr. Sloan is the chief of internal medicine. Every doctor in this hospital seeks out his advice and experience on a daily basis. I don't have to justify the time I spend with him to you or anybody else," Jesse said. "If the ER needs me, they'll page me and I will be there in two minutes."

"Let me be perfectly clear, Dr. Travis, so there's no misunderstanding," Dent said. "When you are in this hospital, you work for me. Your job is downstairs treating patients, not playing detective with Dr. Sloan or discussing autopsies with Dr. Bentley. Unless you are checking on matters that specifically involve one of your patients, there is absolutely no reason for you to be in that pathology lab."

"Dr. Bentley is my friend," Jesse said.

"I'm well aware of that, believe me," Dent said. "I'm also aware that you're sleeping with Nurse Hilliard."

"You're crossing a line here, Dent," Jesse said.

"No, Dr. Travis, it's you who've crossed the line, taking advantage of the trust and authority you've been given by this hospital," Dent replied. "You won't be getting any more special treatment here and neither will Nurse Hilliard. If you want to continue working here, you will adjust your conduct and your priorities. If I see you assisting Dr. Sloan on anything besides patient care, or using our resources to aid in his detecting hobby, I'll fire you immediately. Do I make myself clear?"

And with that, Dent walked out, not bothering to wait for an answer. He didn't care what Jesse had to say, and fully expected the doctor to violate the rules that had just been laid down.

The message hadn't been meant for Jesse anyway. It was meant for Mark Sloan, and Dent knew that Mark's little acolyte would take it straight to him.

# CHAPTER SEVEN

By noon, it was impossible to be a living, breathing member of the civilized human race and not know that Lacey McClure's husband had been shot to death in bed with another woman. The airwaves were choked with news about the shocking, "gangland-style murders" of Cleve Kershaw and Amy Butler. There was continuous, live coverage from outside the gates of Lacey McClure's "Brentwood estate" where, depending on which channel was reporting, she was either "bravely confronting her grief" or "barricading herself in seclusion."

Lacey McClure's publicist, the high-powered and heavily accessorized Randi Lofficier, did reveal that the movie star and her husband, Cleve Kershaw, had been quietly separated for some time, which sparked enormous debate among the shocked entertainment reporters, who couldn't imagine how Lacey and Cleve had managed to keep their marital discord from them.

While the eyes of the world were on that important story, Dr. Mark Sloan and Dr. Jesse Travis labored in the Community General emergency room to save the life of a three-week-old baby who'd been brought in by paramedics.

The baby had been found in an open garbage bag in a dumpster in Mar Vista. She was suffering from exposure and hypothermia, her core body temperature a dangerously cool 85 degrees.

Jesse put the baby on heated, humidified oxygen to warm her lungs and asked Susan to start an IV of heated saline to raise the child's body temperature.

But their efforts weren't raising her temperature fast enough, so Mark was forced to perform a partial cardiopulmonary bypass. He placed catheters in both ends of a coiled tube, then made an incision into the child's groin, inserting one catheter in the femoral artery and the other in the femoral vein that was right beside it. The baby's blood began circulating through the tube, which he placed in a bath of hot water.

Within minutes the bypass showed results, raising the baby's core temperature to 93 degrees, much to the relief of Mark, Jesse, and the rest of the ER team. The baby would survive her horrific ordeal.

There wouldn't be any CNN crews covering her plight, no armies of reporters searching for answers and pressing for prompt action.

There wouldn't be any photographers jostling for position to take pictures of the dumpster where the baby was thrown away.

There wouldn't be any continuous live feeds from the alley.

The baby's story was tragic and unfathomable, but there's wasn't any entertainment value in it. What happened to the nameless child wasn't nearly salacious enough to matter.

After a time, Susan swaddled the baby in blankets and escorted her up to the neonatal intensive care unit for observation. Jesse put a call into the state Child Welfare Office to arrange for foster care after the baby's recovery. And Mark went back upstairs to continue his rounds.

Steve was waiting for the elevator when the doors opened on the third floor, Amanda's autopsy reports under his arm.

"Going down?" Steve asked, stepping in.

"I am now." Mark punched the button for the lobby. "How's the investigation going?"

"If this were anything but a celebrity homicide, I'd say it was going great," Steve replied. "I met with the forensic accountant that Lacey hired to go over her husband's books. There's no question there was some financial sleight-of-hand going on, but there's no evidence that it has anything to do with organized crime."

"But it confirms her husband was laundering money for someone?"

"Sure looks that way," Steve said. "Which means she might be right, and have one more strong motive for killing him."

"Usually we're satisfied if we can establish one strong motive for a suspect, and this time we've got two," Mark said. "Shouldn't we be celebrating?"

"I would if I could explain the time of death problem you discovered."

"Did SID come up with anything at the crime scene house?"

"Tons of stuff. I can tell you the chemical composition of the ChapStick on the nightstand, the thread count of the sheets, but nothing that solves our problem," Steve said. "Lacey's fingerprints are all over the beach house and they found dirt particles in the carpet that can be traced back to her place in Mandeville Canyon."

"Which she can argue makes sense, since she's been to that beach house a thousand times," Mark said. "It doesn't prove she was there yesterday afternoon."

"I know," Steve said, a pained look on his face. "So far there isn't any evidence against her that she can't refute with a reasonable explanation."

"Do you believe her explanations?"

"Hell no," Steve said as the elevator arrived at the lobby. Mark and Steve got out and made their way down the corridor towards the exit to the parking lot. "I don't buy that she and Cleve were separated, either. His clothes and other belongings were still in both houses. It doesn't look like he moved out to me."

"She did say it was a secret," Mark said.

"I'd say that was her weakest argument," Steve said. "If it wasn't for her lousy alibi."

"Sounds to me like an arrest is imminent."

"It's long overdue and it hasn't even been twenty-four hours since the killings," Steve said. "What's amazing to me is that she hasn't made any public statements accusing the Mob of killing her husband. She hasn't lawyered up. And she's going back to work on her movie tonight. Doesn't she realize she's the prime suspect in a double murder?"

"Let's tell her," Mark said.

"And tip our hand?" Steve asked as he stepped out. "What will that get us?"

Mark shrugged. "Whatever her reaction is," he said, "it's bound to be interesting."

And with that, Mark opened the door to the parking lot and ushered his son out with a grand wave of his arm.

In the early days of filmmaking, and through most of the last century, movies were shot on studio backlots where city streets and suburban neighborhoods were recreated in painstaking detail. The storefronts, office buildings, brownstones, and houses were just fake facades, redressed and repainted for each new production.

But as the city grew, the real estate under the backlots became far too valuable to waste on phony buildings when real ones could generate a lot more cash. The studios razed most of their backlots, and production took to the streets, transforming the entire city of Los Angeles into one enormous stage.

Hundreds of productions are shot in and around the city on any given day. For Angelenos, seeing a film crew at work is as common as seeing a road being repaved or mail being delivered, and garners about as much attention—unless the filming involves a car chase, a shoot-out, or an explosion.

Or one of the actors happens to be at the center of titillating scandal involving adultery, sex, money and murder.

Which was why on the night Mark and Steve visited the downtown location of *Kill Storm,* a dozen beefy security guards were scrambling to keep hundreds of onlookers and reporters behind barricades erected a block away from the alley where the crew was shooting.

Although Steve's car was an unmarked detective sedan, it might as well have been emblazoned with the LAPD emblem as far as the security guards were concerned. Most of the guards were off-duty cops and immediately recognized the car for what it was, letting Steve pass through without even asking to see his ID.

Steve parked behind a huge mobile home, which seemed to have expanded itself to cover an area twice its original size. There were four push-out sections adding extra rooms to the floor plan, a massive canvas overhang to provide a shaded patio, and enough satellite dishes and antennas on the roof to allow whoever was inside to communicate with other galaxies.

"Gee," Steve said, motioning to the mobile home, "I wonder whose dressing room that is."

Before Mark could respond, a harried looking young man with a walkie-talkie, two cell phones, and a pager clipped to his belt came rushing up.

"You can't park there," the young man said. "That's Lacey McClure's private guest parking."

"We're her private guests," Steve said.

The young man quickly consulted a sheaf of papers that were folded and crammed into his back pocket. "You aren't on the list."

"I am now." Steve flashed his badge. "Steve Sloan, LAPD. And you are?"

"I'm Morgan," the young man said. "Ms. McClure's APA."

"APA?" Mark asked. "You're her accountant?"

"Her first assistant production assistant," Morgan said, glancing at his watch. "Excuse me one second, I have to bring her water."

Morgan rushed into the mobile home, leaving the door open behind him. Steve and Mark followed the young man inside without waiting to be invited.

Steve took one look at the travertine floors, marble countertops, and leather furniture and let out a low whistle, impressed.

"Is there a *second* assistant production assistant?" Mark asked Morgan.

"And a third. The second assistant production assistant is out getting Ms. McClure a new set of sheets," Morgan said. "She went to take a nap this afternoon and jumped out of bed in a rage. She could feel there were only 250 threads per inch in the sheets."

Steve glanced into the bedroom. The white sheets had

been stripped off the king-sized bed and were piled like a snowdrift against the wall, beneath a massive, flat-screen TV.

"She could actually *feel* the number of threads?" Steve asked.

"Ms. McClure has very sensitive skin," Morgan said, taking bottles of Glacier Peaks water out of the refrigerator and transferring them to a tiny, portable cooler. "She says if she sleeps on anything less than 600 thread count Egyptian or pima cotton sateen sheets, it's like laying on sandpaper."

"Is there something special about that water?" Mark asked. "There's a bottle on her nightstand and, last time we met her, she had one in her hands."

"Glacier Peaks is the only water she drinks," Morgan said, checking a thermometer in the tiny cooler. Satisfied with the temperature reading, he zipped the cooler shut. "It's from a glacier in Antarctica and is shipped directly to her. She demands that it be kept at exactly 68 degrees. She's the same way about carpet. It must be extra heavy, tufted British wool, primarily from Scottish Blackface, Herdwick, and Cheviot sheep."

"She sounds awfully picky," Mark said.

"You mean she's a pain in the ass," Steve said, ducking under the crystal chandelier in the living room to admire her entertainment center.

"She's nothing compared to some actors I've worked with," Morgan said. "A certain Oscar nominee has to have his feet massaged with egg yolks from free-range chickens before he performs a scene."

Morgan's radio crackled and an insistent male voice asked: "What's the ETA on the H2O?"

The beleaguered young man yanked his walkie-talkie from its holster as if he'd been zapped with a cattle prod and quickly responded: "Sixty seconds."

Morgan motioned to Mark and Steve. "Follow me, and I'll take you to her," he said, practically leaping out the door of the mobile home.

Mark and Steve almost had to run to keep up with him, as the APA raced between trucks, over electric cables, and around the enormous lights that illuminated the alley where the night's scenes were being shot.

Morgan edged his way through the intense group of baseball-capped professionals huddled around the cameras and playback monitors and rushed out to Lacey McClure, who stood in the center of the alley in a black leather jumpsuit.

The APA unzipped the little cooler and offered Lacey a bottle. She took a quick drink, put the bottle back in the cooler, and flashed Morgan a superficial smile of thanks. That's when she saw Mark and Steve behind the camera, watching her. Her smile remained, in all its blazing insincerity.

"Is everyone hydrated?" the director asked, his impatience evident in every word.

Lacey glared at him, but it didn't seem to bother the director.

"I'll take that as a yes," the director said, turning to his director of photography, who sat in the canvas chair beside him. "How about you; are we ready?"

"We're set," the director of photography said.

"Great, let's do it," the director said, nodding to his assistant director, who stood in the alley, just outside camera's field of view.

The assistant director took out his walkie-talkie and spoke into it, his voice emanating like a crackling echo from walkie-talkies all over the set. "This will be picture. Everybody settle. Quiet please."

"Action!" The director snapped, then hunched over the monitors to watch the scene unfold.

*Delia Storm walked down the dark alley. Three figures peeled out of the darkness around her like shadows coming to life. There were three men, dressed in black, and they carried baseball bats.*

*One of the men smiled. His yellow teeth looked like they'd been knocked out, mixed together, then shoved back into his mouth in the wrong places. "Didn't anybody tell you it's not safe for a lady to walk alone here at night?"*

*"I'm not a lady," she said with a thin smile.*

*"Then what the hell are you?"*

*"Justice," she hissed, then whirled around and—*

"Hold your positions," the director yelled. "Lacey out, Moira in."

The cameraman didn't move and neither did the three men. Lacey hurried behind the camera and another woman, dressed exactly like her, took her place in the alley, assuming the same position Lacey had been in.

"Who is that?" whispered Mark to the APA.

"Moira Cole," Morgan said. "Lacey's stunt double."

At that instant, the director yelled "Action!"

Moira whirled into a spinning kick, hitting the nearest man in the face with her foot and sending his bat flying from his hands. She caught the bat, twirled it in her hands like a baton, and used it to take out the guy next to her, then froze in a martial-arts stance to confront her lone remaining adversary, her head at an angle that obscured her face from the camera's view.

"Hold your positions," the director yelled again, and Moira rushed out and Lacey assumed her final stance. The director waited a moment, then yelled "Action!"

*Delia gave her adversary a thin smile. "I hope you've got a good dentist."*

*"I hope you picked out your tombstone, Storm," the man growled, swinging his bat at her.*

*Delia ducked under his swing, rammed her bat into his gut, and as he doubled over, whacked him across the face with it. The man went down.*

*She twirled her bat one more time in a self-satisfied show of victory, stepped over the groaning man and continued on her way.*

*"Don't forget to pick up your teeth before you go home,"* she said.

"Cut!" The director yelled. "That's a print. Check the gate. Let's move on."

"What gate?" Mark asked Morgan.

"They're checking to see if there's a hair or lint or anything where the film moves past the lens of the camera," Morgan said. "If there is, they've got to reshoot the scene."

Lacey approached Mark and Steve, the bat still in her hand.

"Good evening, Detective," Lacey said to Steve, then

glanced at Mark. "And Detective's Daddy. Are you making any progress with your investigation?"

"I think so," Steve replied. "You have a minute to talk?"

"Sure," she said, effortlessly twirling her bat again. "They've got to relight for the coverage."

"The coverage?" Mark asked.

"The same shot you just saw but from other angles," she replied. "What we just did was the master, the wide-angle view of the scene. Now we're going to spend the night doing the whole scene again and again and again in different pieces."

"I see," Mark said. "So that's why you could slip out of the scene and your stunt double could slip in. You'll just cut around that moment with the other footage. The action will move so fast, from so many different angles, that no one will ever know you didn't beat up those guys yourself."

"That's movie magic," she said, suddenly whirling around and striking the director across the knees with her bat. Mark caught his breath, but the director didn't even flinch.

"Great scene, Lacey," the director said. "You're Eastwood in a Wonderbra."

"What makes you think he doesn't wear one, too?" Lacey said, then tossed the bat to Mark, who caught it.

The bat was made of rubber.

"I hope I haven't shattered all your illusions," she said to Mark with a mischievous grin.

"Not at all," Mark said. "Seeing through illusions is something of a hobby for me."

"Is that so?" She cocked an eyebrow. "Are we playing cat and mouse, Dr. Sloan?"

"I don't think so," Mark said. "Are we?"

"Why waste the energy?" Steve said, "There's no mystery about who killed Cleve Kershaw and Amy Butler."

"That's good to know," Lacey said, heading for her mobile home, Mark and Steve keeping pace on either side of her. "Who did it?"

"You," Steve said.

She didn't break her stride. "Then why aren't you reading me my rights?"

"I thought you might try to convince me I'm wrong first," Steve said.

"You're wrong," she said.

"Is that the best you can do?" Steve said.

"I don't need to do more," she said, turning to face them as she reached her trailer. "I didn't do it."

"All the evidence says you did," Steve said. "You've also got motive, means, and opportunity, which, according to the detective handbook, makes you the killer."

"I feel like I'm doing the same scene I've already shot, only from another angle," she said. "We had this conversation. The Mob killed my ex-husband, Lt. Sloan. Not me."

"He's already an ex-husband?" Steve said. "You don't waste any time, do you?"

"No, I don't," she said. "So, if you're not going to arrest me, we're done."

"Let me see." Steve glanced at his watch and sighed. "Oh hell, if I arrest you now, I'm going to be up all night filling out reports and fielding questions from the media. I really need my sleep. Tell you what, maybe we'll do it tomorrow. How's that?"

And with that, Lacey McClure went into her mobile home and closed the door on them.

Steve looked at his dad. "Was that interesting enough for you?"

Mark nodded. "Very."

# CHAPTER EIGHT

Steve dropped Mark off at the beach house and continued on to Barbeque Bob's, where he would stay until closing, serving food, ringing up checks, and managing the books.

There was a grocery bag waiting for Mark on his doorstep containing DVDs of Lacey's movies and a note from Jesse, saying he'd ordered her home video at great personal peril and that it would be arriving in a few days.

Mark decided the movies could wait for a while. He made himself some hot tea, settled into his recliner, and started reading through the articles about Lacey McClure that Amy Butler had collected.

He learned all about Lacey's beauty secrets ("Keep your lips moist with ChapStick morning, noon, and night!"), diet tips ("Say no to carbs and trans-fatty acids!") and exercise advice ("you don't need fancy gym equipment—your own staircase can be your StairMaster!").

He read dozens of different retellings of her rather ordinary childhood in Indianapolis before she moved to New York to become an actress. Her parents divorced when she was young and, as she recounted tearfully in many interviews, she grew estranged from them both because they were "emotionally cold" and "emotionally abusive."

Her marriage to Cleve Kershaw was repeatedly described as "one of the great Hollywood love stories" with Lacey frequently referring to their relationship as a "perfect partnership," and praising her husband's creativity, business sense, and "incredible sensitivity." She also referred to him as "a very sexy, masculine man."

She talked tearfully, and at great length, about how he stood by her, providing "enormous emotional support," during her "harrowing cancer ordeal," when a small tumor called a lipoma was removed from her shoulder. The articles, and Lacey herself, described the experience like it was brain cancer when, in fact, Mark knew that a lipoma was merely a common benign fatty tumor beneath the skin, easily excised by laser, cautery, or an incision on an outpatient basis.

But it made good press, allowing her interviewers to portray her heroically as a "courageous cancer survivor" and Lacey to reveal how the crisis "strengthened our marriage" and made them "appreciate each other, and the blessings we have, even more."

She unabashedly compared their romance to such legendary Hollywood couples as Gable and Lombard, Bogart and Bacall, Tracy and Hepburn. And yet, at the same time, she called their relationship "a typical, American marriage," and their lives as "down to earth" and "refreshingly un-Hollywood." They were "just a normal couple" who happened to be incredibly talented, wealthy, famous, and attractive.

The articles that preceded the release of each of her movies were virtually the same. All her films "redefined the action genre" and made "amazing strides for women in Hollywood," putting Lacey at the forefront of "a sexual revolution in the movie industry." Every role she played was a character of "enormous depth and originality" that allowed her to challenge herself and "explore her incredible range as an actress," taking her skills to "astonishing new levels."

Mark finished the magazines knowing nothing more about Lacey than he did before, though he did wonder why people bothered reading celebrity interviews. There were no insights to be gained, no wisdom revealed, nothing new to be learned about anything. Celebrity interviews were the intellectual equivalent of olestra, passing through the mind and leaving nothing to digest.

He wondered what knowledge about stardom, acting, or Cleve Kershaw that Amy Butler had possibly hoped to glean from these vapid articles. Perhaps she had been as disappointed by them as Mark was.

Having read so much about Lacey McClure, Mark was ready to see her movies, and her amazing strides for women, for himself. Ten minutes into *Bloodbath Day Camp for Girls* he hit the FAST-FORWARD button, stopping only occasionally to hear a few lines of Lacey's insipid dialogue. The movie told the story of several sexually adventurous, and barely clothed, young girls terrorized by a disfigured, psychopathic man who systematically killed them with various power tools. Lacey McClure played one of the early victims, who was eviscerated in bloody detail with a pair of electric shears.

*Bloodbath Day Camp For Girls* was easily the most offensive movie Mark had ever seen or, more accurately, fastforwarded through. He couldn't understand what the entertainment value was in watching people being tortured and killed in the most horrific ways imaginable, nor what the artistic interest was in writing, directing, or acting in such a film.

Then again, it was the movie that launched Lacey McClure's career, and as she'd said in one of the interviews he'd read, she had no more regrets about doing it than Renée Zellwegger had about doing *The Return of the Texas Chainsaw Massacre* or Johnny Depp had about being in *A Nightmare on Elm Street*.

Mark took *Bloodbath Day Camp for Girls* from the DVD player and, withstanding the sudden urge to disinfect his hands, placed *Good Morning, Miss Killer* into the machine in its place.

The main titles were just beginning when Steve came home. Seeing what was on, he immediately settled down on the couch to watch.

The movie was just a series of elaborately choreographed fights and fiery explosions, strung together with a few lines of dialogue and an occasional sex scene. Mark tuned out early on, more interested in Steve's reaction to the movie than in the movie itself.

Steve was completely absorbed—laughing, smiling and,

during the action sequences, leaning forward in his seat, eyes fixed on the screen.

When it was over, Steve became aware of Mark staring at him.

"What's wrong?" Steve asked. "It's a great movie."

"But you've met Lacey McClure, you know what she's really like, and you're convinced that she's a murderer," Mark said. "How can you believe her in a role or find her entertaining after that?"

"Two seconds into the movie she just stopped being Lacey McClure to me," Steve said. "She became an ordinary suburban housewife who discovers she's actually an international spy with amnesia."

"It couldn't have been the acting that convinced you," Mark said. "She's not that good."

"It's not about the acting," Steve said. "I grew up watching TV, you didn't. I've been conditioned to immediately suspend my disbelief when looking at something on-screen. It's become an instinct."

Mark thought about that for a moment and decided there might be some truth to it. "Do you think even after you've proven she's a killer and she's been sentenced to prison, you'll still be able to enjoy her movies?"

"Probably," Steve said, then motioned to the TV. "Put *.357 Vigilante* in, it's her best."

Mark put in the DVD and hit PLAY. "Perhaps you'd be interested in reading about some of her health and beauty tips, too?"

"No thanks," Steve said. "I may be screwed up, but I'm not insane."

At ten the next morning, Steve Sloan was in District Attorney Neil Burnside's office, making his case for the immediate arrest of Lacey McClure for the murders of her husband and his mistress. Burnside wasn't paying much attention. The DA quickly got the gist of Steve's argument, so his thoughts drifted to figuring out which assistant district attorney he should sacrifice on this career-ruining prosecution.

Although it sounded to Burnside like Steve had a solid

circumstantial case, the DA also knew how a skilled defense attorney like Arthur Tyrell could turn the evidence into an indictment of the LAPD and, by association, the prosecutors. And if it wasn't Tyrell doing the spinning, it would be some other grotesquely overcompensated, well-tailored lawyer up against Burnside's obscenely underpaid, off-the-rack civil servant.

Whoever Burnside picked to be outmatched in the courtroom had to have a strong personality, somebody who would become so inextricably associated with the case that the DA wouldn't be blamed by the public if the prosecution lost. Conversely, it had to be somebody who, if the prosecution succeeded, could be easily marginalized so Burnside, and his office, could take all the glory.

Burnside was scribbling a shortlist of five names on his notepad as Steve finished his presentation. The DA looked up at Steve and, for a moment, pictured him in the Wal-Mart security guard uniform he'd be wearing when this trial, win or lose, was over.

"You make a good case, Detective," Burnside said, "Just not good enough."

"You don't think she's guilty?" Steve asked.

"It's not what I think, it's what I can prove," Burnside said. "Before I'll sign off on an arrest, why don't you spend a day or two proving she's innocent."

"I thought that was her defense attorney's job," Steve said.

"But if we travel the road first, we'll find the potholes in our case." Burnside smiled, pleased with his metaphor. He wrote it down on a notepad, beneath his shortlist of names. Someday, when he was Chief Justice of the U.S. Supreme Court, quotes like that from his early years in law would become priceless. He had boxes of papers in his garage full of just that sort of invaluable wisdom, waiting for his day to come. "Start by assuming she's right, that this double murder was a Mob hit."

"Do you know anybody who can open some doors for me with the FBI's organized crime unit?" Steve asked.

Burnside got another piece of notepaper, scrawled a name and a phone number, and handed it to Steve. "Special

Agent Larry Bedard, out in West LA. He's coordinating a joint Justice Department, FBI, LAPD passive surveillance operation, monitoring standing wiretaps on key organized-crime figures. Visit him. Maybe he's picked up some useful chatter."

Steve stuck the paper in his breast pocket and studied Burnside for a moment. He knew that Burnside wouldn't be risking his own political capital on this case. The trim, fit, purposely photogenic forty-one-year-old DA didn't try very hard to hide his aspirations to either a higher office or a higher court.

"Who'll be running point for you on this?" Steve asked.

Good question, Burnside thought, glancing again at his shortlist. He did a quick mental calculation of the pros and cons of each candidate, weighing the value they posed as friends and the risk they posed as enemies, before settling on the sacrificial lamb.

"Karen Cross," Burnside said. "A dogged prosecutor. She's perfect for this case."

Steve nodded and walked out, wondering what Karen Cross had done to deserve such a grim fate.

The Los Angeles field office of the Joint Organized Crime Task Force was a tiny room in the basement of the Federal Building, a white concrete monolith rising like a giant tombstone in a patch of dried grass at the junction of Wilshire Boulevard and the San Diego Freeway.

If the building was a tombstone, then the windowless pit Steve entered had to be the coffin. The room was lit with strips of fluorescent light that hummed and flickered, casting a sickly yellow glow over the gunmetal grey shelves that were crammed with CD-ROMs, audio tapes, videos, and bulging binders stuffed with papers. A single fan, placed on a stack of phone books, struggled to circulate the hot, heavy air, the dust and dirt clinging like algae to the metal mesh that enclosed the spinning blades.

In one corner of the room, Special Agent Larry Bedard sat in his shirt sleeves, facing three computer monitors, each showing an EKG-like graphic display of voices being recorded. Bedard looked like a garden gnome disguised as an FBI agent. He was a squat man with a big round face, big round eyes, and a big round body.

"Agent Bedard?" Steve asked.

Bedard spun around in his seat and smiled cheerfully at Steve.

"Detective Sloan, welcome! Welcome!" Bedard said, jumping out of his chair and waving Steve in. "Call me Larry. Sit down; make yourself comfortable."

Bedard motioned to the seat he'd just vacated. There were no other chairs in the room.

"That's okay," Steve said. "I've been stuck in traffic all morning. It's nice to be standing."

"Very well." Bedard plopped back down in his seat. "You must have powerful friends."

"Why do you say that?"

"This is a very hush-hush, vacuum-sealed operation," Bedard said. "You're the first visitor I've had down here in two years."

"What exactly are you doing down here, Larry?"

"Me personally?" Bedard asked, "Or are you asking about the investigative mandate of the JOCTF?"

"How about both?"

"We're maintaining standing remote audio and visual surveillance of key organized crime figures in specified locations within the boundaries set by warrants issued pursuant to several ongoing investigations." Bedard took a breath. "In other words, Steve, we've stuck a buttload of voice-activated listening devices and motion-sensitive hidden cameras in every place these goombahs hang out. We digitally record everything they say, transcribe and index the conversation, then stick the printouts in binders until the powers that be are ready to hand down indictments."

"And what do you do?"

"I'm the tech-head traffic cop," Bedard said. "I coordinate the recording operation. I can come and go as I please, dress the way I want, and nobody bugs me. No more sitting in some cramped surveillance van for days on end, eating fast food and pissing into a Porta-Potty. This is my domain."

Bedard held out his hands expansively, as if they were in

an opulent penthouse instead of an airless room three floors below the Federal Building.

"You've got it made," Steve said.

"I do indeed, Steve. Though, truth be told, I still use the Porta-Potty on occasion," Bedard said. "The heat in this room makes you drink a lot. It's six flights of stairs to the bathroom and all that stomping up steps on a full bladder really—"

"I get the picture," Steve interrupted. "Almost too well."

"I'm guessing you didn't come all the way down here just to admire what a sweet deal I've got going."

"I came to request the impossible," Steve said. "To be honest, I'm almost embarrassed to ask." Though after the Porta-Potty story Bedard just told, Steve wasn't too concerned about his own embarrassment any more.

"I'm looking for two names that might have come up in any of the thousands of conversations you've got here," Steve said. "I can't tell you who was involved in the conversations or when or where the conversations—if they even happened—took place."

"No problem," Bedard said.

"No problem?" Steve asked incredulously.

"Just give me the names."

"Lacey McClure and Cleve Kershaw," Steve said.

"Ah yes," Bedard said. "The movie star and the Mob groupie."

"You're familiar with them?"

"I do get out of this basement some times," Bedard said. "I do see her movies. I am a man."

"I never doubted it for a moment," Steve said. "Why did you call Kershaw a Mob groupie?"

"Kershaw grew up in New Jersey; he's really into the whole 'mobster chic' thing," Bedard said. "He loves to hang out any place you can find pasta and lots of guys wearing gold jewelry."

Bedard typed *Lacey McClure* and *Cleve Kershaw* into one of his computers. A new window opened in the middle of the digital recording display on one of the screens, and a list of names and dates scrolled by. One of the listings was highlighted.

"Here we go. Recorded, January 12, 11:38 P.M., Salvatore 'Daddy' Crofoot's Lincoln Town Car, cruising east on Sunset Boulevard out of Beverly Hills. Crofoot is present, so is Cleve Kershaw. Anthony 'Little Zam' Zambardi is driving," Bedard said. "Would you like a transcript?"

"If it's no trouble," Steve said, truly impressed. "This is an incredible operation."

"This is nothing. The National Security Agency monitors tens of thousands of telephone conversations and millions of e-mail transmissions," Bedard said. "When you read about the government picking up 'chatter' about possible terrorist attacks, where to you think they're picking it up from?"

"I never thought about that," Steve said.

"What we're doing here is rudimentary by comparison," Bedard said. "We're just trying to make our case."

"What is the case?"

"I can't say, Steve. But it's huge, it's nationwide, and it will eventually involve hundreds of indictments."

Bedard hit a key on his keyboard and pages began to spit out of the printer. "Anything else I can help you with? We can run the phrase *bada bing* and see how many times that comes up. Or *hooters*. That's always fun."

"What can you tell me about the guys on this recording? Aside from Kershaw, I'm not familiar with any of the players."

"Tony Zambardi is just a muscle head, a driver, forget about him. Salvatore Crofoot is a real character," Bedard said. "They call him Daddy because he's fathered so many illegitimate children. But he likes the nickname because it makes it seem to people who don't actually know his story that he's some kind of paternal figure in the Mob, a don or something. Fact is, he's got no power of his own, he's just a messenger between Hollywood and the guys back east."

"Is Hollywood that heavily tied to organized crime?"

Bedard shook his head. "They just like hanging out with each other. Goes all the way back to the Rat Pack days."

"So Kershaw and Crofoot weren't doing business together?"

"I didn't say that." Bedard handed Steve the printout. "Read for yourself while I knock off a copy of the tape for you."

# CHAPTER NINE

Recorded: January 12, 11:38 P.M.
Location: Salvatore "Daddy" Crofoot's Lincoln Town Car
Individuals Present: Salvatore "Daddy" Crofoot (DC), Cleve Kershaw (CK), Anthony "Little Zam" Zambardi (AZ)

DC: She told you she's not gonna make the picture?

CK: That's what she said, but she doesn't mean it.

DC: Is she doing the picture?

CK: I'm working on it.

DC: I don't like this, I don't like it at all. You know what I mean?

CK: I'm not happy about it either, Daddy. But that's the way it is.

DC: We're talking about a lot of money here, Cleve. I mean, I understand your situation, you know? We're friends. But this is business. And the guys in New Jersey, they might not be so sympathetic.

CK: Hey. C'mon. Don't get all worked up over this. It's a marriage thing. Haven't you ever had trouble with your wife?

DC: No.

CK: You must have had trouble with your wife. Everybody, sometimes, has trouble with their wives.

DC: There's trouble, and then there's three hundred grand. I've never had three hundred grand of trouble with anyone. Well, anyone who's still alive, that is.

AZ: Anybody want a Krispy Kreme? There's a Krispy Kreme coming up.

DC: It's a donut. Why would I stop for a donut?

AZ: It's a treat.

DC: It a friggin' donut. Keep driving.

AZ: They got the hot light on, Daddy. That means they're hot and fresh.

DC: Forget about the donuts. We aren't stopping for donuts.

AZ: They got a drive-thru. We can drive through.

DC: God damn it, Zam. I'm trying to do some business here.

CK: You didn't have to say that.

DC: Say what?

CK: You know what you said, that little throwaway comment you made about dealing with problems. I don't appreciate the implication.

DC: You'll appreciate the reality even less.

CK: I thought we were friends; friends don't threaten each other.

DC: You don't seem to get it, Cleve. This may be a little marriage problem to you, but it's a major cash-flow problem for us. We've come to rely over the years on this arrangement to free up certain funds. Commitments have been made elsewhere based on the assumption that our arrangement was solid. This has an undesirable ripple effect, up and down the line. It strains a friendship, you know?

CK: Look, Daddy, I think everybody needs to take a deep breath here. Everybody. Lacey is having a tantrum, that's all. She doesn't understand how the business works. She'll come around.

DC: You got to get stars insured, right? Before they do a picture? What kind of insurance payoff you get if she, you know, has an accident that lays her up for a while?

CK: There. That's exactly what I mean. That's not helpful, Daddy.

DC: It might help her come around.

CK: It's counterproductive. She can't work on crutches, can she? I've got leverage against her she doesn't know I have. I can bring her into line without putting her in a hospital bed.

DC: Then why the hell haven't you done it?

CK: She's my wife, first and foremost. I'm trying to save my marriage, Daddy. I was hoping to resolve this business misunderstanding without going nuclear.

DC: Yeah? My friendly advice to you is nuke the bitch before New Jersey decides to nuke you.

Mark set the transcript aside and glanced across the table at Steve, who wore a bib to protect his shirt as he finished up a plate of BBQ Bob's famous spareribs at their favorite corner booth. The lunch crowd was fairly light, giving the small restaurant's two young waitresses plenty of time to gossip behind the counter.

"Lacey was telling the truth about Cleve using her films to launder Mob money," Mark said. "This wiretap and the financial irregularities her forensic accountant discovered proves it."

"All it proves is that she had a strong motive to kill her husband," Steve said. "Besides the fact that he was sleeping with an aspiring actress in their bed."

"But this bolsters her claim that the Mob had reason to kill Cleve Kershaw," Mark said.

Steve licked the tangy sauce off his fingers and wiped his face with a moist towelette.

Mark didn't have to order the ribs to taste them. The restaurant had the permanent, woodsy smell of hickory smoke. The walls had absorbed the thirty years of barbeque that had come out of Bob's kitchen before he retired and sold out to Steve and Jesse.

"You don't believe her now, do you?" Steve asked.

"No, I don't. But whether she's guilty of murder or not, this recording is evidence of an ongoing conspiracy to commit extortion," Mark said. "If the FBI knew what was going on with Lacey's movies, why didn't they do something about it?"

"I asked the same question," Steve said, pushing his plate aside and yanking off his bib. "They are after bigger fish. They don't want to jeopardize their case, and expose the wiretaps, on a such a small-time operation."

"But the Mob could have been laundering millions of dollars through each movie," Mark said. "That's not counting the $300,000 'convenience fee' they were strong-arming out of Cleve. That's small-time?"

"The Feds have their priorities," Steve said. "I guess this money-laundering scam will come out with everything else when the rest of the indictments are handed down."

"But in the meantime, the extortion continued," Mark

said. "And two people got killed. It might not have happened if the FBI had acted on what they knew."

"I can't argue with you on that," Steve said. "But I do know those are the kinds of trade-offs you have to make when mounting a major undercover or surveillance operation. Do you act immediately on every crime you see, or wait until you have the evidence to make a more substantial arrest? It's a tough call."

"Did you get this transcript officially?" Mark asked.

"The DA called in a favor, and got me the transcript and a tape," Steve said. "If you're asking me whether we can use it in court, I'm guessing no, not unless the FBI is ready to reveal the existence of their massive covert wiretapping operation."

"So you can't use the wiretap as leverage against Daddy Crofoot to get him to talk."

"I'll just have to ask him nicely," Steve said.

Mark picked up the transcript again and flipped through it. "Cleve mentioned he had leverage against Lacey that she didn't know about. I'd sure like to find out what it was. That leverage may be what got him killed."

"Then she'd have *three* motives for murder. That might be a record." Steve's cell phone trilled. He unclipped the phone from his belt and flipped it open. "Sloan."

He listened for a moment, then met his father's eye. Mark could see from the expression on his son's face that it was important news.

"I'll be there in half an hour," Steve said, then listened to the response. "Okay. I'm at BBQ Bob's restaurant on the Westside. I'll stick around for dessert." Steve snapped the phone shut and looked at his Dad. "That was Lacey McClure. She wants to talk."

"She's coming *here*?"

"She's afraid if I show up at her place, the reporters camped outside will get the wrong idea," Steve said. "So I guess she isn't coming to confess."

"Isn't she afraid they'll follow her here?"

"She's got three cars," Steve said. "She and her staff are gonna drive all three out of her compound at once and go in three different directions. When the press goes off to follow them, she'll slip out the back on foot and borrow her neighbor's car."

"Very resourceful," Mark said. "She's given this some thought."

"She watches her own movies," Steve said. "Her security-consultant character ran the same scam in *Body Armor.*"

A half-hour later, a dark-haired woman wearing impenetrable sunglasses, an oversized, well-worn UCLA sweatshirt and faded blue jeans walked into BBQ Bob's carrying a heavy gym bag.

Mark was surprised just how effective a simple wig, a pair of sunglasses, and unremarkable clothes could be as a disguise. Anyone expecting to see Lacey McClure would have recognized her, but with the exception of Mark and Steve, no one eating in BBQ Bob's had that expectation. She came in unrecognized and strode directly to the booth in the back, where Mark and Steve were eating thick slices of pecan pie.

Mark slipped the wiretap transcript into his jacket pocket as she approached. Lacey dropped the gym bag on the floor at the edge of the table and slid into the booth beside him so she could face Steve.

"Care for a piece of pecan pie?" Mark asked. "It's quite good here."

"No thank you," Lacey McClure said.

"You'll regret it," Steve said. "This is the best grub in LA."

Lacey gave the restaurant a quick, appraising glance, taking in its scraped linoleum floor, cracked red-vinyl booths, red-and-white checked tablecloths, and vintage, rusted-tin soft drink placards nailed to the faded, paneled walls.

"You eat in this dump a lot?" she asked.

"I own this dump," Steve said. "Want to autograph an 8x10 for the wall? If you don't have one on you, maybe you can sign your mug shot for me later."

Lacey slid the gym bag over to Steve with her foot. "There's $300,000 in cash in that bag."

"Is that a bribe?" Steve asked.

"It's not for you," Lacey said. "Unless you were the man

who called me an hour ago on my private line, offering to sell me evidence that would keep me out of jail."

"It wasn't me," Steve said. "What kind of evidence did he say he had?"

"He didn't. All he told me was that it would cost $300,000," Lacey said. "That seems to be the going rate for a shakedown these days."

"So why not just pay him? Why come to me?"

"Because I don't pay extortion. That's why I left Cleve. This money is bait; I want it back," she said. "And if this guy really has evidence that clears me, I want it to go directly to the police so there's no question about where it came from."

"You had $300,000 in cash just lying around your house?" Mark asked.

"I toss my spare change in a jar every night," she said. "Don't you?"

"How many people have your private number?" Steve asked.

"Just my agent, my manager, and Cleve," she said. "Until today, nobody else ever called me on it."

Steve lifted up the bag and unzipped it just enough to peek inside. It was filled with neatly wrapped bundles of hundred-dollar bills. "Where and when is the meet?"

"The Santa Monica Pier." She glanced at her watch. "In forty minutes."

"That barely gives us time to get there," Steve said, "and no time to put a wire on you or mount a proper surveillance."

"He knew what he was doing," Mark said, then glanced at Lacey. "Is he expecting you to deliver the money yourself?"

She nodded. "He told me to wear this sweatshirt."

Mark frowned. "He knows your private number and that you own a UCLA sweatshirt? He's either someone close to you or he's been watching you for some time."

"I know," she said. "And it creeps me out."

"Let's move." Steve slid out of the booth and picked up the gym bag. "We'll figure out a plan on the way."

\* \* \*

Compared to the elaborate attractions at any of the half-dozen amusement parks in Southern California, the carnival rides at the Santa Monica Pier were about as exciting as the quarter-a-ride kiddie cars found outside of grocery stores, only twenty times more expensive.

The brightly painted midway with its arcade games and cotton candy and loud music tried to capture the energy of a county fair, but it was like trying to energize a decomposing corpse by slathering it with make-up and sticking a Gameboy in its mouth.

Instead of lovingly evoking a bygone era, the pier exuded desperation and decay, which was also an apt description of the thin, wiry man who approached Lacey McClure as she sat at a table in the food court, $300,000 in cash in the gym bag under her chair.

The man was unshaven, with long, greasy hair tied into a ponytail. It looked like a squirrel had crawled onto his head and died. He wore an untucked flannel shirt over baggy cargo pants and a crusty pair of Timberlands.

"You're Lacey McClure, aren't you?" the man said, his thin smile showing only a hint of his nicotine-stained teeth.

"Yes, I am," Lacey said.

"I love your movies," he said.

"How nice," she said. "Which one is your favorite?"

He reached into his shirt pocket, pulled out a Hi8 camcorder cassette, and tossed it on the table in front of her. "This one."

She stared at the tape as if it were a dead rat. "I can buy that for $29.95 on the Internet. What makes you think I'd pay you $300,000 for it?"

"It isn't that one," he said. "Think of this as an unauthorized sequel."

"How do I know I'm not buying a blank tape?"

He took a camcorder the size of a box of cigarettes out of his pocket, slipped the cassette into it, then placed it on the table, the tiny screen facing Lacey. What she saw made the color drain from her cheeks.

"You bastard," she hissed.

He grabbed the camcorder, ejected the tape, and handed

the cassette to her. "You got a funny way of saying thank you."

The man pocketed the camcorder, reached under Lacey's chair, and dragged out the gym bag. "But this will make up for it."

He unzipped the bag, glanced at the cash, then closed it again.

"Did you make any copies of that ugly little tape?" she asked.

The man only grinned, giving her a good look at his teeth this time, before turning his back on her and walking away.

That's when he saw Steve Sloan standing at the mouth of the food court, arms held loosely at his sides, staring at him with the flinty determination of a frontier marshal waiting to draw on a gunfighter.

The man turned around the way he came, realizing only then why Lacey McClure, who now had a smug smile on her face, had chosen that table. He was being herded into a bottleneck. The only other way out was a crowded, narrow pathway between the arcade games and the bumper cars.

But he had no choice. He weaved quickly among the tables toward the pathway, his eyes scanning the crowd ahead of him for adversaries.

He should have been looking at his feet.

Mark Sloan stuck out his leg as the man passed, sending the blackmailer tumbling to the ground. A ponytailed wig flew off the man's head into the bumper car arena, where it became roadkill.

Steve was on the man an instant later, yanking the black-mailer's arms behind his back and slapping on handcuffs before pulling him to his feet. The man's fake yellowed teeth were knocked loose, revealing the pearly whites hidden underneath.

"Nice move, Dad," Steve said to his father, who sat at one of the tables, casually enjoying a bag of popcorn.

"Sometimes the simplest methods are the best," Mark said with a smile, drawing his leg back under the table.

# CHAPTER TEN

Mark and Steve watched the video on a television set they wheeled into the captain's office. The man Steve apprehended at the pier sat in an adjoining interrogation room while Lacey McClure sat out in the squad room, giving her statement to a detective.

The video was taken outside the Slumberland Motel, a purple-painted cinderblock eyesore near the intersection of the Pacific Coast Highway and Kanan Dume Road. Mark and Steve had driven past it a thousand times and wondered how it had survived on such a valuable piece of "Malibu-adjacent" property. The Slumberland had always looked like the kind of place that had condom vending machines in the front office and vibrating beds in each room.

The date and time the video was shot was stamped in the corner of the screen. It was the day of the double murders. The time was 3:13 P.M.

Lacey McClure drove up in her vintage Mustang and parked beside a huge Cadillac Escalade in front of the last room at the far end of the low-lying, one-story building. The number on the room door was 16. She got out wearing the same tight black tank top and gray shorts she'd been wearing when Mark and Steve first met her. The only slight attempt she made to obscure her identity was a pair of dark sunglasses and a baseball cap.

There was an excited, girlish bounce to her step as she hurried to the room and knocked on the door. It was opened an instant later by a man in his late twenties with the chiseled, blow-dried good looks of an aftershave model.

The man swept Lacey up in his arms, lifting her off her feet as they embraced in a deep, passionate kiss. She wrapped her legs around him and they tumbled back into the room, the man closing the door with a swift kick.

There was a quick cut in the film, and then they saw the motel from a different angle. The cameraman was on a hillside at the end of the building, looking down on the back window of the last room on the end. The shades were half-drawn, leaving just enough of the window open to see Lacey, her naked back to the camera, straddling her lover on the bed and grinding rhythmically against him. When she bent over to kiss him, her body resembled the poised tail of the scorpion that was tattooed on her lower back.

The time was 3:47 P.M.

There was another cut, and then the motel room was seen from the front again, only from an angle that also showed the gas station across the Pacific Coast Highway and an LAPD patrol car speeding past, lights flashing.

Lacey emerged from the motel room, gave her lover a long, languorous kiss, then got into her car and drove off. The time stamp was 4:35.

The tape ended. Mark stared at the blank screen as if he still saw images flickering past. He was replaying the video again in his mind, time stamps and all. Steve studied the rigid expression on his father's face. It was an expression Steve had seen many times before. His father had become a guided missile locking on to its target. The only way to stop him now would be if he self-destructed.

"Now I *know* Lacey McClure killed Cleve Kershaw and Amy Butler," Mark said.

"Why are you so certain?"

"Because now confusing facts of the murder make perfect sense," Mark said. "It was all contrived to give her this airtight alibi."

"This video doesn't prove anything. Whoever made this could have stamped any time and date on there if he wanted," Steve said. "It could have been taken two days, two months, or two years ago."

Mark shook his head. "The time and date are accurate, I guarantee it. You'll be able to corroborate everything. I'd start by checking the number of the patrol car we saw going by. I'll bet it was the two officers responding to my 911 call."

"If you're right, and the time stamp on this video is accurate, then there's no way Lacey McClure could have fired the shots you heard," Steve said. "Or even the shots you *didn't* hear an hour earlier."

"That's why there's no question she did it."

Steve stared at his father. "I'm not sure that's the best argument to make in front of a jury, assuming this case ever gets that far."

"It will," Mark said, his eyes blazing with determination. "I'd like a copy of that tape."

"No problem," Steve said. "You think she arranged everything at the pier today to get this tape into our hands?"

"Not directly, but I'm sure she manipulated events to her advantage," Mark said. "Lacey McClure is very shrewd, Steve. It would be a big mistake for either one of us to underestimate her intelligence."

"Then let's start with Nick Stryker," Steve said. "Maybe we'll learn something from him that will help us crack her."

"Who's Nick Stryker?"

"The guy who supposedly tried to shake down Lacey at the pier with this video," Steve said, tossing an evidence Baggie onto the table containing Stryker's driver's license and other ID. "He's a licensed private detective."

"I should have guessed from the name," Mark said, examining the IDs.

"Maybe that's why he picked it," Steve said. "Somehow Zanley Rosencrantz doesn't evoke the same rugged image, does it?"

Nick Stryker looked a lot healthier without the wig and false teeth. His tall, lanky frame fit uneasily into the rigid metal chair he was sitting in, prompting him to shift constantly in a futile effort to get comfortable.

The fact was, nobody could get comfortable in the seat. It was designed that way. One leg was also shorter than the other, to keep whoever was sitting in the seat off balance throughout their interview.

The seat was also positioned so that Stryker was forced to look at his own reflection in the mirror, which hid observers on the other side. It had been crafted, like a funhouse mirror, to narrow and stretch his face, to make him appear to himself as weak and sickly.

Changing his seat to one of the two across from him wasn't an option. He was handcuffed to the armrest.

Steve came in alone, careful to take a seat that wouldn't obscure Mark's view of Stryker from the observation room.

"How you doing, Zanley?" Steve asked.

"The name is Stryker, Nick Stryker. And I don't appreciate being handcuffed to this chair."

"Lacey McClure doesn't appreciate being blackmailed," Steve said.

Stryker snorted with derision. "Blackmail is the extortion of money or something of value from a person by threatening to expose embarrassing information or criminal acts. I didn't make any threats. Therefore, I didn't commit blackmail. Therefore, you got nothing on me."

"Then what would you call demanding $300,000 in cash for that video?"

"A bargain price," Stryker said. "I could have sold it to the tabloids for twice as much. But I felt I owed her first crack at it."

"Why's that?"

"Out of respect for Cleve. He was the one who hired me to follow her. He suspected she was having an affair. Ironic, huh?" Stryker said. "Cleve is banging some bimbo and he's worried his wife isn't being faithful."

"I thought they were separated."

"If they were, why would he care who she was boinking?"

"They weren't living apart?"

"He went home every night," Stryker said. "And so did she, except when she was shooting a movie someplace else."

"So how is it you're respecting Cleve Kershaw by selling Lacey the video you made of her cheating on him?"

"She's his next of kin," Stryker said. "I'm making sure

the dirty laundry I found for him is staying in his family. I'm being discreet, ergo, respectful."

"As long as you're being so respectful, why not just give the tape to her?"

"There's a matter of my fee," Stryker said. "Cleve got killed before he could pay me. I incurred expenses."

"Three hundred thousand dollars' worth?"

"You keep talking like I did something wrong," Stryker said. "I conducted an investigation and uncovered information that was of value. I'm exchanging it for something of equal or greater value. That's business."

"If this was all so innocent, why were you wearing the Halloween costume?"

"I'm known as a master of disguise," he said.

"You aren't known at all, Zanley."

"Not outside the trade, so to speak. To the criminal element, and the general public, I'm invisible. It's why I'm so good. So obviously, I didn't want her to know who I was," Stryker said. "I felt if she knew my identity, it might compromise my future investigations."

"There won't be any future investigations," Steve said. "Your license is being shredded, ergo, you're out of business."

"C'mon, Lieutenant, let's be reasonable," Stryker said. "You see me lawyering up? No. Why's that? Because I want to be cooperative with my colleagues in law enforcement. You tell me what I need to do to keep this amicable between us and I'll do it."

"You can start by giving me a full, signed statement repeating everything you told me today. Then I want all the material you gathered during your investigation for Cleve. Videos, photos, reports, invoices, the works," Steve said. "Then, maybe, we'll talk again about your license."

Steve got up and walked out.

"Hey," Stryker called after him, "What about these handcuffs?"

Steve closed the door, pretending not to hear him, and went into the observation room, where Mark was watching the private eye stew.

"What do you think?" Steve asked.

"It explains how he got Lacey's private number and how he knew she had that sweatshirt."

"Do you believe Cleve hired him?"

Mark nodded. "I also believe Lacey knew she was being watched and used it to her advantage. Proving it is going to be another matter."

"Ready to talk to her?" Steve asked.

"Not as ready as she is to talk to us," Mark said, frowning. "Lacey is still directing this show. We're simply actors in her movie, following a script she wrote a long time ago."

"At least now we know it," Steve said, opening the door and leading Mark into the squad room, where Lacey was sitting at his desk, pretending not to notice the sideways stares she was getting from starstruck detectives.

Steve took a seat at his desk and made a show of going over her signed statement. Mark pulled a chair over and sat next to Lacey.

"Why didn't you tell us you had an alibi?" Mark asked. "It would have saved us all a lot of trouble."

"I wasn't interested in your trouble or mine," Lacey said. "My concern was sparing Titus a lot of unnecessary embarrassment and attention."

"Titus?" Steve asked. "I take it he's the boy toy in the motel."

Lacey gave Steve a cold look. "It's that kind of attitude that kept me from telling the truth. I wanted to keep his name out of this. He shouldn't have to lose his privacy, and become the butt of jokes, because he made the mistake of loving me."

Steve winced. "That's worse than the dialogue in one of your movies—not that anyone actually cares what's being said."

"Titus Carville," Lacey said.

"Who started cheating on whom first?" Mark asked. "You or Cleve?"

"We were separated, Dr. Sloan," Lacey said. "But we still had needs."

Steve looked at her skeptically. "Your husband didn't tell Nick Stryker you were separated."

"Who's he?" she asked.

"The guy who tried to shake you down today," Steve said. "He's a private eye your husband hired to find out if you were cheating on him with some boy toy with a ridiculous name like Brock or Thor or Titus."

"I told you, we were keeping our separation a secret until the movie came out," she said. "It's probably the same reason he didn't tell this so-called private eye."

"So why did Cleve care who you were sleeping with?"

"I don't know," Lacey said.

"We're going to have to talk to Titus," Steve said. "I'll need his address and phone number."

He passed her a paper and pencil. While she wrote out the information, she said, "Do you really have to involve Titus in all this, or are you just doing it out of prurient interest?"

"My prurient interests were satisfied by that tape," Steve said.

Mark knew his son was being purposely offensive to spark a revealing reaction from Lacey. But she wasn't taking the bait.

"If that's what you get off on, I've shown more and done more in my movies. I'm sure the camera work and lighting are better, too." She rose from her seat. "I trust you'll make sure I don't see that tape on TV tonight or the Internet tomorrow?"

"You won't see this one," Steve said, patting his breast pocket. "But I don't know how many copies Stryker made. And let's face it, Lacey, the man is pissed off after what you did to him today. There's no telling what he might do to get back at you and make a little money."

"You could stop him," she said.

Steve shrugged.

Lacey gave Steve a long look. "I can see you're going to make this difficult."

"As difficult as I can," Steve said.

"Even though that tape proves I'm innocent," she said.

"Does it?" he replied.

"It's a good thing you have that restaurant, Detective," she said. "At least you'll still have one job when this is over. Now where can I find my bag of spare change?"

# CHAPTER ELEVEN

"What they had wasn't a marriage," Titus Carville said, dabbing the sweat off his face with a towel. "It was a business relationship masquerading as love. It was never really love. What we have, *that's* true love."

Titus was shirtless and sweaty. He'd been working out with his weight set in the living room of his Venice bungalow when Mark and Steve arrived. Even though Lacey had called ahead to warn him they were coming, he apparently didn't see any reason to interrupt his workout and get dressed.

"Oh yeah, that's what people go to the Slumberland Motel for," Steve said. "True love."

"You don't think Lacey and Cleve ever loved each other?" Mark asked Titus.

"I think they loved what they could *do* for each other. I think they loved the success they were having," Titus said. "But that was as far as the love went."

"Is that what she told you?" Mark said.

"She didn't have to," Titus said. "Anybody could see it if they spent any real time with them."

"And you spent real time with them?" Steve asked, throwing a casual glance over at his father. With that look, Steve conveyed a message. He'd keep asking questions and occupying Titus' attention, freeing Mark to roam around largely unobserved, gathering whatever clues he could.

"Cleve hired me as her personal trainer," Titus said, tossing the towel aside and moving to his treadmill. "Then my job naturally evolved into being her personal assistant, too."

"Naturally," Steve said.

"I saw how they talked, how they looked at each other, how they touched. I could see there was no love between them," Titus said. "It was obvious."

"But not to Lacey."

Titus turned on the treadmill, set the program, and started running.

"She came to realize it through my little acts of devotion," Titus said, a comment that gave Steve an unsettling feeling in the pit of his stomach. This guy was sounding more and more like a stalker with every word.

Mark felt the same uneasiness, only much more acutely. At the moment Titus made that comment, Mark stepped into what he thought, at first, was a teenage boy's bedroom. A teenage boy with a healthy, adolescent interest in scantily clad women. But all the posters and pictures on the wall were of just one scantily clad woman: Lacey McClure. There were filing cabinets, stacks of DVDs and videos of Lacey's movies, pile of scripts, and desktop computer with a large monitor with bikini-clad Lacey McClure as a screen saver.

"I made sure she got her Glacier Peak water, her 600-thread-count sheets, her special vitamins, her ChapStick—whatever she needed or wanted, before she knew she needed or wanted it," Titus said, as the treadmill slowly sped up. "I managed her needs because I cared about her needs. Not as a job, as a calling, the way it should be when you're in love."

Mark tapped the space bar on the computer. The screen saver blinked off and the "Official Lacey McClure Home Page" appeared, framed within a window of a website-administration program. Titus apparently was her webmaster, as well.

"Don't take this the wrong way," Steve said, moving in front of the treadmill. "But you sound like one of those obsessed, lunatic stalkers, the kind of whackos who camp outside a star's house hoping to get a glimpse of them, or, failing that, steal a whiff of their garbage."

Mark smiled when he heard that. Steve often said what others only thought, and it frequently got him in trouble. But it was also a good technique for unnerving witnesses and suspects.

"I won't take offense at that," Titus said, "because it's a very thin line between devotion to someone you love and obsession. I've seen her stalkers. I've talked to them. And, in a few cases, I've had to hurt them."

"So you're also her personal bodyguard?"

"I'm everything to her I can be," Titus said, beginning to breathe hard now, the treadmill simulating a steep hill. "I run her website, answer her fan mail, and coordinate her personal appearances."

"Like the one she made at the Slumberland Motel?" Steve asked.

"That's a cheap shot," Titus said.

"It's a cheap motel," Steve said.

Titus' bedroom was spare, but neat, lit with pinpoint halogen lights, his clothes crisply folded on open shelves, almost as decoration. The bed minimalist, merely a mattress on a box spring, no headboard, runners, or footboard. Mark untucked a corner of the bed and ran the edge of the top sheet between his fingers.

"The paparazzi watch the big, five-star hotels, waiting to see stars. They don't wait outside places like the Slumberland," Titus said. "Lacey wanted to keep her marital problems quiet until her new movie was out for a while; that's why we were there."

"You could have gone to her house," Steve said.

"There are paparazzi camped outside there, too," Titus said.

"What's the big deal?" Steve asked. "You're her personal trainer and personal assistant, wouldn't you be expected to come and go?"

"She also has a cook, a housekeeper, a gardener . . . Where do you think the rags get all their information? We were being discreet."

"Not discreet enough," Steve said.

Mark stepped into the hallway and opened the linen closet. There were some towels, an extra blanket, and two extra sets of sheets. He felt those, too.

"How long have you and Lacey been lovers?" Steve asked.

"A few weeks. But we didn't consummate our love until she and Cleve were separated, if that's what you're asking," Titus said, struggling up the imaginary hill his treadmill was simulating. "This isn't a sleazy affair. Lacey is as devoted to me as I am to her."

"Is she fetching your water now and counting the threads in your sheets?"

"She wants me to take over as her manager and producer. She knows I won't betray her the way Cleve did. I'm doing this for love, not money."

"Uh-huh," Steve said. "So let me see if I've got this straight. Cleve was only in it for the bucks. And Lacey, she got swept up in her own success and went along for the ride. What you and Lacey have, that's true love. You take care of everything for her out of genuine devotion."

"Is that so hard to understand?" Titus asked.

"No, I think I understand," Steve said. "You insinuated yourself into Lacey's life and seduced her. Now, with Cleve dead, you get his woman and his job. Sounds to me like a motive for murder."

Titus was huffing now, hands on the rails of his treadmill. "I suppose it's a good thing I have an alibi."

"Same one as Lacey's, as a matter of fact," Steve said, as his father returned to the living room. "Funny how that worked out. Whose idea was it to go to the Slumberland Motel that day?"

"Mine," Titus said. "I think it's kitschy."

"That's one word for it," Steve said. "Who picked the time?"

"The production coordinator of her movie," Titus said. "Lacey's a slave to the production schedule. We get together whenever Lacey can spare the time."

"Did you know you were being watched by a private eye?" Mark asked.

Titus turned, a bit startled. Apparently he'd forgotten Mark was even in the house.

"Of course not," Titus said. "The whole idea was to avoid being seen."

"I suppose so," Mark nodded. "Did Lacey know her husband was having an affair, too?"

"I don't know," Titus said. "I doubt she would have cared, anyway."

Mark stepped beside the treadmill and looked at the console's elaborate graphic display of Titus' recent ascent.

"Look like you've reached the top of a pretty steep mountain here," Mark observed.

"It was a hard, fast climb," Titus said.

"Well, now that you're there, I'd be careful if I were you," Mark said with a friendly smile. "You don't want to fall off a cliff."

They were leaving Titus Carville's house and walking back to the car when Steve asked Mark if he'd found anything interesting in his search.

"It's what I didn't find that was interesting," Mark said. "He had ordinary sheets on the bed, nothing approaching 600 threads. The sheets in his linen closet weren't any fancier."

"I guess she never slept at his place," Steve said. "Or they never used the bed."

"Makes me wonder," Mark said. "How many threads do you suppose the sheets at the Slumberland Motel have?"

"However many they have on a piece of canvas," Steve said, walking around to the driver's side of the car and unlocking the door.

"I'm asking myself why someone so sensitive would let her bare skin touch those sheets."

"True love conquers all?" Steve said, then saw the skeptical look on his father's face. "Okay, maybe Titus brought some sheets with him."

"If he did," Mark said, opening his car door. "Where are they now?"

"He's either got them hermetically sealed and is keeping them as sacred heirlooms," Steve said, getting into the car, "or he's selling them on eBay."

Steve drove back to BBQ Bob's so Mark could retrieve his Saab convertible and return to work at Community General, where the doctor hoped his afternoon-long lunch had gone unnoticed by Noah Dent, the new hospital administrator.

This was the first Steve had heard about Dent. From what Mark told him, Steve was pretty sure the administrator knew how long his father was gone to the minute, if not the second. Dent sounded like another adversary Mark would do best not to underestimate.

Steve went from BBQ Bob's to Nick Stryker's office in West Los Angeles, a second-floor storefront above a corner mini-mall. He arrived just as the private eye—his wig and false teeth in a paper bag—was unlocking the iron security gate over his door.

"Hope I'm not catching you at a bad time," Steve said. "But you were on my way back to the station."

"I suppose you've come for stuff you asked for," he replied irritably.

Stryker unlocked the door and motioned Steve inside. It was a five-hundred-square-foot, one-room office dominated by a woodoleum-veneered office desk covered with papers, two guest chairs, and an overpadded leatherette couch. One wall was lined with file cabinets of different sizes and colors, obviously bought individually as the need for storage space arose. There were thick, metal straps across each row of drawers, the straps locked in place with fat padlocks.

"Very classy," Steve commented. "So when a client comes in, do you offer them coffee, or do you run downstairs to the 7-Eleven and spring for a Big Gulp?"

"My clients don't come to the office," Stryker said. "My office is the streets. I go to them. This is a home base for me, that's all, a place to store my files and hang my hat."

"Don't you mean your wig?" Steve said, motioning to the Baggie. "I wouldn't want to meet the poor dog you took that from."

"Did you come here to ridicule me, Steve, or are we going to do some business?"

"What happened to all that friendly cooperation you were promising me back at the station?"

"I don't think you appreciate just how cooperative I'm being." Stryker took a seat behind his desk. "Giving you my files on an investigation I conducted for a client violates the sanctity and privacy of our relationship. My business is built on discretion. If word got out about this, my career as a private investigator would be over."

"Look on the bright side: without a license your career as a private eye will be over anyway," Steve said. "It's your choice, Zanley."

"It's *Stryker,* Nick Stryker," he said, glaring at Steve as he unlocked his desk and pulled out a huge key ring. "You don't need to be demeaning. We're both professionals here, doing our jobs. It doesn't have to be personal."

Steve didn't see how Stryker's attempted shakedown of Lacey McClure qualified as professional conduct, and doubted the licensing board would see it that way, either, but he decided not to provoke the guy any more than he already had.

"You're awfully touchy for a hard-boiled detective," Steve said.

Stryker found the key he was looking for and unlocked one of the file cabinets. He slid open a drawer, pulled out a stack of files, and passed the pile to Steve. "That's everything."

"You want a receipt?" Steve asked.

"I'll settle for my license," Stryker replied.

"I'll get back to you about that," Steve said. "You going to be around if I have any questions?"

"Just look over your shoulder," Stryker said. "That's where I'll be. That's my motto."

"Catchy," Steve said, and walked out.

# CHAPTER TWELVE

The press conference outside the gates of Lacey McClure's Mandeville Canyon compound was timed to coincide with the evening news so it would be carried live on all the local stations, turning it into an event rather than a mere sound bite.

The movie star stood in front of the cameras, her publicist, Randi Lofficier, at her side, to make a major announcement involving the murder of her estranged husband and his lover. Lacey began by saying that she and Cleve were separated, and that the public deserved to know the reasons why.

Her jaw trembling with emotion, Lacey revealed that Cleve secretly used her films to launder Mob money and that once she found out about it, she threw him out of her house and her life.

Lacey's revelations sparked a flood of questions, prompting her publicist to step forward like a grade-school teacher about to admonish her unruly class.

"As you can see, this is a harrowing ordeal for Lacey," Randi said, the flashbulbs and camera lights glinting off her heavy charm bracelets. "It's hard enough for her to stand here, facing the entire world, and talk about painfully intimate details of her marriage. If you'd like her to continue, you'll have to show some basic human decency by not pestering her with questions."

Randi gave them one more chastising look, wagged a heavily ringed finger at them as a warning, then stepped back so Lacey could resume her remarks.

Lacey cleared her throat and continued, expressing the

shame and the horror she felt when she discovered that her movies had been used to enrich the bank accounts of the same "criminal scum" she fought on-screen.

She extended her heartfelt sympathies to the family of poor Amy Butler, an innocent victim caught up in this "senseless act of Mob violence," and promised to work closely with authorities to bring the killers to justice.

Lacey put special emphasis on the word *justice*—the same emphasis she'd used to such dramatic effect in the thirty-two different takes of the action scene she filmed the previous night.

And then Lacey looked into the camera, her eyes ablaze with righteous fury, and made a vow. She would find the cowardly bastards who killed Cleve Kershaw and Amy Butler. There was no where on earth the killers could hide. And if the Mob didn't like it, she dared them to come after *her* this time.

After the press conference, nearly all of the stations took a commercial break. And in most cases, the first commercial up just happened to be for *Thrill Kill,* the soon-to-be-released movie starring Lacey McClure as a woman who singled-handedly takes on organized crime in a city gripped by terror.

"What an amazing coincidence," Jesse noted, watching the broadcast in the Community General doctors' lounge, where he sat at a table with Susan. "It's disgusting how she's turned her husband's murder into the promotional campaign for her movie."

"I thought she was the woman of your dreams," Susan said.

"But you're my dream come true," Jesse said, switching off the TV with the remote.

Susan gave him a smile. "Nice save."

"I thought so," Jesse said and gave her a kiss. Over her shoulder, he could see Noah Dent just outside the door, about to come in. "Uh-oh."

Jesse straighten up in his seat. Susan turned to see what he was looking at just as Dent opened the door.

"Good evening, Doctor," Dent said. "Nurse Hilliard. Enjoying a little break?"

"We *were*," Jesse said pointedly.

Dent went to the coffee pot and poured himself a cup. "It's fortunate that you've both found some time to relax. Funny, I don't see any other doctors in here. They must be busy."

"They must be," Jesse said.

"It's odd how there's enough work to keep them busy, and not quite enough for you two," Dent said. "Maybe it means we're overstaffed."

"Or it means that after eight solid hours of trauma cases in the ER, things have finally slowed down for a minute so we can catch our breath," Jesse said. "You ought to get out of your office once in a while, and see how hard the doctors and nurses are working around here."

"The strange thing is, whenever I do get out of my office, I see the two of you in the pathology lab or in the doctors' lounge. I guess it's just a coincidence," Dent said. "Speaking of my office, I have to get back. I'm wrestling the budget into line. I'm afraid it looks like there may have to be some layoffs. But don't spread that around. I wouldn't want people to start getting nervous."

Dent smiled and walked out, Jesse and Susan staring after him.

"If he had a mustache, he would have been twirling it," Susan said. "Why does he hate us so much?"

"It's not us he hates," Jesse said. "It's Mark. It's been like this with every new administrator."

"Not like this," Susan said. "No one ever came after us before."

The more Jesse thought about it, the more he realized Susan was right. Why *did* Dent hate Mark so much?

Steve was at his desk at the police station, sorting through Stryker's files, when the press conference aired. The only time he'd seen so many officers and detectives gathered around the TV was to hear the O. J. verdict come down.

But he was only half-listening to the TV; most of his attention was on the files in front of him. Stryker was a sleaze-bag but he kept surprisingly detailed records. Among the papers was an investigative contract, signed by Cleve Kershaw, and a photocopy of a $5,000 retainer check, apparently drawn from Kershaw's private account.

When the press conference was over, Steve called Special Agent Bedard and asked him if he could monitor the "Mob chatter" for mentions of Lacey McClure. He also asked if Bedard knew where Steve could find Daddy Crofoot.

Bedard said Crofoot liked to eat at Filippo's Restaurant in Westlake, but that the wiretaps hadn't picked him up in a few weeks. Perhaps he was back east, Bedard suggested, meeting with his masters. Steve asked if Bedard could check into it for him.

"I don't work for you," Bedard said. "You do realize that, don't you?"

"Maybe I can do a favor for you someday," Steve said.

"How about getting me Lacey McClure's autograph?" said Bedard, laughing as he hung up.

Steve set the telephone receiver back in its cradle just as a woman marched up to his desk. She was an exceedingly thin mix of Asian and Caucasian background wearing a sheer blouse that only underscored her frailty. But there was a hardness to her expression that conveyed a toughness and strength in sharp contrast to her physical appearance.

"Have you proved Lacey McClure innocent yet?" she asked, her lips barely edging into a smile.

"You must be Karen Cross," Steve said, rising from his desk and offering his hand.

"What gave me away?"

"I figured Burnside must have asked you to go looking for potholes on the road to justice, too," Steve said, careful not to squeeze her hand too hard as he shook it, which made him all the more surprised by how firm her grip was.

"He used the same metaphor on me," she said, "but I don't think the road led anywhere when I heard it."

"I'm embellishing," Steve said, sitting back down and offering her the guest chair usually occupied by suspects—the only guests he ever had. "You're not what I was expecting."

"With a name like Cross, you were expecting to see an

all-American girl," she said, taking a seat. "Not a white woman with an Asian face and delicate features."

"I was expecting a hard-charging, ambitious, politically ruthless prosecutor with a take-no-prisoners attitude."

"What makes you think I'm not?" Karen asked.

"I'm a crack detective, for one thing. For another, the woman I imagined wouldn't refer to her features as delicate."

"I wouldn't have referred to my features at all if you hadn't jumped to conclusions about my character."

Steve smiled. "Now you sound like a lawyer. We've only been talking two minutes and you've tripped up my testimony."

"I wouldn't criticize lawyers if I were you," Karen said. "You studied law for a while."

"Half-heartedly. I went to night school, but I gave it up after a few months," Steve said. "As you know."

"Why?"

"Because you insist on knowing everything about the cops who gather the evidence that your prosecutions depend on," Steve said. "You wouldn't want another Mark Fuhrman on your hands."

"I meant why did you quit studying law?" she said, knowing full well that he knew what she meant the first time.

"That wasn't in whatever file Burnside put together on me?"

"Nope."

"Then I think I'll keep it to myself," Steve said.

"Why?"

"I'd like to maintain a little mystery to my character. It makes me harder to resist," he said. "You sure like to ask 'why' a lot."

"It's how I got into this profession," Karen said. "And it's the reason I'm stuck with this case. I ask Burnside 'why' too often for his comfort, and if he doesn't give me the answers, I go out and find them. I prosecute cases for justice, not politics. He's not quite as discerning."

"How do you feel about this case?"

"I feel two people were murdered and whoever did it has

to be prosecuted to the fullest extent of the law," she said. "I don't particularly care about the politics."

"Even if trying the case means you might lose your job?"

"Cases like this *are* my job," she said. "I don't think about anything beyond the verdict."

Steve grinned. "I can see why he assigned you to this. If you stay on his staff, he may never get elected or appointed to whatever the hell it is he wants to get elected or appointed to."

"So back to my original question, Detective," Karen said. "Have you proved Lacey McClure innocent yet?"

"I don't have to—she's doing a pretty good job of that herself," Steve said, then filled Karen Cross in on his version of everything that had happened since the bodies were found, putting special emphasis on the discrepancy between the time of death and when the gunshots were reported.

He detailed Lacey's three viable motives for murder: her husband's affair, her husband's money laundering, and whatever leverage her husband had to force her to cooperate with his financial schemes.

It was that final motive that led Steve to bring up the wiretapped conversation, where the leverage was first mentioned, and the forensic accountant's report, all of which supported Lacey's charge that the Mob was responsible for the murders.

"You have any working theories about what really happened?"

"It's elaborate, and a little difficult to follow," Steve said.

"Try me."

"She did it," Steve said.

"That's your theory?"

"Uh-huh," he replied.

"What about her airtight alibi?" Karen said.

"That's the part that makes my theory elaborate and difficult to follow."

"I see," she said. "Has it occurred to you that the Mob might actually be responsible?"

"Nope."

"Even though all the evidence points that way."

Steve nodded. Karen took a deep breath and let it out slowly before she spoke again.

"You think Lacey is guilty because she has a perfect alibi and you think the Mob isn't involved because there's so much evidence of their involvement."

"That pretty much sums up my investigative approach," Steve said. "Can I arrest her now?"

"Oh boy," Karen said, rising from her seat. "This is going to be quite a ride."

# CHAPTER THIRTEEN

Steve came home at midnight to find his father sitting in front of the TV, watching Stryker's video for what was probably the fiftieth time. Steve would have been shocked if Mark had been doing anything else. The video was not only the strongest piece of evidence of Lacey's innocence, it was, at least in his father's mind, absolute proof that she was guilty. And Steve knew his father would keep watching the video until he could find the fault in it.

Unfortunately, there wasn't one.

"There's something wrong with this tape," Mark said, as if reading his son's mind. "I just can't see it."

"If it's any consolation to you, neither could the experts in the crime lab," Steve said. "I was convinced the video had to have been digitally altered in some way. But it checks out. What you see is real."

"Were you able to confirm when it was shot?"

"You were right. The police car in the background was responding to your 911 call," Steve said. "I had some experts check out the weather, the position of the sun, and the angle of the light in the earlier scenes. It's all consistent with the day and hour the film was shot. The time and date stamps are accurate."

"I knew they would be." Mark shut off the television and went out on the deck to get some air. Steve followed him out.

The moon was bright enough so they could see the waves crashing against the shore, and the light breeze off the water brushed their faces with sea mist.

"You okay, Dad?"

"I feel like we're seeing this case from a forced perspective," Mark said. "One meticulously designed by Lacey McClure."

"Forced perspective?" Steve said. "Like the little cardboard airplane and the midgets they used at the end of *Casablanca* to make the plane in the background look far away when, in fact, it was right behind Bogart?"

"Exactly—but the illusion isn't just used in movies, but in architecture as well," Mark said. "The ancient Greeks made the columns of their buildings slightly smaller at the top to create the illusion of greater height. In Disneyland, Main Street USA is designed to look longer as you enter the park, so you'll hurry in, and shorter as you exit, so you'll linger as you leave. In order for the illusion to work, you have to control how your audience views the environment. Lacey McClure has done an expert job of that on us and I don't like it."

"She didn't figure that the person who found the bodies would be a doctor, or would be clever enough to determine the actual time of death."

"But it hasn't broken the forced perspective," Mark said. "We all still see a distant door at the end of a long hallway, instead of realizing it's actually a tiny door at the end of a very short hallway."

Steve just looked at him. "What door?"

"In other words," Mark said, "she's still getting away with two murders, unless you've uncovered a mistake I don't know about."

"I wish I could say that I have. I've gone through Stryker's files, receipts, and reports," Steve said. "His story checks out. Stryker followed Lacey for a few weeks. He got a lot of shots of her with Titus, but nothing incriminating until their rendezvous at the Slumberland Motel."

"Unfortunately, that's not quite as incriminating as we would like," Mark said. "So what's your next step?"

"In light of Lacey's perfect alibi, and pressure from the media, the incredibly attractive ADA wants me to concentrate on the Mob angle. I'd like to talk to Daddy Crofoot,"

Steve said. "Though I suspect that after that press conference today, he's going to be a hard man to find."

"You'll find him," Mark said. "He just might not be breathing anymore when you do."

"That would work out well for Lacey, wouldn't it?" Steve said.

"Why do you think she held the press conference?"

Steve studied his father, though it was hard to read his face in the moonlight. "You're not usually this cynical."

"I'm being pragmatic." Mark stared out at the surf. "Lacey McClure knows exactly what she's doing. We're the ones who are lost."

Mark couldn't sleep, tossing and turning, unable to get comfortable. After a few hours, he got up and went to the couch, where he sat in his bathrobe, staring at the dark screen of the TV. He didn't have to turn it on to watch the video again. Stryker's tape was on a feedback loop in Mark's mind, replaying over and over.

It was getting him nowhere, and since he knew sleep was hopeless, he decided to watch another one of Lacey's movies. He decreased the volume to a low hum and watched *Sting of the Scorpion,* with Lacey McClure as an exotic dancer, known as the Scorpion because of the distinctive tattoo on her back. In addition, she's a masked vigilante, also known as the Scorpion, who goes after sexual predators and kills them, usually after luring them into bed first. Despite the fact that the mysterious avenger and the stripper shared the same name, and moved in the same underworld of the sex trade, none of the cops or bad guys in the movie ever made the connection.

Mark finished the movie feeling pretty stupid himself, wondering if there was an obvious connection he wasn't making. He sat in the shadows, wondering. And wondering. The house was very still. The rhythmic crashing of the surf was like the tick of a clock, measuring the slow passing of the hours until morning.

At the first hint of sunrise, Mark showered, dressed, and made a quick breakfast for himself and Steve. They ate in silence, Mark avoiding the newspaper. He didn't need to read any more about Lacey McClure and be reminded that she was not only orchestrating how the investigation unfolded, but was setting the agenda for the media coverage, as well.

Once again, he thought about forced perspective and wished he could figure out how to break Lacey's hold on how he was seeing the case.

He went to the hospital for a few hours, but found himself too tired and distracted to work. He canceled all his appointments, rescheduled his meetings, and went home, claiming to be sick. It wasn't entirely untrue. He was suffering from a troubling affliction—a mystery he couldn't solve.

On his way out, Mark passed Noah Dent, who glared disapprovingly at him.

"Another early day, Dr. Sloan?" Dent asked.

Mark pretended not to hear him and continued on to the parking lot.

The drive home from Community General took him west, through Santa Monica, and then north, up along the Pacific Coast Highway and past the Slumberland Motel. Somehow, on his way to the hospital that morning, the motel had just dissolved into the blur as he drove, and he hadn't even noticed it. But now, stopped at the red light at Kanan Dume Road, he couldn't avoid it.

The Slumberland Motel rested on a narrow shelf carved out of a hillside, tucked into the shadows, and out of view, of the sprawling mansions set back on the hilltop above. Below the motel, just over the edge of its cracked blacktop parking lot, was a deep ravine blanketed with iceplants, clogged with overgrown plumbago bushes, and littered with fast-food garbage tossed from passing cars.

It was hardly a location that inspired romance. But as Mark knew from personal experience, it was a place that people passed without really seeing, which made it a good spot for illicit trysts.

He parked his car across from the last room at the end of the building, looking over his shoulder and backing his car up carefully so he didn't tumble into the ravine. When he turned around and faced forward again, he saw room 16 from roughly the same perspective that Stryker's camera had.

Mark got out of the car and walked to the edge of the parking lot, overlooking the ravine. He could see where Stryker had probably crouched, behind the flowering plumbagos, to get his view of the room. There were several soft-drink cans and potato-chip bags discarded in the brush. If it wasn't Stryker's trash, Mark figured it belonged to some other spy hoping to photograph a lover's betrayal. It was a comfortable hiding place that offered good cover and a clear view of most of the motel. There was even a rough trail through the brush, leading around to the back of the building.

He followed the trail, moving carefully so as not to get too scratched up. The trail ended on a slight rise behind a fenced-in enclosure for the trash bins. From there, Mark could see down into the window of the last room, where the blinds were still only half-closed.

The room was empty, so Mark could keep studying the view without feeling like a Peeping Tom. He noticed that the window frame and the bottom of the blinds created a frame of their own, limiting how much of the room he could see. All he could see was the bed from above and a section of the carpet between the bed and the window. Everything else was blocked by the blinds. He didn't know if that was significant or not, but anything that hinted at a forced perspective nagged at him now. The half-closed blinds didn't change what the camera saw, but it did limit what the camera *could* see.

Mark stepped out from behind the trash area and went down to the motel-room window, peering in from up close. He saw a sagging bed with a thin, flowered bedspread with a busy pattern meant to camouflage stains. The pattern wasn't busy enough. The carpet was a faded red with the thick, luxurious pile of a napkin. There was a single vinyl armchair, a bathroom, closet, and a door to the adjoining room. If Stryker had been standing right outside the window with his camcorder, Mark wasn't sure it would have changed anything.

He went around to the front of the motel and walked the

length of the purple building toward the office at the far end. Along the way, he could hear the urgent, labored moans of people and bedsprings behind the closed doors and drawn blinds.

The office reminded Mark of the waiting area at an automobile repair shop. A single vinyl couch, a coffee table covered with auto magazines, and a soft-drink vending machine. The only thing there that one didn't usually see at an auto mechanic's garage was a condom vending machine. As a doctor, though, he was glad the management of the Slumberland Motel was at least making a token effort at disease prevention. Having seen the bedspread in room 16, he had his doubts.

The paunchy manager wore a Hawaiian shirt and Bermuda shorts, and was sitting behind the counter, watching *The Young and the Restless.* He was about sixty, with short, spikey hair held upright by heavy application of a gel with a scent so strong Mark smelled it as soon as he stepped in.

The manager swiveled around on his stool to greet Mark. "May I help you?" he asked, with a faint trace of a Southern accent.

"Yes," Mark replied, flashing his friendliest, most ingratiating smile. "I'm here about a guest who rented room 16 three days ago. His name is Titus Carville, but he might have used a different identity when he checked in."

The manager sighed wearily. "So who are you? The husband, the father, the boyfriend, or the private investigator?"

"None of the above," Mark said. "I'm a doctor."

"I get it," the manager said, holding up a halting hand. "Say no more."

Mark was glad to oblige, since he hadn't figured out what to say next, anyway. Getting information from people who were under absolutely no obligation to give it to him was just one of the difficulties of investigating a murder without any authority whatsoever.

"You can lead a horse to water but you can't make him drink," the manager said, motioning to the condom machine. "I wanted to put one of those little vending machines in each of rooms, but my wife wouldn't go for it. She said it would kill the charm of the place."

"I appreciate your attention to public health," Mark said, almost adding that he'd appreciate it even more if they'd also burn all the bedding.

"What does my wife know about charm? She doesn't see the people who come in here," the manager said. "She doesn't see some of the bizarre combinations either, if you catch my drift. Her thing is the décor. The style. The ambience."

"It is a lovely place," Mark said. "Now, about Titus Carville—"

"We don't get the family or tourist trade anymore. But what we've got is a steady business, we have our niche in the marketplace. But do you know how many times I've been subpoenaed by divorce lawyers to testify?" the manager plowed on, oblivious to Mark's attempt to interject. "You know how many times guys have come in here waving guns and knives at me, looking for their cheating spouses?"

"I can imagine," Mark said. "I'm interested in the room Carville rented and if he's been here before with—"

"Love is a battlefield, as the song says, but I don't need to tell you, do I, Doc? I don't even want to think about what you have to see." The manager opened the check-in register and flipped back a couple of pages. "How many of this guy's sex partners are you and the health department looking for?"

"As many as we can find," Mark said.

The manager turned the book around so Mark could read it. Mark was mildly surprised to see that Titus had checked in under his own name. It didn't show much discretion, but it did help anyone checking up on Lacey's alibi. What he found odd was that Titus had signed twice.

"Why did Mr. Carville sign the register twice?" Mark asked.

"He ended up renting rooms 15 and 16. They're adjoining rooms at the very end of the building," the manager said. "He said that he wanted more privacy, since they liked to have a very good time and didn't want any complaints about the noise."

"I see," Mark said, digesting this new piece of information. "Has he ever been here before?"

"Not as far as I know," the manager said. "You're welcome to look through the register if you like."

"Did you see who was with Mr. Carville?"

"I didn't see anybody, but then again, I try not to," the manager said. "Less chance I'm going to have to testify to anything. They don't compensate me for testifying, you know, and I've got to pay someone to fill in for me while I'm stuck in the courtroom."

Mark closed the register and passed it back to the manager. "You've been very helpful. Thank you."

"I had the clap once while I was in Vietnam," the manager said. "The waterworks have never run quite right since then."

Mark smiled politely, not quite sure of the appropriate response to a disclosure like that, and hurried for the door before the manager decided to ask for a free exam.

Perhaps if he'd been in less of a hurry, and if his mind wasn't occupied with the new information he'd learned, Mark might have noticed the Dodge Ram pickup that was backed into the parking spot directly across from the office. He might also have noticed the gun the driver was aiming at him out the window.

# CHAPTER FOURTEEN

The first gunshot shattered the glass beside Mark, who dived onto the vinyl couch for cover. The next shot tore a chunk off the couch right above Mark's head. He peered over the edge and saw the truck speeding straight for the office and the couch he was lying on.

There was nowhere Mark could go and no time to do it if he could. He ducked down again, covered his head with his arms, and braced himself for a lot of pain—not that he had much hope of being alive to feel it.

That's when he noticed the manager standing in front of him, legs apart, holding a sawed-off shotgun in both hands, facing the oncoming truck.

The manager fired, blasting open the truck's hood, which flew up, completely blocking the driver's view through the windshield.

The driver wrenched the steering wheel hard to the right, his bumper clipping the edge of the office, shattering the remaining windows and smashing the condom vending machine.

The truck burst into traffic on the Pacific Coast Highway, where it was immediately sideswiped by a Ford Explorer, which went spinning into oncoming cars, colliding with an Impala that had a pair of surfboards strapped to its roof. The Impala jumped the curb and careened into the gas station, slamming into a car parked at the pumps, the impact launching the surfboards like missiles. The boards sailed through the windows of a minivan and became lodged inside, the ends sticking out of either side of the empty vehicle.

The shooter's truck veered out of control in a screeching U-turn that took it across the motel parking lot again and straight over the edge of the ravine. The truck tumbled down and disappeared into the dense brush below, kicking up a huge cloud of dirt and leaves.

Mark sat up and gaped at the destruction. The floor was covered with broken glass, bits of cinder blocks, and condom packets from the smashed vending machine. The motel manager hadn't moved. He stood in place in his Hawaiian shirt and shorts, bleeding from dozens of wounds caused by the flying glass, the shotgun still smoking in his hands.

"I need you to sit down for a moment," Mark said, leading him to the couch, using a copy of *Road & Track* magazine to brush away the broken glass. "My name is Dr. Mark Sloan. You didn't tell me your name."

"Phil," the man said, taking a seat and holding the shotgun across his lap. "Phil LaLonde."

"Phil, I'm going to examine you." Mark wiped blood out of his eyes, suddenly aware of the sting of his own injuries. "Are you feeling any pain?"

"Mostly in my wallet. I had this window replaced two weeks ago," the manager said. "That guy is going to pay for it."

"I think he already has," Mark said, then noticed a steady stream of blood spilling from inside the bend of Phil's left knee. The popliteal artery had been cut, and the blood loss had to be stopped fast.

Mark gathered up some condoms, tore open the packets, stretched out the prophylactics, and quickly tied them together into a band.

"What are you doing?" Phil asked.

"Making a tourniquet." Mark placed the tourniquet above the wound and twisted it tightly enough to stop the blood flow. "Now you can tell your wife that the condom machine really does save lives. Stay here until the EMTs arrive."

Mark stepped through the frame that once held the office windows and hurried to his car, popping open the trunk and yanking out his medical bag. He took a roll of gauze and wrapped it like a sweatband around his head to keep the blood from his scalp wounds from running into his eyes.

Then he put on a pair of surgical gloves, picked up his bag, and went to the edge of the ravine, peering over cautiously in case the shooter was on his way back up to finish the job.

The truck lay at the bottom, upside down, its wheels spinning, the dust still settling around it. There was no sign of the driver. Mark wasn't about to go down and check on him. Not only would Mark be presenting himself as a target, he also didn't want to risk injuring himself going down the steep hillside, especially when there might be people on the street who needed his immediate attention. The shooter, whatever his medical condition, would have to wait for help from the fire department and the EMTs.

Mark hurried out onto the highway, where traffic was snarled around the accidents. The SUV that had sideswiped the shooter's truck was in the center of the intersection, dented on all sides. Several cars that had collided with the SUV were stopped haphazardly around it, the drivers staring at the damage to their vehicles and talking ferociously into their cell phones. Mark hoped one of the people thought to call 911 before their insurance agents. In his rush to treat the injured, he'd forgotten to make the call himself and his cell phone was back in his car.

He leaned into the crumpled S.U.V., where the driver, a woman in her thirties wearing a seatbelt, was lifting her face from the airbag that had deployed from her steering wheel. She seemed slightly dazed, but otherwise he didn't see any obvious signs of injury.

"I'm Dr. Mark Sloan," Mark said, giving her a quick visual examination. "Can you tell me your name?"

"Mary White," she said.

He didn't see any blood or deformities that might indicate fractures, but that didn't mean there weren't injuries obscured from his view. "Do you feel any pain or discomfort?"

"No," Mary said.

"Do you feel any tingling, burning, or numbness in your arms or legs?" he asked, gently steadying her chin with one hand while checking her neck for tenderness with the other.

"No," Mary said, studying his face as he examined her. "I'm just a little shaken up. How about you? You're all bloody."

Mark smiled. "It looks worse than it is. Stay still, Mary. Help is on the way."

He looked in the backseat for other passengers, then went to the check on the driver of the Impala that had careened into the gas station.

The driver of the Impala was shirtless, in his late twenties, and had the dark, even tan and sun-bleached hair of a surfer. He wasn't wearing a seatbelt and was slumped over the steering wheel, which was bent out of shape, indicating the surfer had hit it hard with his chest.

As Mark got closer, he could see the surfer was conscious, that his breathing was labored, and that he was in considerable pain.

"I'm a doctor; don't try to talk," Mark said, gently easing the surfer back from the steering wheel. "I'm going to help you."

It was immediately obvious to Mark that the impact had broken several of the surfer's ribs, separating the sternum and loosening a segment of the chest wall, impairing his ability to breathe. He explained the injury to the victim while checking him for telltale signs of traumatic asphyxia, but didn't see the bulging eyes, swollen tongue, and purple discoloration of the head, neck, and shoulders that were symptoms of the emergency condition.

Mark was concerned that the victim might have suffered a possible neck injury, but the danger posed by the chest and lung trauma was far greater. He couldn't wait for help to arrive with a neck collar or a carrying board.

"I need to get you out of the car and lay you down on your back so I can help you breathe," Mark explained, then rose from the car and motioned to the nearest person he could see, which was the gas station attendant. "I'm a doctor, I need some help lifting this man out of the car."

The attendant came over and, following Mark's directions, he carefully lifted the surfer out of the car while the doctor held the victim's head in both hands to prevent it from moving. They moved the victim a short distance from the car before slowly setting him on the ground. Mark gently raised the surfer's arms above his head.

"Keep your arms over your head," Mark said. "I'll be right back."

Mark returned to the car, removed several large beach blankets he'd spotted earlier in the backseat and brought them back with him to the surfer. The doctor rolled up two of the blankets, placed them on either side of the victim's head, then used tape from his medical kit to create a make-shift splint. It wasn't much, but Mark figured it was the best way to keep the surfer's head from moving until the para-medics got there and replaced it with a cervical collar.

With the neck braced, Mark quickly folded another blan-ket into a heavy square, set it over the depressed area of the surfer's chest, then taped it tightly into place. The pressure created by the tension of the tape against the blanket kept the loose section of the surfer's chest from moving, creating a stable cavity for respiration.

With the surfer's breathing noticeably improved, Mark sat beside him and took stock of the situation around them. Traffic was gridlocked on the highway. Several Good Samaritans were scrambling into the ravine to help the driver of the truck. He heard sirens approaching from Kanan Dume and he saw a police helicopter streaking across the sky towards the scene. It was while looking at the chopper that Mark saw something interesting that he hadn't noticed before.

High atop a light pole, positioned for the best possible wide-angle view of the gas pumps, was a security camera. And from where it sat, it also had a nice, wide-angle view of the entrance to the Slumberland Motel parking lot.

By the time Steve made it through the dense traffic to the scene of the shooting, an hour and a half had passed since the incident. He arrived as the driver of the truck was being brought up the hill in a body bag and the cars blocking the intersection were being towed to the side of the road.

After conferring with the uniformed officers at the scene, Steve found his father in the office of the gas station, sitting at the security monitor, watching the playback of a video tape.

Mark was still wearing his bloody headband and his

blood-spattered clothing, refusing treatment for his own wounds in his eagerness to watch the security footage.

Steve took one look at his dad and yelled, "I need a medic, now!"

"Is somebody hurt?" Mark asked, transfixed by what he was watching.

"Dad, you're covered in blood." Steve put his hand on his father's shoulder. "You need to see a doctor."

"I am a doctor," Mark said. "I've seen myself and I'm fine."

"Dad, you're covered in blood."

"You keep saying that," Mark said. "It's nothing that can't be cured with a few cotton balls, some antiseptic, and a bandage."

"So let an EMT do it," Steve said as one came in, as if on cue.

Mark smiled at the EMT. "Don't bother, I'll go to the hospital and have these lacerations treated there. Go help somebody who needs it."

The EMT hesitated. "You really should let me examine you, Dr. Sloan."

"I appreciate your concern, Willy, but I assure you I'm okay and that my son here will transport me directly to the hospital for treatment."

The EMT shrugged at Steve, as if to say "I did my best," and left again.

Steve looked at his father, sitting there bloodied in front of the video screen, seemingly oblivious to the fact he'd nearly been killed, more interested in solving the murder than in his own well-being.

He'd only seen his father hurt like this once before, in the aftermath of the bombing of Community General Hospital. It was a miracle Mark had escaped that tragedy with his life. And now, today, there had been another assassination attempt that Mark emerged from bloodied, but alive. Steve wondered just how many miracles his father had left in his account.

"I'm taking you to the hospital now," Steve said.

"In a minute." Mark turned his attention back to the

screen. "Have you identified the man who was trying to kill me?"

"Not yet. His ID is fake and he was driving a stolen truck," Steve said. "It may not have been you he was after. The motel manager says he's been the target of a lot of irate husbands lately."

"I was the target—the security camera caught it all," Mark said, picking up a cassette and handing it to Steve. "The shooter was tailing me, but I took him by surprise when I made a U-turn in front of the motel. He had to drive up a block and turn around, but got caught up in traffic. By the time he got back, I was already in the manager's office."

"If this is the tape of the shooting that just happened, what are you watching?"

"Lacey McClure's tryst, unedited," Mark said.

"Does it punch a hole in her alibi?" Steve asked.

"Just the opposite. It corroborates Stryker's tape. You can see Lacey's car driving in at 3:12." Mark advanced the tape past the coming and going of several vehicles before, then paused the playback on the image of Lacey's car on its way out. "And there, you can see her driving out again at 4:35."

"We're screwed," Steve said.

"You'd think so." Mark popped the tape out of the VCR and handed it to Steve. "But if that's the case, why does someone want me dead?"

# CHAPTER FIFTEEN

Mark sat in a medical gown on the edge of an examination table in the ER, wincing as Jesse carefully plucked glass shards out of his flesh with tweezers. While Jesse removed the glass, Susan thoroughly flushed the wounds with saline, applied disinfectant, and bandaged him up.

"With all these tiny bandages," Jesse observed, "you're going to look like you nicked yourself all over trying to shave your body hair with a cheap razor."

"Have people done that?" Susan asked incredulously.

"I haven't seen it," Jesse said, "but this is what they'd look like if they did."

"Do you have to dig so deep?" Mark winced again. "It feels like you're using garden shears."

"I got my technique from you, so you only have yourself to blame. Have you ever considered wearing Kevlar?" Jesse asked, shooting a mischievous smile at Susan. "Considering how often people try to kill you, you could use the protection. If you'd been wearing it today, you'd have half as many cuts."

"I'll keep that in mind," Mark said, hearing a *plink* as Jesse dropped another shard into a metal pan full of bits of broken glass.

"Any idea who the shooter was?" Jesse asked.

Mark shook his head. "Steve is busy trying to figure that out. The shooter was carrying false ID and was crushed to death in the accident."

"I wouldn't call what happened an accident," Susan said.

"Did you learn anything at the motel?" Jesse asked.

"Titus Carville rented two adjoining rooms," Mark said. "He supposedly did it for increased privacy, but I'm wondering if there was another reason."

"Like what?" Susan asked.

"I don't know," Mark said.

"Doesn't sound like you found out anything worth someone killing you," Jesse said.

"Maybe I did and don't realize it," Mark said. "I have this nagging feeling that the answers are right in front of me and I just can't see them."

"I hate it when that happens," Jesse said.

"When has that ever happened to you?" Susan asked.

"Every time Mark solves a murder and reveals to me how it was done," Jesse said. "Lacey's new movie *Thrill Kill* opens tonight; want to see it with me?"

"No thanks," Susan said. "I don't like seeing a grown man drool in public."

Jesse looked at Mark. "How about you?"

"I think I'll pass," Mark said. "I heard the manager of the Slumberland and the surfer were brought here. Did you treat either of them?"

"They're doing fine," Jesse said, "thanks to you."

"I've never seen condoms and a beach blanket put to such clever use before," Susan said.

"You haven't gone to the beach with me lately," Jesse replied.

Susan laughed. "Jesse!"

"What?" Jesse replied innocently.

Noah Dent was passing by in the corridor, when he spotted Mark through the exam room window, and doubled back.

"Here comes trouble," Jesse mumbled, motioning to the door just as Dent invited himself in.

"Dr. Sloan," Dent said. "I heard you had a nasty scrape."

"More like a couple dozen," Mark said. "But I'm receiving excellent care."

"You certainly are," Dent said. "Which is why I couldn't help noticing that you didn't register with the front desk."

"It's not like we don't know who he is," Jesse said.

"But do you know who his insurance carrier is? What his

deductible covers?" Dent asked, looking from Jesse to Susan, then back to Mark. "I didn't think so. When you are done with your treatment, Dr. Sloan, I expect you to fill out the payment forms like every other patient is required to do before receiving medical care."

"This is basic first aid," Jesse said. "We aren't doing open-heart surgery here."

"We charge for all the services rendered at this hospital, including services performed on our own staff," Dent said. "Your time, and these supplies, are costing us money, regardless of who you're treating."

"He just saved two people on the street," Jesse said. "You don't see him presenting them with bills."

"He's right, Jesse," Mark interjected quickly, eager to stop the dispute before it escalated. He turned to Dent. "I apologize, this is entirely my fault. I should have filled out the forms. I'm afraid I wasn't thinking clearly when I came in."

"Of course you weren't. You shouldn't be expected to be thinking about paperwork under the circumstances," Dent said, then glared at Susan. "But I expect more from our nursing staff. Sadly, they don't have any excuse."

And with that, Dent marched out.

"What a lovable guy," Jesse said.

"I'm sorry if I got you or any of the ER staff in trouble," Mark said. "I'll fill out the forms and issue a memo tomorrow taking full responsibility for whatever procedures weren't followed."

"He's really out to get you," Jesse said.

"It certainly seems that way," Mark sighed. "Maybe I should consider wearing Kevlar in the hospital, too."

Jesse and Susan gave Mark a lift back home, stopping at the Slumberland Motel along the way so Susan could pick up Mark's car for him.

It was barely evening, but Mark went straight to bed, slipping between the cool sheets and falling instantly asleep.

He awoke at eight a.m., having slept a full fourteen hours, his body making up for the sleepless night the day be-

fore and the stress of nearly getting killed at the Slumberland Motel.

Because of his injuries, Mark opted for a delicate sponge
bath so as not to aggravate his many cuts. Shaving also presented a challenge, his face already scratched from the flying glass. All in all, though, he thought he looked pretty
good for a man who should be dead.

He wouldn't admit it to anybody himself, but he found
the brush with death invigorating. It energized him and
kicked him out of the doldrums he'd been feeling over his
inability to solve the case. The attempt on his life not only
made him feel more alive, it gave him a sense that he'd engaged the enemy. The game was on, and he was ready to
play.

Mark went into the kitchen just as Steve came in from his
morning jog on the beach.

"Hey, how are you feeling?" Steve asked.

"Great," Mark said.

*"Great?"* Steve asked incredulously.

"It's amazing what a good night's sleep can do for you,"
Mark said.

"I wouldn't know," Steve said. "I've been up all night
following up leads from the Slumberland shooting. I just got
back."

"And you went for a run?"

"I needed to clear my head," Steve said. "Now I'll be so
exhausted that I can't help but fall asleep."

"Did your all-nighter yield any new information?"

"Yeah, and you're not going to like it." Steve went to the
fridge, pulled out a Gatorade, and drank it straight from the
bottle. "The guy who tried to kill you was Albert 'Fresh'
Frescetti, freelance muscle for the Mob."

"The Mob?"

"I wish everybody would start calling them something
else, because I feel silly every time I say it," Steve said.
"Not that *the Syndicate, the Organization,* or *the Mafia*
sound any better."

"Why would anybody in organized crime want to shoot
me?" Mark asked. "Wouldn't it make more sense to shoot
Lacey McClure?"

"Speaking of Lacey, officially she's no longer the focus of our investigation."

"She *is* the case," Mark said. "She murdered her husband and his lover. This whole Mob thing is a smokescreen."

"It doesn't look that way now," Steve said. "We recovered Frescetti's gun and the bullets he shot at you. They match the bullets we pulled out of Cleve Kershaw and Amy Butler. It's the murder weapon."

"He *kept* the gun? Why would he do that?" Mark asked. "If he was a professional killer, he would have ditched it right away, not saved it to use in another killing. The last thing a killer wants is to keep any evidence—especially the murder weapon—that could tie him to his crime."

"Frescetti isn't known as a great intellectual," Steve said. "He is known for being a violent sociopath."

"But even sociopaths don't want to get caught," Mark said. "And if he killed them, who drugged them first and why?"

"Maybe Jesse's theory was right," Steve said. "Maybe the drugging and the shooting aren't related."

"If it's a simple execution, why bother trying to disguise the time of death? Who came back at four thirty and fired the shots I heard?" Mark said. "And more importantly, why?"

"We can ask Daddy Crofoot that," Steve said, "when we find him."

"Why was Frescetti tailing me and not you or Lacey?" Mark continued. "I wasn't the one who accused the Mob of being responsible for the killings. I don't think they had anything to do with them."

"Yeah, but *they* don't know that," Steve said. "You do have a reputation for being tenacious. Once they found out you were involved, maybe they got afraid you would eventually find evidence that linked them to the murders."

"Which wouldn't be too hard to do if the idiot killer was still carrying around the murder weapon," Mark said. "This doesn't make any sense, Steve."

"It does to everybody else," he said. "From the chief of police and the DA on down. Everything we've found so far confirms Lacey's story: her accountant's report, the FBI wiretaps, Stryker's video, the gas station surveillance tapes, and now a Mob killer taking shots at you with the murder weapon."

Mark shook his head. "The shots didn't even sound the same."

"What shots?"

"The shots I heard yesterday and the shots I heard the day Cleve Kershaw and Amy Butler were killed," Mark said. "They didn't sound the same."

"You heard the shots in entirely different situations," Steve said. "The first time, you were sitting out there on the deck on a peaceful afternoon when you heard shots coming from fifty yards away. Yesterday, you heard the shots while diving to the floor, windows shattering and cars crashing all around you. Of course they didn't sound the same."

"I don't think that's it," Mark said. "The gunshots had a different pitch."

"How can you possibly remember the pitch?"

"I do."

"Dad, the bullets all came from the same gun."

"But that's not what I heard."

"It's what the evidence proves," Steve said. "There isn't any doubt."

"So now you're convinced she's innocent, too?"

Steve looked at his dad and wondered why this felt like a betrayal. The evidence was overwhelming and undeniable. He couldn't continue pursuing a line of investigation on gut feeling alone, not with the entire police hierarchy and the national media watching his every move. If he ignored the evidence and followed his instincts, his career would be torched. He knew he was playing politics but he was also facing reality. It didn't mean he didn't trust his father or have faith in his instincts. Steve was just doing his job.

He wanted to tell his father all those things, and he found a simple way to do it.

"I'm only going where the evidence takes me," Steve said.

"That's just it," Mark replied. "You're being taken."

\*    \*    \*

"She was this cute little furball," the woman said, wincing. "Just sitting outside the Starbucks this morning, waiting for her master to return with a latte."

Jesse's patient was a plus-sized woman in her forties. From the numerous bloodstains on her blouse, she looked at first to be far more injured than she actually was. Her only wound was a mild dog bite to her left hand. She got blood all over herself trying to shake her hand free from the dog's jaws, waving the beast around until he finally let go.

"Didn't your parents ever tell you not to pet strange dogs?" Jesse said, examining her wound.

"The dog didn't look strange to me," the woman said.

"Well, you must have looked strange to him," Jesse said. "Do you know if the dog had a rabies shot?"

"You can call the vet and find out," she said, handing him a slip of paper with her good hand. "I wrote the number down. They might still be there."

"The dog got hurt, too?" Jesse asked.

"He wouldn't let go until I whacked him against the wall a couple of times," the woman said, then noticed the way Jesse was looking at her. "I had no choice. It was self-defense."

"I'll call the vet. You're going to need a tetanus shot and some antibiotics." Jesse pocketed the note. "I'll be back to clean and dress the wound in a few minutes."

"Are the shots really necessary?" the woman asked. "The dog seemed clean to me."

"You also thought he was friendly," Jesse said. "Besides, think about where even the friendliest dogs like to lick themselves."

Jesse left the exam room and was on his way to the phone at the nurses' station when Susan caught up with him. She handed him a piece of paper.

"Take a look at this," she said.

He glanced at it, bewildered. "This looks like your resume."

"I've spent the last few years in the nursing field, but I worked a little in the food-service industry when I was in college," Susan said. "As a nurse, I'm told I have a comforting and supportive bedside manner, so I'm sure my table-side manners are good, too. I've had to work very fast in the ER, taking doctors' orders, treating patients. Add that all up, and it's obvious I could be the fastest, friendliest, hardest-working waitress you've ever hired."

Jesse set the paper side and looked at her with concern. "Susan, what are you talking about?"

"I'm talking about a job." She ran a hand across her cheek, wiping away a tear. "I'm suddenly in the market."

"You've been fired?" Jesse asked incredulously.

"It's part of a new 'austerity program' to cut hospital spending. One nurse from every department is being cut, based on seniority," Susan said. "And since I have the least seniority of any of the ER nurses, I'm the one who has to go."

"Dent can't fire you—we've got too few nurses as it is," Jesse said.

"And still more than the hospital can afford," Susan said, "at least that's what Dent said as he gave us our severance checks. I have to clean out my locker and turn in my ID at the end of my shift."

"This isn't about the budget," Jesse said. "This is about Dent trying to get at Mark."

"I'm not that close to Mark, and neither are the fifteen other nurses who got fired," Susan said. "This is about corporate greed and the bottom line."

"Dent knows how close you are to me, and how close I am to Mark, that's the bottom line," Jesse said. "You said it yourself, he's been gunning for us. Dent knew he couldn't just single you out and get away with it. Next he'll find a way to get rid of me, and then Amanda."

"I'm not so sure," Susan said.

"I am," Jesse said, "and I'm going to do something about it."

# CHAPTER SIXTEEN

Mark was the lone figure strolling on the beach in the early-morning fog. There was an eerie, unreal quality to the light, the mist, and the long, broad expanse of empty sand. It seemed appropriate. His thoughts were on the killings, and the atmosphere matched the isolation he felt as the one person who still believed Lacey McClure was guilty.

The facts were on Lacey's side. Mark simply doubted the facts. Everything fit together too neatly, the revelations unfolding in an almost choreographed way.

*Like a movie.*

Lacey McClure was using the techniques of her profession to commit the perfect murder. Careful plotting of the story. Actors performing their scenes according to a detailed script. Forced perspective to fool the audience into seeing what she wanted them to see. Revelations of characters and plot timed for maximum dramatic impact.

But it was more than a double murder produced like a feature film. It was also a carefully orchestrated promotional campaign for Lacey McClure's new movie.

Her press conference, in which she accused the Mob of killing her husband, and the very public attempt on Mark's life just happened to coincide with the release of her new movie, a story about a woman pitted against organized crime.

It was all so clear to Mark. Unfortunately, there wasn't any evidence to prove it.

So why was he so certain? Why was he the only person unwilling to accept the facts?

It was a feeling—the kind that had never failed him in the past—the kind he had learned never to ignore when investigating a homicide. Although he didn't ignore his instincts, he wasn't beyond questioning them. Often the questions would reveal new paths of inquiry he hadn't considered before.

He asked himself what Lacey McClure had said or done that had convinced him on some deep level that she was guilty. The answer came to him almost immediately. It was how she'd described her deteriorating marriage to Cleve, and the reasons for keeping their supposed separation a secret.

She'd said they agreed to hide their marital separation, and the reasons for it, because the publicity would overshadow the premiere of their movie. Her explanation gave Mark a clear picture of her mind-set. It revealed her priorities, the importance she placed on marketing, and the amount of premeditation that went into her actions. More importantly, it revealed her unabashed desire to manipulate the media to her own advantage.

News about her marital difficulties might have trumped the coverage of her movie if it had been revealed before the murders. But now, with her husband dead and herself cast as both victim and heroine, it was a marketing dream.

It was too good to be true.

And it made his feelings about Lacey's guilt even stronger. Despite the evidence. Despite logic. Despite it all.

To others, he might be seen as arrogant, defiant, and stubborn in his refusal to let go of his belief in her guilt. Maybe even to his own son. But Mark wasn't going to give up. He *couldn't*. It was beyond his control now.

Which was, perhaps, why he found himself standing outside Lacey and Cleve's beach house, where the mystery began for him. The yellow police tape that surrounded the house fluttered in the breeze like decorative streamers for a party. He was alone on the beach. The media flotilla in the bay was long gone; the story wasn't here anymore.

But it was for Mark.

When all else fails, he thought, go back to the beginning. He strode up to the house, looking around to see if anyone was watching him. There was no one. He lifted up the tape, stepped under it, and tripped over a boulder in the dune grass.

Mark staggered, regaining his balance and managing not to fall. He glared back at the rock resentfully, as if it was a person playing a prank on him.

The rock was granite, barely peeking out of the wavy dune grass that delineated the property lines of the house. But as he studied it, he realized it wasn't a rock at all. It was a stereo speaker designed to look like a boulder.

He turned and looked at the other side of the property and saw a matching speaker. In fact, there were several hidden amidst the sparse plantings.

The sight was like a key slipped into a deadbolt. Mark could almost feel the tumblers falling in his mind, unlocking a memory and, with it, a revelation.

He hurried up the stairs to the deck and tried the French doors. They were locked. He took another quick look around, smashed one of the panes with his sleeve-covered elbow, then reached in and opened the door.

Mark slipped inside, closed the door behind him, then glanced around the living room. The champagne glasses, the bucket of melted ice, and the woman's shoes were gone. But one thing was exactly as it had been the first time he'd come through the door on the day of the shooting.

*The power lights on the entertainment system were on.*

He examined the elaborate components which, combined, looked like something from the cockpit of a jetliner. But he saw a button with a right-pointing arrow on it, the universal symbol for PLAY, and pressed it. There was a whirring sound as the disc in the CD player began to spin. A counter appeared on the CD player display, ticking off the number of tracks, the seconds as they passed, and the total running time remaining on the disc. There was only one track and sixty minutes of running time.

Using the toggle control, Mark advanced the CD to the last two minutes of the track, then went to the front door and opened it, leaving it slightly ajar.

Two gunshots rang out, startling Mark even though he

was expecting them. Almost immediately, two more shots cracked the silence.

Mark glanced at his watch, sat down on the arm of the couch, faced the door, and waited.

It didn't take long.

Three minutes later, almost to the second, a shirtless Steve Sloan burst through the half-open door and sprang into the room, his gun leveled at Mark.

"Convincing, isn't it?" Mark said, smiling at his son, who was in his bare feet, wearing only a pair of gym shorts.

Steve lowered his gun, gave his father a furious look, and went straight to the phone. He dialed the emergency operator, identified himself, and told her to cancel the patrol cars responding to the scene. It was a false alarm, and they could ignore the dozens of other calls they were bound to get reporting gunfire. When he hung up, he turned angrily to his father.

"You were asleep, but you still beat my time getting here," Mark said. "You must have been running, which couldn't have been easy barefoot."

"You want to explain to me what the hell it is you're doing here?" Steve said irritably, holding his gun at his side. There was no other place to put it.

"Answering one of the unanswered questions that's been nagging at me about the murders."

Mark went to the entertainment center and ejected a CD. There was no label on the disc, but it was obviously a CD-R, the kind used in computer drives to copy data, music, and video files. He took the disc out, holding it carefully by the edges.

"This is a recording of sixty minutes of silence and then four gunshots," Mark explained. "Lacey shot her husband and his lover with a silenced gun, then on her way out put the CD in the stereo, cranked up the volume and hit PLAY, so everybody would think the murder happened an hour later than it did."

"How do you know it was Lacey McClure?"

Mark held up the disc. "Does this seem like the kind of thing that Albert 'Fresh' Frescetti, a guy who shot at me from a truck in broad daylight on the Pacific Coast Highway, would think of doing?"

"No, but that doesn't mean it's Lacey McClure, nor does it explain how she could have been in two places at once."

"Let's get this CD analyzed first," Mark said, handing Steve the disc, "and we'll worry about the rest later."

"I have to worry about it now."

"If I were you," Mark said. "I'd be worrying about walking home in your underwear."

Steve glared at his father. "When, exactly, did it occur to you that the killer might have used this CD ploy?"

"While I was walking on the beach."

"You could have come home and told me what your hunch was. Then I could have gone to the police station, picked up the key to this house, and returned here to recover the CD," Steve said. "Instead, you thought it was a better idea to break in and play the CD at the highest possible volume, waking up the entire beach and getting me to run down here in my shorts to point a gun at you."

"Yes, but it proved my theory far more effectively than simply explaining it would have," Mark smiled, walking past Steve to the door. "And besides, it was a lot more fun."

Special Agent Larry Bedard slipped the CD from Cleve's entertainment center into his computer and played the gunshot at low volume. He didn't want a hundred FBI agents rushing down to the Federal Building basement and drawing their guns on him and Steve.

The sound of the gunshot was represented by an EKG-like display on his computer screen, much like the voices Bedard recorded on his wiretaps.

"Okay, that's one of the gunshots from the CD-R you found," Bedard said. "What kind of gun was the murder weapon?"

"A .45 ACP," Steve said. An Automatic Colt Pistol.

Bedard typed furiously on his keyboard. The screen with the readouts of the gunshots was reduced to a smaller window, and another, identical window opened, only without a soundtrack displayed.

He did some more typing, and a third window opened up,

this one with a program Steve recognized. It was Internet Explorer.

"Checking your e-mail?" Steve asked.

"Snagging a recording off the web of a .45 being fired," Bedard said as a website came up, offering thousands of sounds in hundreds of categories.

"You can do that?" Steve asked.

"You can do anything on the web," Bedard said. "Buy your groceries, get a medical exam, talk to friends, do your taxes, read a book, spy on your neighbor, watch a movie, have sex with a stranger . . ."

Steve wondered how much of that Bedard knew from personal experience, working alone down here in this cave. It was an unsettling thought.

With a few key clicks of his mouse, Bedard found a .wav file of a .45-caliber gunshot and downloaded it in seconds.

"Okay," Bedard said. "Let's see how they match up."

Again, keeping the volume low, Bedard played the gunshot, the sound depicted as a series of sharp peaks and valleys on the graphical display.

Mark was right: There was a difference in pitch between the gunshots. Steve heard it himself. Then again, he'd heard the other shot only seconds ago, so the comparison was easier for him to make. What stunned Steve was that his father could remember a detail like that after a number of days.

Bedard highlighted the .45 readout with his cursor, then moved it across the screen to the other window, laying it on top of the readout from the CD-R. Sure enough, the two didn't match.

"I'm not a ballistics or audio expert, but my guess is that the recording on the CD-R is a rifle shot, which has a higher frequency than a bullet fired from a handgun," Bedard said. "The guy probably didn't know the difference. To most civilians, a gunshot is a gunshot—they all go *bang*. He probably snagged this file off the web someplace, just like I did."

"So it's a dead end I can't trace," Steve said. "What about the disc?"

"It's a recordable CD," Bedard said. "You can buy them anywhere and burn them in any computer."

"Is there any way to identify the computer that burned this CD?"

"Yes and no," Bedard said, beginning to type again. A different window opened up, strings of commands and responses that made no sense at all to Steve. "The studios and music companies are all pissed off about people copying songs and swapping them on the Internet, so they've come up with some sneaky ways of tracking these pirates down. You know the biggest weakness all criminals share, right?"

"They like anything they can get for free," Steve said.

The LAPD had mounted several contest cons, luring wanted criminals out of hiding by tricking them into thinking they'd won free trips, cars, and cell phones. It amazed Steve that a guy on the run from a $700,000 jewelry heist would come in from hiding for a free weekend in Lake Tahoe.

"Same goes for your basic pimply-faced teenager who wants to burn CDs of songs he's ripped off from file-swapping services," Bedard said, still typing and clicking away. "So the studios and record companies have started offering CD-burning software for free on the web."

Steve smiled, already seeing the genius of the plan. "The software leaves a trail that leads right back to the copyright violator."

Bedard nodded. "Anybody on a network, or using high-speed Internet services, has an Ethernet card or adapter in their computer. Each adapter has a unique, twelve-byte, hexadecimal serial number hardwired into it that can't be changed. It's known as the MAC-address, short for media access control. The free CD-burning software scribbles that MAC address onto every disc it formats and every file it rips."

"What if our guy didn't use one of these programs?"

"That's something you don't have to worry about," Bedard said. "Because he did. The MAC address of his network card is 00-A0-B7-A9-C8-4C."

Steve wrote the number down on his notepad. "Okay, now what does that mean?"

"It identifies the manufacturer and the serial number of the specific card."

"This is terrific," Steve said excitedly, a smile on his face. Finally, a real break in the case. "All I have to do is contact the manufacturer, he'll tell me which computer this card is in, and a few phone calls from now, I'll be knocking on the killer's door."

"I don't think so," Bedard said.

"Why not?" Steve said, his smile evaporating.

"Remember when you asked me if you could trace the CD-R and I said yes *and* no?" Bedard said. "Well, here comes the *no* part. There are literally tens of millions of these cards out there in tens of millions of desktop and laptop computers. I'm not even counting tiny Ethernet cards you can carry in your shirt pocket and use in any computer that's handy."

"So what good is this MAC address to me?"

"If you find the right computer, you can match it to this CD-R."

"If I knew where the right computer was," Steve said, "I wouldn't need to trace the CD-R."

Bedard shrugged. "Nobody said this job was easy."

# CHAPTER SEVENTEEN

Jesse was armed for war. His weapons were a laptop computer, a high-speed Internet connection, a bowl of Nacho Cheese Doritos, and a huge bottle of Coca-Cola.

The Pentagon was his one-bedroom, Marina del Rey apartment. The kitchen table was his command center. His objective: to acquire operational intel on the enemy's strengths and weaknesses, then use that information to develop an attack strategy.

The enemy was Noah Dent. The hospital administrator had crossed the line when he fired Susan.

Jesse had been at the computer since his thirty-six-hour shift ended that morning. He was too angry to sleep, unwilling to rest until he found a way to stop Dent from destroying the people close to him.

Dent's animosity toward Mark Sloan went beyond office politics or an administrative power grab. There had to be another reason Dent was out to get him, and Jesse was determined to find it.

But after several hours of work, all Jesse had been able to find was a list of the schools Dent attended and the degrees he'd received, along with details of his various jobs before landing at the healthcare subsidiary of Hollyworld International, the amusement-park company.

If there was a clue to Dent's hatred of Mark in all that material, Jesse hadn't spotted it yet. Then again, he was having trouble focusing his eyes on anything. He needed some sleep, and then he'd take a fresh look at the reams of material he'd printed out.

He heard Susan fumbling with her key at the door, so he got up and let her in. She stood there with two bags of groceries in her arms.

"You're supposed to be asleep," she said, edging past him into the living room which, in his apartment, also happened to be the kitchen, dining room, and den.

"Yeah, but I couldn't sleep with Dent on my mind," Jesse replied, closing the door and padding into the kitchen after her. "I'm gonna figure out what that guy's problem is and then I'm going to find a way to fight back. I've printed out a ton of stuff about him, but I'm too tired to make any sense of it right now. I can't see straight."

"My plan was to wake you up with a wonderful lunch." Susan unpacked chicken legs, vegetables, cheese, a cake, and two bottles of wine from a grocery bag and set them on the kitchen counter. "But you've ruined it."

"What did I do to deserve such a nice surprise?"

"Nothing," Susan said, a little too strongly. "It was to entice you into hiring me at BBQ Bob's until I can find a new job."

"The job is yours, as long as you want it. Consider yourself the new senior vice president of worldwide operations. You don't have to entice me," Jesse said with a smile, slipping his arms around her waist from behind. "Though you do it naturally, without even trying."

Susan stifled a smile and pushed him aside. "I'm impervious to your charm."

"Since when?"

"Since I picked up your mail." She reached into a grocery bag, dumping several bills and a box on the counter.

Jesse ignored the bills but picked up the box. He knew what it was without opening it. The Lacey McClure sex tape.

"Now wait a minute," Jesse said. "You know I didn't buy this for me, it's for Mark."

"Uh-huh," Susan said, neatly folding the empty bags and sticking them in the cupboard under the sink.

"It's for legitimate investigative purposes only," Jesse said. "I have no interest in it myself."

"Really?" she said with a teasing grin. "So why didn't you have it delivered to Mark's house instead of yours?"

"They didn't give me that option on the website," Jesse said. "You had to send it to the billing address on your credit card."

"You weren't planning to watch it first?"

"Of course not." Jesse hoped he sounded convincing. "I'm going to drop it off, that's all."

"But you're exhausted from your long shift and all that research," she said. "Hey, I have an idea. You go to bed and I'll take the tape to Mark for you."

"No, no, no," Jesse said, looking for his wallet and his keys. "I couldn't ask you to do that. It's my duty as his investigative assistant. He may have other critical sleuthing tasks for me to perform."

"I thought you were dead tired," she said. "I thought you couldn't see straight."

"The sight of your beauty has revived me," he said, flashing a smile he hoped was irresistibly charming.

"Yuck," she said. "So, what are you going to do if he asks you to watch the tape with him?"

"Avert my gaze and run out of the house as fast as my legs will take me?" He scooped up his keys and his wallet and headed for the door.

"Nice answer," she said.

"Do you believe me?"

She gave him a smile. "Not for a second."

Mark sat on the deck of his beach house, a yellow legal pad on his lap. On the pad, he'd written down all the evidence that had been collected so far and broke it down into four columns: EVIDENCE OF HER GUILT, EVIDENCE OF HER INNOCENCE, EVIDENCE AGAINST THE MOB and THE UNEXPLAINED.

They looked like titles for a handful of cheesy thrillers, exactly the kind of thing Lacey McClure would star in. And appropriately enough, she was at the center of each of these stories, too.

Under EVIDENCE OF HER GUILT, he wrote:

Three Motives to Kill Cleve: 1) He was cheating on her with a younger actress he was grooming as her replacement. 2) He was using her films to launder Mob money. 3) He had some kind of leverage against her (hinted at in the FBI wiretap).

She had a key to the beach house.

She had gunpowder residue on her hands and clothes.

The gunshots on the CD were created to help corroborate an alibi. So far, she is the only one who has an alibi that needs corroboration.

The PI following her saw no evidence that she and Cleve were separated.

The killings create an amazing promotional opportunity for her new film.

She has an airtight alibi.

It wasn't a very persuasive list of evidence—even he could see that. Under *Evidence of Her Innocence,* he wrote:

She was separated from her husband, so adultery was not an issue. In fact, she was having an affair herself.

The fact that no one knew they were separated only proves how intent she and Cleve were on keeping their marital troubles a secret.

FBI wiretaps confirm that Cleve was using her films to launder money for the Mob and that Lacey was angry about it.

Gunpowder residue on her was from firing weapons during the shooting of an action sequence in front of one hundred witnesses. Also captured on film.

Two videos, independently made by separate parties, prove Lacey was at the Slumberland Motel at the time of the killings.

Ordinarily, that would be enough evidence to scratch her permanently off the list of suspects. Not this time. Under *Evidence Against the Mob*, he wrote:

Cleve and Amy were killed "execution-style."

The report by Lacey's forensic accountant confirms that Cleve was laundering money.

The FBI wiretap confirms he was laundering money

for the Mob and that the Mob was contemplating violence against Cleve and Lacey.

A Mob shooter tried to kill me with the same weapon used to murder Cleve and Amy.

Lacey's airtight alibi rules her out as a suspect.

All that was missing in the case against the Mob was a signed confession from Daddy Crofoot. It was a slam-dunk. Open and shut. A no-brainer. Which is exactly why Mark didn't believe any of it.

Under *The Unexplained,* he wrote:

Why were Cleve and Amy drugged?
Who recorded the gunshots on the CD?
Why did the Mob gunman try to kill me and not Lacey?
How did Lacey pull this off?

He set his pencil aside and stared in frustration at the notepad. Setting all the facts on paper made the case much clearer. There was absolutely no justification for him to believe Lacey McClure was guilty. He didn't blame Steve for pursuing the Mob angle. Any rational detective would.

If Mark continued to investigate Lacey McClure, he would be doing it on his own, without the support of the LAPD and, by extension, his own son.

The media scrutiny of Steve's investigation would only be getting worse. His every move was under a microscope. If Steve helped Mark, in direct opposition to the official police stance on the case, his son would be jeopardizing his career. Mark couldn't ask him to do that.

Alone and without the benefit of Steve's authority, Mark would never be able to get close to Lacey McClure, her family, friends, or business associates. They certainly had closed ranks by now to avoid the media, who were undoubtedly hounding them for information, sound bites, and footage. They would all be safely behind walls, real and symbolic, protected by armies of spokesmen, attorneys, and armed security. Getting himself onto Lacey's property again, or onto her movie set, would also be impossible.

Perhaps it was time, Mark thought, to concentrate on his duties at Community General, especially now that Dent was out to get him, and leave the homicide investigation to Steve. His son was a good cop; he'd get the truth without Mark's help.

Mark tore the sheet of paper off the notepad, rolled it into a ball, and was about to toss it in the trash, when he realized he didn't have a trash can nearby.

Frustrated, he shoved the paper into his pocket and went into the house. The DVDs of Lacey McClure's movies and the magazines with articles about her were still scattered all over the living room. He started to gather the material up to take downstairs to Steve's room, out of sight and out of mind. It was time to start thinking of other things.

He was heading for the stairs, his arms full of DVDs and magazines, when Steve walked in with Jesse at his side.

"Look who I ran into out front," Steve said, then noticed all the stuff in Mark's arms. "What are you doing with all of that?"

"Taking it downstairs for you," Mark said. "It's time for me to stop intruding on this case."

Those were words Steve had never heard before. He only got a few seconds to savor them before Jesse ruined it.

"Then I guess you aren't interested in seeing this." Jesse held up the tape. "It's the home video of Lacey and Cleve having sex."

Mark hesitated, shifting his weight between his feet, trying to decide whether to go back the way he came, or continue on downstairs.

Steve could almost see the mental tug-of-war being waged between Mark's sharply conflicting interests.

His father had just decided to bow out of the case, and here was a chance to see the victim and his likely killer in an unguarded moment. And yet . . .

It was a stolen, explicit video of Lacey and Cleve making love. Watching it made Mark a voyeur or worse. What he was going to see was bound to be distasteful. And yet . . .

It might provide some insight into their relationship and, possibly, the murder.

Mark's curiosity was piqued, but was his interest prurient or professional?"

The conflict was etched in Mark's face, in his inability to take a step forward or backward. Steve watched, knowing exactly the decision his father would make.

"It couldn't hurt to look at a few moments." Mark did an abrupt about-face and returned to the living room.

Steve turned to Jesse. "Thanks, I was almost free."

"Sorry," Jesse said.

The two men followed Mark into the living room. As Mark set down his stuff on the coffee table, he asked Steve if he'd found out anything about the CD. Steve told Mark what he'd learned from Larry Bedard while Jesse put the tape in the VCR and turned on the TV.

"Think Lacey would let you check out the MAC address of her Ethernet card?" Mark asked.

"Not without a search warrant," Steve said, taking a seat on the couch. "And I don't know if I could convince the DA or a judge to give me one based on the evidence we have."

Steve glanced at Jesse, who stood indecisively in front of the TV.

"What's your problem?" Steve asked.

"I promised Susan I wouldn't watch it," Jesse said.

"Did she believe you?" Steve asked.

"No," Jesse confessed.

"Then you won't be disappointing her," Steve said. "So sit down, you're blocking my view."

Jesse sighed with resignation and took a seat on the couch next to Steve, who aimed the remote at the VCR and hit PLAY.

There was a rough title card, apparently made with some cheap, off-the-shelf editing software. The titles read "LACEY MCCLURE IN THE RAW!" in bold, white letters, with some cheesy electronic music in the background.

The title card stayed on screen for five seconds, and then there was a jarring cut to Lacey and Cleve already energetically making love. The angle was that of a stationary camera on a tripod, the only movement in the scene was from the couple, the only sounds were their moans and heavy breathing. The two of them were uninhibited, moving into a variety of positions, acknowledging the camera with playful grins.

Although there was no date or time stamp on the video, the scorpion tattoo on Lacey's back made it clear when the footage was shot. It had to have been produced some time during or after the making of *Sting of the Scorpion*, her second movie.

"When did this video come out?" Mark asked.

"About two years ago," Jesse said.

"How long after *Sting of the Scorpion* was released?" Mark asked.

"Around the same time," Steve said, glancing at his dad. "I know what you're thinking. Everybody thought it. The video couldn't have been stolen, distributed, and released at a better time. The publicity was huge."

"That scorpion on her back is like an ad for the movie," Jesse said. "It's also really sexy. What do you think Susan would say if I suggested she get something like that?"

"I don't think she'd say anything," Steve said. "It's what she might *do* that should worry you."

Mark took the remote from Steve and paused the image on the screen, Lacey's back arched in passion. He studied the image.

"You'd think Lacey would have insisted on a temporary tattoo rather than a permanent one," Mark said. "Doesn't it get in the way in her other movie roles?"

"Sure it does. Every time you read an article about one of her movies, the directors complain about having to hide the tattoo or airbrush it out," Jesse said. "Lacey made a big deal out of getting the tattoo at the time. She did all these interviews where she said it was essential to have a real tattoo to genuinely inhabit the role and portray all its complexity."

"She still talks about it in all her interviews. You'd think she was the first person to ever get a tattoo," Steve said. "She made it sound like she'd had open-heart surgery."

Mark gazed quizzically at Steve for a moment, then aimed the remote at the VCR and turned it off.

"Seen all you can stand?" Steve asked.

"Could you grab *Sting of the Scorpion* for me?" Mark asked.

"Apparently he hasn't," Jesse mumbled to Steve.

Steve found the DVD in the pile on the coffee table and tossed it to his dad, who put the disc into the player and picked up the appropriate remote control.

The movie's main menu appeared on the TV screen. Mark clicked his way to the scene selection menu, then moved quickly through the vidcaps of the various sequences, settling on the first lovemaking scene. He selected the scene and hit PLAY.

Jesse turned to Steve. "See? We aren't the only guys who go straight to the sex scenes."

Steve ignored Jesse and studied his father. The expression on Mark's face had changed. The sense of frustration and resignation Steve saw a few minutes ago was gone. Now Mark had the look of a hunter engaged in pursuit, eyes intense, focused on his prey.

Mark watched the stylized love scene unfold, full of quick cuts, percussive music, and dramatic lighting. The scene wasn't nearly as explicit as the home video. The camera lingered on Lacey's face, on the muscles tensing in her bare back, and on her hands gripping the sheets.

He stopped the playback, ejected the DVD and stared for a moment at the black screen, feeling the flush of realization. The millions of scattered pixels in his mind came together to become one dazzlingly sharp picture.

When Mark turned around, there was a sparkle in his eyes and a cunning smile playing on his lips. Steve and Jesse had seen the look before and knew exactly what it meant.

"Lacey McClure is a killer," Mark said. "And I can prove it."

# CHAPTER EIGHTEEN

The deck of a penthouse apartment, several stories above the glittering Los Angeles skyline, had been recreated on the Pinnacle Studios soundstage.

The nighttime cityscape was an immense photograph hung like a curtain and draped in a half-circle behind the set to create the illusion of height and distance.

Smoke filled the air to diffuse the light and heighten the illusion. Fans blew to mimic a night breeze, so the leaves rustled on the potted plants arrayed around the penthouse deck.

Lacey McClure, dressed in a black leather jumpsuit, climbed over the railing, as if she'd just scaled the side of the building. She crouched, catlike, and spotted a man in a tuxedo standing with his back to her at the opposite edge of the patio, smoking a cigar and admiring the view. She crept up behind him, removing a large knife from a sheath on her belt as she advanced.

In one smooth move, she grabbed his chin with one hand and slit his throat with the other. As the blood seeped out of his throat and spilled over her hand, she whispered in his ear: "You can't escape justice."

She released him, and as his body fell, the director yelled "Cut!"

A bell rang, signaling that the shot was complete, and that it was safe for people to move around and talk. The murder victim got up, opened his shirt, and removed the "blood bag" that fed his latex wound. A prop man took the rubber knife from Lacey while other crew members began to wipe the fake blood off the floor for the next take.

"That was great, Lacey," the director said, rising to meet Lacey, pulling his headphones off and letting them rest around his neck. "A wonderful starting point."

"Starting point?" she asked.

"I think you have the chops to give it even more levels of intensity," he said. "I want to see the rape of your sister, the firebombing of your house, and the kidnapping of your son on your face when you slice that bastard's throat. I saw the rape and the firebombing, but I didn't sense the kidnapping."

"We've already done six takes," she said.

"Think of your performance as a staircase and each take as one tiny step," he said. "Each step gets you closer to the top, to where you want to be."

"And with one shove you could tumble all the way down those stairs and land at the bottom," she said. "With a broken neck. If I were you, I'd hold on to the railing, and think about moving to the next shot. I'll be in my trailer."

She pushed past him and left the soundstage. He looked after her for a moment, and suddenly saw a horrific vision of himself freezing in a soundstage in Canada, directing episodes of *Sue Thomas F.B.Eye*, trying to get intensity from a deaf FBI agent and her hearing-ear dog.

He cleared his throat and turned to his assistant director.

"She really hit it out of the park with that performance," the director said. "I think we're ready to move to the next shot."

Lacey's trailer was parked right outside the soundstage door. She rushed in without even noticing the two uniformed police officers standing a few yards away, or the bland Crown Victoria sedan parked behind her vintage Mustang.

Perhaps if she had, she wouldn't have been so surprised to see Mark Sloan sitting on her couch, his feet up on her coffee table, watching television. Or his son, Steve, standing in her kitchen, helping himself to one of her Glacier Peaks bottled waters.

"Look who's here. It's Lt. Sloan and Dr. Sloan, too. I don't think I've ever seen the two of you apart," she said, turning to Steve. "Tell me Lieutenant, is this relationship reciprocal? Do you go into the operating room with your dad and offer him pointers during surgery?"

Steve shook his head. "I don't have an interest in medicine. But my father has a definite interest in homicide."

"I bet you're thrilled about that, aren't you?" she said to Steve, a malicious twinkle in her eye.

"It depends," Steve said. "Sometimes he sees things everybody else missed."

"I've seen something on Stryker's tape that might interest you," Mark said, holding up her remote. "I've got it cued up for you."

"Sure, why not?" She walked over and stood beside the couch. "This is the only film of mine I haven't seen."

Mark aimed the remote at the TV and hit PLAY. They watched the screen and saw Lacey driving up to the Slumberland Motel and parking in front of room 16. He paused the playback.

"That's a very nice Mustang. It's a classic, isn't it?" Mark said. "I couldn't help noticing it parked out front the first time we visited your house. It really stands out."

"I'm glad you like it," she said. "Is that why you're here, to talk about my car?"

"No, no," Mark said. "I just thought it was interesting that you'd chose such a distinctive car to go on such a discreet rendezvous."

"It's my car," she said. "It's how I get from place to place."

"Of course," Mark said, starting the tape again.

The film showed Lacey getting out of her car, embracing Titus Carville, and then tumbling into the room in his arms.

Mark paused the film again. "I should warn you: The next scenes may make you a little uncomfortable."

"I think I can handle it," she said.

He shrugged and hit PLAY. The next scene up was shot through the window of the motel room, showing Lacey straddling Titus, her back to the camera. Mark paused the film.

"That's a pretty distinctive tattoo you've got there," Mark said. "It really stands out."

"Is there a point to this, Dr. Sloan?" She said.

"There are a few little things that bother me about this shot," he said. "For one thing, I understand you like sheets that have at least 600 threads."

"I have sensitive skin," Lacey said. "What does that have to do with anything?"

"The sheets at the Slumberland have maybe five threads," Steve said. "On a good day."

"When you're caught up in passion, Lieutenant, you don't notice little discomforts," she said. "Are we done here?"

"Did you know your TV has a split-screen feature?" Mark said. "And multiple inputs?"

"No," she said. "I didn't know that."

"It's a wonderful feature, especially if you have two things you want to watch at once, and two VCRs." Mark hit a button on her remote. The screen split in two, with the image from the Slumberland Motel on one half, and a still image from her stolen sex tape on the other. "We can watch two videos at the same time. I never understood why anyone would want to do that until now."

"Do you get off watching me have sex, Dr. Sloan?" she asked.

"I didn't notice the sex, to tell you the truth," Mark said. "I was paying attention to other things."

"Don't tell me," she said. "You were admiring my performance."

"I was thinking about how clearly I can see your face in this home video you shot," Mark said. "And how I can't in this bedroom footage at the Slumberland Motel. You're photographed from behind. I can see your unique tattoo, but your head is turned in such a way that I can't quite see your face."

"Now you know why Stryker is a PI instead of a cameraman," she said. "But you know that's me. You saw me go into the motel room."

"And I saw you leave an hour or so later. But you know what I kept thinking about? Your harrowing brush with cancer. And the benign tumor you had removed from your shoulder. I read all about it, and your brave struggle," Mark said, motioning to a magazine he'd brought along and set on the coffee table. "The thing is, I can see the scar on your shoulder in your home movie, but not in the video of you at the motel."

She stared at the screen. "That doesn't prove anything."

"It proves that's not you having sex in the motel room," Steve said. "Add that to the fact that Titus Carville rented adjoining rooms and it's pretty clear what happened."

"You knew your husband hired Stryker to follow you, and you used that to create your alibi. Your body double, Moira Cole, was in the other room Carville rented, waiting for you to show up," Mark explained. "You allowed yourself to be clearly seen arriving, then you slipped out of the adjoining room in disguise while your double and Carville made love. You used the car she came in, drove to Malibu, and shot your husband and his lover with a silenced gun."

"You wanted to be sure they'd be there and that they'd be helpless," Steve said. "You drugged their champagne so they'd just be laying there for you, waiting to get shot."

"You also made a sixty-minute recording with four gunshots at the end, burned it on a CD, and left it to play in Cleve's stereo system after the murders," Mark said. "You returned to the motel, slipped into the adjoining room, and took off your disguise. You made absolutely sure you were clearly seen on film coming out of the room with Carville and driving away at the same time the shooting was reported. Your double stayed behind in the adjoining room until she was sure Stryker was gone."

Lacey glowered at Mark. "I suppose you expect me to break down and confess."

"I'd rather you waited until I read you your rights," Steve said, getting out his handcuffs. "You're under arrest for the murders of Cleve Kershaw and Amy Butler."

While Steve cuffed her and informed her of her Miranda rights, Lacey stared at Mark, her eyes blazing with fury.

"This isn't over, Dr. Sloan," Lacey said as Steve led her to the door, her arms cuffed behind her back. "It's only the beginning."

When Lacey stepped outside, she was shocked to see the entire crew standing there. From the expressions on their faces, it was obvious that they knew what had happened. That's when she realized she was still wearing the wireless microphone for her scene. Everything that was said in her trailer was heard by the sound engineers, the director, the assistant directors, the producers, and everyone else who had a headset on the stage to monitor her performance.

The director stepped up to Lacey and smirked. "Now you've got the intensity on your face I was looking for."

Lacey was handcuffed, but she wasn't defenseless. She kneed the director in the groin with all her might.

The director crumpled to the ground, clutching himself in agony.

Steve hustled her through the crowd to a black-and-white squad car, where Lacey saw her stunt double, Moira Cole, was already sitting in the backseat, hands cuffed behind her back. She'd been arrested, too.

Everyone's eyes where on Lacey, so when Mark stepped out of the trailer, the only one who seemed to notice him was the director, who was still doubled over at the steps.

"Great performance in there," the director said through gritted teeth.

"Thanks," Mark replied, helping the director to a seat on one of the steps. "Take a deep breath and try to relax. There's really nothing else you can do. The pain will pass in a few minutes."

"I came in a little late and missed the opening credits," the director said. "Who are you, anyway?"

Mark glanced at Lacey in the backseat of the police car, turned to the director and smiled playfully.

"You can call me Justice."

# CHAPTER NINETEEN

The scent of death is unmistakable. Even if someone has never smelled it before, the recognition is immediate, as is the instinctive revulsion and fear that comes with it.

Mark and Steve were outside Titus Carville's front door, a half-dozen uniformed officers behind them, when they smelled it.

The odor was like a physical barrier and it provoked a physical response. The gag reflex. The Sloans had encountered the rotting aftermath of death before and had long since learned to control their reactions. The police officers with them weren't as experienced. They staggered back, their chests heaving.

While the officers tried to control themselves, Steve took out the pocket-sized container of mentholated cream that, as a homicide detective, he always carried with him for exactly this kind of encounter. He dabbed a little of the strongly scented solution under his nose to dull the smell, and offered the container to Mark, who did the same.

Steve took pairs of rubber gloves from the inside pocket of his coat, handed one set to Mark, and put on the other. Given the smell, it was a safe bet that they were about to enter a crime scene. Once his gloves were on, he tried the doorknob. It was unlocked.

"This is the police," Steve yelled, on the slim chance that somebody was still inside despite the overpowering stench of decomposing flesh. "We're coming inside."

He motioned his father to step back, drew his gun, and proceeded into the house.

It was oppressively hot inside, the odor of death even more intense. The air wasn't circulating at all and felt heavy enough to touch. The living room was empty, except for the flies. They were everywhere.

Steve moved down the hall to the office and found Titus Carville's swollen corpse on the floor in front of his computer. Carville was curled on his side, his desk chair in the center of the room, Lacey McClure smiling down at him from a dozen different posters.

He unclipped the radio from his belt and notified the officers outside. "This is Sloan. We're clear. Secure the location, this is now a crime scene. Notify SID and the medical examiner that we have a decomp."

The desktop computer was still on. He tapped the space bar on the keyboard and the monitor snapped to life, revealing a Microsoft Word document.

It was a suicide note.

> *Forgive me, Lacey, for everything I have done. I'll be waiting for you in heaven.*

Mark came in behind Steve and read the note over his shoulder.

"That's convenient," Mark said, waving away the flies buzzing aggressively around him.

"Amazing, isn't it?" Steve said. "Everything seems to happen just at the right moment."

"For Lacey McClure, though I doubt she was expecting her alibi to fall apart," Mark said, then noticed the coffee mug and CDs scattered on the desk. "Did your friend at the Bureau teach you how to find out a computer's MAC address?"

"I was going to use what I learned on Lacey's computer, but I might as well get some practice now." Steve took out his notebook, referred to his notes, then used the mouse to minimize the Word document and click his way to a DOS command prompt. He typed "ipconfig /all" and hit RETURN. The screen displayed a list of the computer's configuration details. He compared the MAC address on screen with the one in his notes.

"That's one mystery solved," Steve said, diminishing the DOS window and restoring the Word screen to full size. "Titus made the CD with the gunshots on it."

"He was certainly devoted to Lacey," Mark said. "He was willing to help her establish an alibi by making the CD and having sex with her stunt double at the Slumberland Motel."

"I don't know if that last part was such a big sacrifice," Steve said. "I understand his motivation, but I don't see what was in it for Moira Cole."

"Neither do I," Mark said.

Steve motioned to the fly-covered, bloated corpse on the floor. "What do you make of this?"

Mark glanced at the office chair in middle of the room, then crouched beside Titus Carville's decomposing body and examined it. The squirming maggots were newborns, about the size of rice, which gave Mark a rough idea how long Carville had been dead. But what was the cause of death? The only sign of trauma he could see was a superficial scrape on Carville's forehead. Otherwise, there were no wounds, no broken bones, nothing that obviously indicated violence. Even so, it wasn't difficult for Mark to make an educated guess about what had happened to Carville.

"I'd say Carville was sitting at his desk about two days ago, drinking whatever was in that mug, when he lost consciousness," Mark said. "He slumped forward, hit his head on the edge of the desk, and then fell, his chair rolling out from under him into the middle of the room."

Steve nodded. He'd come to pretty much the same conclusion. "If I was going to off myself, though, I don't think I'd do it sitting in my home office staring at my computer."

"Perhaps you would if you didn't think of it as an office, but as a shrine to the woman you love," Mark said, glancing at all the posters of Lacey that covered the walls. "And if it was her face you were looking at, not the computer."

The incessant buzzing of the flies seemed to be increasing. It was bothering Steve even more than the smell. "So you believe it was suicide?"

"I believe Titus Carville would do just about anything for Lacey McClure," Mark said. "But I wonder if even he would have drawn the line at taking his own life."

Mark wandered out and went to the bedroom, Steve following after him. The sheets were turned down, as if a maid had come in. All that was missing were the chocolates on the pillows. With a glance, Mark could see they were nicer linens than Carville had on his bed before. He touched the folded-over top sheet. It was soft and silky, 600 threads or better.

He turned to Steve, who was standing in the doorway. "Carville was expecting Lacey."

Steve glanced at the bed. "He was expecting a lot more than that. Apparently, she never showed up."

"Or she did, and it never got this far, because she poisoned him first."

"Looks like Lacey was cleaning up after herself," Steve said. "It's a good thing we arrested her when we did or Moira Cole could have been the next one to die."

"Maybe you can use this as leverage to get Moira to testify against Lacey."

"Wouldn't that be nice," Steve said.

Jesse woke up on the couch at Mark's house. It took a minute before he realized where he was and why he was there and then he felt stupid. He'd begged Steve and Mark to let him come along for the arrest, but he must have fallen asleep while Steve was on the phone, finding out where Lacey McClure was shooting her movie that day.

He'd missed all the action. His thirty-six-hour shift and the hours he spent awake immediately afterwards doing research on Noah Dent had taken their toll. His body decided to close for business without consulting him first.

Jesse checked his watch. It was a little after six p.m. He'd only been asleep a few hours, but he knew a lot had gone down in the meantime, and it was probably on the early evening news. He grabbed the remote and turned on the TV. Lacey McClure's surprise arrest for the double murders of Cleve Kershaw and Amy Butler was the top story on every network and local channel, as he knew it would be.

But he wasn't expecting to hear Mark Sloan doing the play-by-play. Over the footage of Lacey being led into the county jail downtown, CNN played a tape, made without her knowledge, of part of her conversation with Mark and Steve in her trailer. The sound engineer only began recording after Lacey accused Mark of getting off on watching her have sex. Jesse didn't know what came before that, but as far as he was concerned, the engineer got the best part. Mark's step-by-step explanation of how she committed the murder, and all the mistakes she made, was all there.

The guys at CNN knew they had some good stuff to work with, and used it well. Over the shot of Lacey McClure walking into jail, the big doors slamming shut behind her, the camera panned up to one of the barred windows and played her final, taunting words: *"This isn't over, Dr. Sloan. It's only the beginning."*

Jesse loved it. He'd been with Mark in so many similar situations that he could easily imagine the expression on his face as every word was said. It was like Jesse was right there, in middle of it all. It was so good that Jesse decided that Mark should consider recording all his confrontations with killers.

When the CNN report was over, Jesse felt like he hadn't slept through a thing. It was easily the most accurate reporting he'd ever seen on television.

He grabbed the phone and called Susan.

"I hope you weren't too worried about me," Jesse said.

"Mark called me and told me he made you take a nap," she said. "He also told me the video you brought him was the key to solving the case."

"So you forgive me for buying it?"

"I never had a problem with you buying it," she said. "I had a problem with how much you wanted to watch it."

"Have you seen the news?" Jesse asked.

"No."

"You've got to turn the TV on," he said. "You're missing all the great stuff they've got on Lacey McClure. They've even got a tape of Mark nailing her with everything."

"I've been too busy to watch the news," she said.

"What have you been doing?" Jesse asked, with worry in his voice. The last time he'd left her alone for a while in his apartment, she'd rearranged his closet and thrown out his favorite pair of old socks.

"I've been going through all this stuff you printed out about Noah Dent," she said. "I think I found something. Buy me dinner at BBQ Bob's and I'll tell you all about it."

Moira Cole sat glowering across the table at Steve from the same lopsided chair Nick Stryker sat in not so long ago.

While Moira Cole and Lacey McClure shared some obvious physical similarities, they projected a very different presence. Moira's facial features were as sharp, but came across as harder, less feminine. Lacey effortlessly radiated an intensity, with her eyes and with her body language, that Moira simply couldn't match. It was easy to see why Lacey was the movie star and Moira was the stunt double. She was Lacey McClure at half the wattage.

Steve wondered if Moira would be more attractive if she didn't try so hard to look like Lacey, which only invited comparisons. But being the lesser Lacey was Moira's profession and, if she wasn't careful, it would also be her downfall. He was there to remind her of that.

"You've taken being a stunt double to a whole new level," he said. "You don't just stand in for Lacey McClure in movies, but in real life, too."

"I don't get it," she said.

"I'm talking about being an accessory to murder," Steve said. "I'm talking about helping her fabricate an alibi so she could shoot Cleve Kershaw and Amy Butler."

"Huh?" she asked, acting confused. Her acting made Lacey McClure look like Meryl Streep.

Steve held up a video tape. "We know this is you having sex with Titus Carville, not Lacey McClure."

"I didn't know having sex with a guy was a crime," Moira smirked.

"It is if you're doing it to help someone commit murder," Steve said.

"I'm, like, totally lost," Moira replied. "So I hooked up with a guy in a motel. All we killed was an hour and a few calories."

"We know you were in the adjoining room that Titus rented. We know you slipped in and had sex with him after Lacey left," Steve said. "You knew there was a private eye outside with a camcorder. So you positioned yourself with your back to the camera to be sure he'd see the tattoo on your back, but not your face. You wanted him to mistake you for Lacey."

"I positioned myself that way because I like it," she said. "Sure, I've got a scorpion tattoo because I want people to mistake me for Lacey. That's what I do for a living. I get people to think I'm her. But I had no idea some pervert was outside the window filming us."

"So you were just there having a romantic rendezvous with Titus Carville," Steve said.

"Yeah."

"Lacey's boyfriend."

"He's not her boyfriend," Moira said. "He's mine."

"That's not what he told us," Steve said. "He said Lacey was his true love. So you can see why I am bit confused."

"So am I," Moira said. "I suggest you ask him again."

"I'd like to," Steve said. "But he's dead."

Moira's whole body stiffened and she blinked twice, as if trying to clear her vision. Again, not a very convincing performance.

"What happened?" she stammered.

"It looks like suicide," Steve said. "But as you know better than anybody, looks can be deceiving."

"I'm tired of this," Moira said. "I want to leave now."

"You want to go? There's an easy way to walk out this door," Steve said. "Tell us everything that happened. Testify against Lacey."

Moira gave him a cold look. "I have nothing to testify about."

"Lacey murdered two people and you helped her do it by trying to create an airtight alibi for her," Steve said. "Tell us how she planned it and I'll get the prosecutor to cut you a deal. Who knows, maybe you'll even get immunity."

"I told you, Titus and I were lovers," Moira said. "The two of us hooking up at the motel had nothing to do with any killings."

"So why was Lacey there?" Steve said. "And why did she drive off in your car, then come back and leave in hers again?"

"She didn't go anyplace."

"We have surveillance footage from the gas station across the street," Steve said. "We know that you arrived in a rented Ford Taurus. Ten minutes after Lacey showed up, kissed Titus, and went into the room, the car you rented was driven out of the lot. Forty minutes later it came back, and a few minutes after that, Lacey came out of the motel room and drove out again in her Mustang. She was followed out by Titus in his pickup truck and then you in the Taurus."

"I didn't rent a car," Moira said.

"We traced the license plates on the Taurus back to the rental company," Steve said. "The car was rented by a woman using a stolen credit card—another felony by the way, Moira. We looked at their security-camera footage. The woman was wearing a large hat and sunglasses, but we're sure it's you."

"It wasn't," she said.

"Why did you rent the car?"

"I didn't," Moira said. "Don't you listen?"

"So you're saying you met Titus Carville at the motel for sex."

"Right."

"And that Lacey showed up and didn't leave," Steve said.

"Uh-huh."

"What was Lacey doing there?" Steve asked. "Are you saying it was a threesome? Or does she just like to watch?"

"You're a sicko, you know that?" Moira said. "It wasn't anything like that. We were rehearsing a scene."

"I thought you met Titus there for some afternoon delight."

"That wasn't exactly how it started," she said. "I double for Lacey in sex scenes that involve nudity. But since I'm still portraying her, she wants to be sure I look right, you know? That I evoke the essence of who she is, or people won't believe it's her. So she asked me to rehearse what I was going to do, with Titus, my boyfriend, and she'd give me pointers on how she wanted me to perform."

Steve gave her an incredulous look. "You've got to be kidding."

"I'm a method actress," Moira said. "Since Titus is my

boyfriend, we kind of got into it, so Lacey went into the next room to give us some privacy."

"Why did you do this in a motel instead of Lacey's house, your place, or his place?"

"Lacey was afraid of how it might look," Moira said. "She wanted to go someplace where we wouldn't attract attention."

"That's the dumbest story I've ever heard," Steve said. "It makes no sense."

"Like yours does?"

"I'm not telling stories," Steve said.

"Sure you are. You're twisting everything to fit this stupid fantasy of yours, anyway," she said. "It's pathetic."

"I don't understand something, Moira. What's in this for you? Why are you protecting her?" Steve said. "She killed Titus Carville. She would have killed you, too, if we hadn't arrested her first."

"See, you're doing it again," Moira said. "Twisting everything around. I'm done. You have any more questions for me, talk to my lawyer."

"You don't have one yet."

"I will," Moira said.

"Is Lacey providing one for you?" Steve said.

"Is that a crime, too?"

"No, just not very smart." Steve got up from the table. "Do you really think your interests and hers are the same? She will sell you out. But I guess that's an improvement over what she did to Titus."

He left the interrogation room, hoping she'd think about what he'd said, but he didn't have much hope. For whatever reason, Moira Cole was willing to go down with Lacey McClure.

Fine, he thought, let 'em both go to prison. Moira didn't deserve any breaks, anyway, and he certainly didn't need her testimony to convict Lacey.

His beeper went off. He looked at the number and felt a pang of anxiety in his stomach.

Chief Masters wanted to see him.

# CHAPTER TWENTY

Jesse slid into the booth across from Susan at BBQ Bob's. The printouts Jesse made off the Internet were spread all over the table between them, only now the papers had color-coded tabs, and sections of text were highlighted.

"Aren't you organized," Jesse said.

"I get that way the more disorganized the rest of my life becomes," Susan said.

"You've only been out of work for a few hours," Jesse said.

"And see how I am already?" Susan replied. "Imagine what I will be like in a week."

"You can start work here tonight," Jesse said. "If that will make you feel better."

"We haven't talked about my salary," she said.

"I need to consult with Steve about that," Jesse replied.

"You haven't talked to him yet?"

"He's been kind of busy with his day job," Jesse said. "I'll catch him tonight or tomorrow."

"But what if he doesn't want to hire me?" Susan said. "What if he thinks I'm not qualified?"

"Susan, you've already been working here for years," he said. "The only difference is that now, instead of taking advantage of you, we're going to pay you."

"It's just until I find another nursing job," she said.

"Then we'll be lucky if we can keep you until this time tomorrow," Jesse said. "Hospitals will be lining up to have you. That is, if Community General doesn't beg you to come back."

"They won't," she said. "Not as long as Noah Dent is there."

"Which may not be long if you found something."

"Don't get your hopes up," she said, turning some papers towards him to read. "It's interesting but I'm not sure what it means. Check out his work history since he graduated from business school, and tell me what you see."

Jesse scanned the documents. "Dalberg Enterprises, Deon Worldwide, Mediverse Corporation, Healthcorp International, Davis & Laurin Properties, Hollyworld International." He looked up, bewildered. "Mediverse, Healthcorp and Hollyworld have all owned Community General at one time."

"It gets creepier than that," Susan said. "Dent left Mediverse as soon as they sold Community General to Healthcorp. He worked briefly at Davis & Laurin while Healthcorp went through bankruptcy liquidation, then went straight to Hollyworld the moment they acquired the hospital."

"How come we never heard of him before?"

"Because until now he never worked in divisions of the company that gave him any control over Community General," she said. "He's been in finance, not in administration. It's almost like he's been working his way up, waiting for his chance."

"You're amazing." Jesse leaned across the table and gave Susan a kiss. "I thought you weren't interested in being a detective."

"I never had a reason before," she said. "You know what? It's kind of fun. I felt a real charge when I saw the pattern in his work history. It was like the feeling I get when I win at the slot machines."

"Why do you think I've been helping Mark out?" Jesse said. "It's because I like that little thrill of discovery when you unearth a clue."

"We still don't know why Community General means so much to Dent."

"It doesn't," Jesse said. "Mark does."

"How do you know?"

"It's a hunch," Jesse said. "Now all we have to do is prove it."

\* \* \*

Police Chief John Masters had the largest office in Parker Center and, perhaps, the largest office of any Los Angeles public official. But with Masters, DA Burnside, and ADA Karen Cross waiting for him in the room, it felt very cramped to Steve.

The mood was hardly congratulatory or festive when he walked in. It was an atmosphere of barely controlled rage. Steve felt like he was a lit match in a room full of explosives.

"Lt. Sloan, we understand you've arrested Lacey McClure for murder, along with her her stunt double," the chief said.

"Yes, sir," Steve said. As long as the chief was going to state the obvious, Steve figured it was best to follow his lead.

"Did you consult the district attorney or Ms. Cross before you made the arrest?"

"No, sir," Steve said.

The chief's face was as lifeless and cold as a statue. "You want to tell me why?"

"Because new evidence came to light that torpedoed Lacey McClure's alibi and established her guilt," Steve said. "There's no question she's the killer."

"Would the evidence have changed if you waited an hour or two?" Burnside asked. "Would the evidence have evaporated, would Lacey McClure have fled, if you'd consulted with us first before making an arrest?"

"I didn't see the point of waiting," Steve said. "Or why she should get special treatment because she's a movie star. If this was anybody else, you wouldn't care if I arrested her or not and we wouldn't be having this conversation."

"But it isn't anybody else, Detective," the chief said. "And this is no ordinary case."

"It's tragically ordinary, sir," Steve said. "She murdered her husband over love or money or both. I see it every day."

"You may not be seeing it much longer," The chief said. "You acted alone. You disregarded procedure and willfully defied your superiors. I ought to take your badge right now and flush it down my toilet."

The chief was right and Steve knew it. The fact was, he'd gotten caught up in the energy of the moment. His father had cracked Lacey's alibi and Steve couldn't wait to slap the cuffs on her after that. He was tired of being manipulated by her. But now, as Steve stood in Chief Masters' office, feeling the angry glares of his superiors, he realized another reason why he'd done it.

"But you're not going to do that, Chief, because the way you figure it, you'll have my badge when this is over, anyway." Steve glanced at Karen Cross. "You'll probably be rid of her, too. This case is a career-killer, no matter what happens. If my career is going to end over this, then I want as much control over how I'm going to go out as I can get. I'm not going to be a pawn in anybody's political game."

"It's all about you, isn't it, Sloan?" Burnside sighed with disgust. "What about the department? What about the city? Do you care about what will happen in the wake of your thoughtless actions? There will be lasting repercussions."

"Each day she is on TV, manipulating the press and directing this investigation, the LAPD suffers and the city suffers," Steve said. "Which is why she needed to be taken down the instant we had the evidence to do it. I hope this arrest has repercussions, and that the message is that murderers will be prosecuted, no matter who they are."

"You shouldn't have given up law school," Karen said. "You obviously enjoy playing to an unfriendly jury. I've only got one question for you. Do you have the evidence to back up your arrest?"

"She's got so many motives, you can pick the one you like best." Steve handed her the videos Mark had shown Lacey. "And we've cracked her alibi wide open and exposed the cold calculation that went into it."

"You mean your father did," Masters said.

"Yes, he did," Steve said. "Does it matter?"

"Perhaps it wouldn't if Dr. Sloan's entire conversation with her hadn't been recorded and broadcast all over the globe," Masters said. "If we win the case, the message is that a doctor solved a crime that you, and this department, couldn't. It makes us look incompetent. If we lose, the message is that we're a bunch of fools who let some doddering old civilian run our investigation. And we will look incompetent. Do you see the theme here, Detective?"

"I do." Steve took a step forward and looked the chief in

the eye. "And you've just explained, better than I ever could, why I didn't call anybody in this room for their approval. I'm not interested in the politics. I'm interested in who shot Cleve Kershaw and Amy Butler to death while they were laying unconscious and helpless in bed. That person is Lacey McClure. She has to pay. Everything else is irrelevant."

"If you think that, Sloan, then you're a bigger fool than I thought," Burnside said. "Context is everything. You made a big mistake here today."

Steve turned to go. There was no point to listening to this garbage any more. But before he reached the door he stopped, replaying everything that had been said. Suddenly the whole meeting suddenly took on new meaning to him, a new context, as Burnside might say. Now there was one more thing Steve had to say. He looked back at the three of them.

"You're right. I broke the rules. I disrespected your authority. So fire me. Go ahead," Steve said, holding his badge out to them. "C'mon, why wait? It's what you want to do, isn't it? Take my badge and flush it down your toilet, Chief."

He stared at them, daring them to act. None of them said a word. Steve shook his head and put his badge back in his pocket.

"You can't do it, can you?" Steve said. "Because it will look like you're punishing me for arresting a famous movie star for murders that she obviously committed. And what message would *that* send about *you?* What repercussions would *that* have for the department and the city? So unless you're ready to take my badge now, I guess I'm pretty much free to do whatever I want and not care what you think."

Karen Cross smiled. "I thought you didn't play politics."

"I'm a quick study," Steve said, and walked out.

Arthur Tyrell's new home theater sat across from him in a bright orange prison jumpsuit, a sullen expression on her famous face.

Despite her predicament, her wardrobe, and her sour mood, Lacey McClure still looked terrific, and still radiated her undeniable star power. But all Tyrell saw when he looked at her was a loving recreation of one of LA's grand, Art Deco theaters, most of which had either been torn down or were decaying in obscurity, relegated to screening bad Spanish movies and providing shelter for drug addicts.

His home theater would be small, a mere one thousand square feet, but the plans included a concession stand, a ticket booth, and a marquee. If this case was as lucrative as he expected it to be, he would honor Lacey McClure by having her movie posters on permanent display in his home lobby. Perhaps he'd even ask her to autograph one of them.

"I hear you're the best," Lacey said.

"You heard right," Tyrell said.

"I want you to represent me and Moira Cole," Lacey said. "She's my stunt double."

"I'll need a $500,000 retainer to start," he said, realizing he'd yet to choose a pattern for the curtains over his movie screen. "That is by no means the limit to what it might cost to adequately defend you and Ms. Cole in this case."

Lacey nodded. "My accountant will have a cashier's check waiting for you in your office when you return."

"Very well," Tyrell said, patting his briefcase. "Then let's get started. First off, my job is to prove you're innocent, so all I want to hear are facts that support that position. Don't tell me more than I need to know, but don't hold back anything they could spring on us in court."

"Can you get me out of here on bail?" she asked softly.

"No," he said bluntly. "I'll try, of course, but it's a multiple homicide case, so it's unlikely I'll prevail. But it will give me a chance to make a statement to the media about the injustice you're enduring, which will only help you down the road after I get the entire case thrown out in the preliminary hearing."

Lacey's expression brightened considerably. "Do you think you can do that?"

Tyrell gave her a smile that conveyed confidence, amusement, and more than a little cunning. It was a complex smile, practiced and refined over the years to justify any doubts a client might have about Tyrell's stiff retainer.

"I don't think they have a case," Tyrell said.

"They think the video that PI shot proves I'm guilty."

"I think the tape can prove whatever you want it to

prove," he said, maintaining his smile. "Tell me why Dr. Sloan was in your trailer when you were arrested."

"He lives a couple doors down from our beach house," she said. "He's the one who found the bodies, and he's the father of Steve Sloan, the homicide detective investigating the case."

"Interesting," Tyrell said, making a note on his legal pad. "So Dr. Sloan was alone with the bodies before the police arrived."

"I don't know," Lacey said. "The first time I met Dr. Sloan was when he and his son showed up at my house to tell me that Cleve had been killed."

"Dr. Sloan was there, too?" he asked in disbelief.

"I've never seen the two of them apart," she said, "Lt. Sloan brings his father with him everywhere."

"I want to know the details of each meeting you had with them," Tyrell said. "I need to know exactly what you told them and what their responses were."

Lacey recounted her first conversation with the Sloans, about her separation from Cleve and the money-laundering scheme she'd discovered. While she talked, Tyrell wrote quickly on his legal pad, filling page after page with indecipherable scrawl.

"Lt. Sloan practically accused me of murder right then," Lacey said, concluding her account. "And then he did this gunshot-residue test, which turned out positive because I'd been firing a gun all night on the set. He didn't believe me, of course."

"Did he have a warrant to perform the test?"

"He talked to a judge over the phone, then delivered a copy of the executed warrant later."

"Tell me about your next meeting," Tyrell said without even looking up from his pad.

"It was on the set. They came down while I was doing an action scene with Moira. Dr. Sloan had lots of questions about the movie-making process and how stunt doubles are used. He was obviously trying to play some kind of cat-and-mouse game with me. When I called him on it, his son came right out and called me a murderer."

"Did he read you your rights?" Tyrell asked.

"I dared him to arrest me, but he refused," Lacey said. "He said he didn't want to spend the night dealing with the media."

"I wish that conversation had been recorded," Tyrell said, still writing. "We could have used it to establish a pattern of harassment."

"Titus told me the Sloans came to his house to harass him, too," she said, "but that Dr. Sloan spent most of his time out of sight, creeping around the house."

"They were both at his house before his suicide?" he asked.

She nodded. "Is that important?"

"This gets better and better." Tyrell kept writing, even more furiously now, as if his hand couldn't keep up with his thoughts. "How did the videotape of Moira and Titus come into play?"

"The guy who shot it called me on my private line, saying it would cost me $300,000 to stay out of jail," she said. "I called Lt. Sloan right away and asked for his help."

"Excellent," Tyrell said, again not looking up from his pad as he wrote. "Go on."

"The Sloans went with me to the drop and caught the guy who was shaking me down. Turns out it was a PI who Cleve hired to follow me," she said. "The first time I saw the tape was today when the Sloans showed it to me. You've heard the rest. So has the entire world."

Tyrell stopped writing, cracked his knuckles, and leaned back in his chair. He thought for a long moment. Lacey seemed perfectly at ease with his silence. Unlike his other clients, she didn't fidget or needle him with questions as he let the facts snap into place, like bullets being loaded into an ammo clip.

"I have a lot more questions to ask you, and some detective work of my own to do, but I can tell you with absolute certainty that you will be cleared of all the charges against you," he said. " And you're going to enjoy the preliminary hearing immensely."

"I'm not looking forward to being put on trial," she said.

"Think of it as a show you're attending. Because you're not the one who's going to be on trial," Tyrell said. "It's going to be Mark Sloan."

# CHAPTER TWENTY-ONE

When Mark woke up in the morning, he looked out the back window and saw the flotilla of reporters offshore again—only now their cameras were aimed at his house instead of Cleve Kershaw's. Out the front window, he saw a thicket of satellite dishes rising from television news vans crowding the parking lot of Trancas Market on the other side of the Pacific Coast Highway.

He'd been preparing himself for a media assault since last night, ever since Larry King called to ask him about the audiotape CNN had acquired of his confrontation with Lacey McClure. Mark declined comment and disconnected the phone. Steve wisely spent the night at Parker Center and arranged to meet Mark at Community General the next morning to fill him in on the latest developments and to get Amanda's autopsy report on Titus Carville.

Mark got through the night undisturbed, thanks to the police officers Steve sent to keep reporters off the private street they lived on, just as Steve had on the day of the murders. The way things were going, Mark expected that his secretive, publicity-shy neighbors would soon start up a petition asking him to move.

Community General Hospital was walled in by television news trucks when Mark arrived, and a crowd of reporters was waiting for him at the entrance to the parking structure. The reporters were held back by private security guards, and Mark was able to drive through without having to face a single microphone or camera.

Once he was inside the hospital, Mark immediately noticed how unhappy and tense all the nurses and doctors seemed to be. At first he feared it had something to do with him, but then he learned from one of the nurses about the layoffs Dent had imposed during his brief absence. It was an outrage, and Mark promised to take the issue up with the administrator at the earliest opportunity.

That opportunity came a lot sooner than Mark anticipated. Dent was waiting outside the pathology lab, which doubled as the adjunct county medical examiner's office, where Titus Carville's body had been taken.

"Just the man I want to see," Mark said. "We need to talk."

"You could have seen me yesterday," Dent said. "But you didn't come in, did you? You called in sick—too shaken from your injuries to treat patients, yet, tellingly, not too shaken to play detective."

Mark ignored the dig. "You didn't consult me, or any other department heads, before laying off nurses. What were you thinking? We don't have enough nurses in this hospital as it is. Most of them have been working double shifts just to keep up with the workload. We should be hiring more nurses, not laying off the ones we have."

"We have a budget to balance, Dr. Sloan," Dent said. "Some sacrifices are inevitable."

"We're a hospital, those sacrifices should not come at the expense of patient care," Mark said. "You can't run Community General like one of your company's amusement parks."

"Your concern would be a lot more compelling if you had the slightest interest in patient care."

"I've been a doctor in this hospital for more than forty years," Mark said. "I've treated thousands of patients."

"Only lately, most of them have been dead. Take today, for example. You're not here to treat patients, are you? You're here to see a corpse. And look at what it's costing the doctors, nurses, and patients of this hospital."

Dent marched to the window and pointed to the media trucks outside. "Look outside, Dr. Sloan. Everybody in this hospital has to run a gauntlet of reporters because of you.

You've not only inconvenienced the staff of this hospital, but also the relatives of the patients we are caring for."

"I am not responsible for what the news media does," Mark said. "Go outside and take it up with them."

"You're the reason they're here, Doctor."

"Lacey McClure is the reason they're here," Mark said. "She murdered two people. All I did was help catch her."

"And by doing so, once again Community General suffers. Who do you think is paying for the security guards outside? We are. And we're going to have to recoup it somewhere, either with cuts in staff and services or in higher fees to our patients," Dent said. "So before you complain to me about layoffs, look at your own behavior and the costs incurred by this hospital because of it."

Mark sighed heavily. "What do you want from me, Mr. Dent?"

"I want you gone," Dent said.

"I'll be glad to take a few days off until the media attention dies down," Mark said.

"I was thinking of something more permanent." Dent offered Mark a manila envelope. "Take a look at your severance package. I think you'll find it very reasonable in light of the current situation."

The elevator opened behind Mark and Steve emerged, looking very tired. Mark glanced at Steve, then back at Dent.

"I'm not interested," Mark said, ignoring the envelope in Dent's hand.

"This is a limited-time offer, Dr. Sloan, reflecting Hollyworld's respect for your years of service," Dent said. "But that respect is significantly diminishing with each passing day, along with the cash settlement we're willing to provide."

"Give the settlement to the nurses you laid off," Mark said. "It will tide them over until I can get their jobs back."

"The only way you can do that is by leaving," Dent said. "And letting us use your salary to hire a few of them back."

"I'm not leaving," Mark said.

"Not voluntarily, anyway," Dent said, and walked off, dumping the envelope in the trash on his way.

Steve joined his father. "What was that all about?"

"The hospital administration wants to get rid of me," Mark said.

"So what else is new?"

"They laid off a bunch of nurses," Mark said. "Susan was one of them."

"Can you get them back?" Steve asked.

"I don't know," Mark said. "But I'm going to try. Anything new on the Lacey McClure case?"

Steve motioned to the path lab. "I'll fill you in after I get the autopsy results."

Mark opened the door and walked in to find Amanda in her scrubs, leaning over the corpse of a young man, rope burns around his neck.

"Hanging?" Mark asked.

Amanda nodded. "Rigged up a noose to the garage door opener, then sat on a stool, reading old *Goodnight Moon* until his wife came home. When she drove up and opened the garage with her remote, she hung him. Lifted him two feet off the ground."

"My God," Mark said. "He must have hated her."

"I heard about this one," Steve said. "Tanis Archer is working it. Turns out the wife was having an affair."

"Why was he reading *Goodnight Moon*?" Mark asked.

"They've been going through infertility treatments," Steve said. "It wasn't working."

"It's horrifying how far people will go to hurt one another," Mark said.

"Which I suppose brings us to Titus Carville," Amanda said, peeling off her gloves and going to her desk. She sorted through the files on her desk until she found the one she was looking for, then gave it to Steve. "He died of an overdose of rohypnol."

"The date-rape drug that was used to knock out Cleve Kershaw and Amy Butler," Steve said. "Cute."

"It was mixed in with the coffee in the cup on his desk," Amanda said. "I'm guessing he's been dead two days."

"Around the time someone was taking a shot at you," Steve said to his dad.

"Is there a connection?" Mark asked.

"We checked Titus Carville's phone records," Steve said. "And guess who he called the night before the attempt on your life?"

"Albert Frescetti," Mark said, then added, for Amanda's sake, "the shooter."

"I know, he's behind you. Third drawer on the right," Amanda said, then turned to Steve. "You think Carville arranged for the attempt on Mark's life to make you think the Mob was involved?"

"I think Lacey arranged it," Steve said, "and had Carville do the dirty work. It was a stunt to implicate the Mob and get rid of dad, who she was worried might punch a hole in her alibi."

"And when the hit failed, Carville killed himself," Amanda said. "That would explain the suicide note. He was distraught over failing his Lacey."

Mark shook his head. "He was expecting Lacey to show up. He'd made his bed with her special sheets because he expected her to sleep with him. That's not the act of someone about to kill himself."

"Unless she wouldn't sleep with him because of his failure," Amanda said. "What if she showed up and berated him until he had a complete breakdown. She stormed out, then he went into his little Lacey shrine and swallowed a bunch of roofies."

"That's exactly what Lacey wants us to think," Steve said. "Lacey couldn't risk turning Titus against her, he knew too much. He had the power to send her to prison with one phone call. Burnside would have given him immunity in a heartbeat and Titus could have sparked a multimillion-dollar bidding war over the rights to his story. She had to kill him."

"It's all speculation," Mark said. "We don't have any evidence to back it up."

"We don't need any. She'll go down for Kershaw and Butler," Steve said. "How many life sentences can she serve, anyway?"

Moira Cole's tiny bungalow had a leaf-covered, wood-shake roof and was nestled deep in an overgrown corner of Topanga Canyon. Her home was destined to be kindling in one of the next big Malibu fires. It wasn't a guess on Mark's part, it was a certainty. Wildfires scorched the Santa Monica Mountains with frightening regularity, propelled by the hot Santa Ana winds and consuming hundreds of homes in a relentless march to the sea.

Several years ago, Mark had seen the fires up close, not very far from where he and Steve now stood outside Moira Cole's bungalow. That fire incinerated sixteen thousand acres and turned day into night under dense clouds of smoke. He'd treated victims of the inferno and hunted a killer who hoped the flames would mask his crimes. But the lasting memory Mark had from that experience was the horrific sight of wild rabbits scrambling aflame out of the blazing chaparral, starting new fires wherever they fell.

Steve glanced at his father and seemed to sense what he was thinking. "Living in this house is like dousing yourself with gasoline and then lighting a cigarette."

"I don't know how this place has survived this long," Mark said, judging the house to be at least thirty years old. Nobody who lived in this fire zone dared to have a wood shake roof or allow dry brush so close to their homes.

"Maybe whoever lived here before maintained a firebreak," Steve said approaching the front door. He had Moira Cole's house key in his hand and a search warrant in his pocket. "It doesn't take long for the brush to get overgrown if you don't cut it back."

"Not something we have to worry about," Mark said. "One more benefit to living on the beach."

"Let's see how you feel when the big one hits, and liquefaction turns the sand underneath our house into soup."

"What a cheerful thought," Mark replied.

Steve unlocked the door and stepped inside, his father following behind him. They both stopped a few steps inside the door and stared in shock at the décor. It wasn't that the furnishings were outlandish or bizarre. In fact, the décor was understated and traditional. What was unnerving was where they'd seen it before.

Tile floors. Exposed beams. Vintage, ranch-style furniture made of rough wood and well-worn, cracked leather.

The bungalow was decorated just like Lacey McClure's

Mandeville Canyon home, only on a far smaller scale and budget.

"Is this creepy or what?" Steve said, slipping on his rubber gloves.

Mark found it far more disturbing than Titus Carville's home office. Titus was fixated on Lacey McClure, turning a room into a virtual shrine, covered with photos of Lacey and Lacey memorabilia. But Moira had taken the fanaticism way beyond that. Not only did Moira replicate Lacey's home, she replicated Lacey herself, remaking her own body in Lacey's image.

"Now we know why Moira was willing to help Lacey establish an alibi for murder," Mark said. "Both Moira and Titus were obsessed with her."

"So you'd think they'd hate each other, that they'd be competing for her attention. But no, they slept together," Steve opened the refrigerator. It was filled with bottles of Glacier Peaks water. "How were they able to do that?"

"It's not so hard to figure out, psychologically," Mark said. "For Titus, it was like sleeping with Lacey's identical twin—another opportunity to act out his Lacey fantasies. For Moira, having sex with Lacey's lover was just one more way to *be* Lacey. They both got something out of it that fed their obsessions. And they were both pleasing their idol by doing it."

Mark stepped into Moira's bedroom. There was ChapStick and a bottle of Glacier Peaks water on the nightstand. He didn't have to touch the sheets to know they were 600 threads or more. On top of the dresser, there were several framed pictures of Lacey and Moira together, taken on the sets of their various movies.

"It's still pretty sick," Steve said.

"That's an understatement," Mark replied.

Moira Cole looked like Lacey, lived like Lacey, even performed the same movie roles as Lacey. And now she would spend her life in prison, just like Lacey. It was obsession taken to an astonishing extreme. Mark began to wonder if perhaps it was Moira who killed Titus just so she could have Lacey all to herself.

Steve joined his father in the bedroom. "Yikes. This is one scary lady. The ultimate date from hell."

"Maybe she was," Mark said. "For Titus Carville."

"You think she killed Titus?"

Mark shrugged. "Seeing this, I'm surprised Cleve and Titus survived as long as they did."

# CHAPTER TWENTY-TWO

Assistant District Attorney Karen Cross returned from Lacey McClure's bail hearing to find Steve Sloan waiting in her office, her tiny TV set on and tuned to one of the local stations for the evening news.

Teetering stacks of bulging files covered every available surface in her office, including the guest chairs. Steve had moved one of the piles off one of the chairs and set it on the floor, braced against her desk, so he'd have a place to sit.

The sight of the stack on the floor unnerved her, and Steve sensed it.

"Did I just screw up some incredibly complex filing system?" he asked.

"It's not complex," she said, "It's *idiosyncratic*."

"What does that mean?"

"It means the files are organized by geography and chronology," she said. "It's a system I could never explain. It's a combination of sight, memory, and familiarity. Even the height of the pile tells me something. Move a couple of stacks, though, and the whole system crumbles into anarchy."

"All I moved was the stack on this seat," Steve said. "I promise I'll put it back. I'd swear on a stack of Bibles, but I'd be afraid to move them."

"What are you doing here, Detective?"

"I came to tell you that Moira Cole is a nutcase who'd slit her own throat for Lacey McClure, but other than that, I didn't find out anything at her house," Steve said, jacking up the volume on the TV just as Karen Cross herself appeared on camera, outside the courthouse.

Karen stood behind Steve's chair, watching herself being surrounded by reporters thrusting microphones in her face.

"We have charged Lacey McClure with two counts each of murder and conspiracy in the shooting deaths of her husband Cleve Kershaw and his lover, Amy Butler," Karen Cross told the reporters. "Additionally, we have charged Moira Cole with conspiracy to commit murder. Due to the heinous nature of these crimes, bail was denied and the defendants will remain in custody pending the outcome of a preliminary hearing. Thank you."

And with that, Karen walked away from the reporters, refusing to answer any of the dozens of questions they shouted in her wake.

Steve looked over his shoulder at her. "Don't like talking to reporters much, do you?"

"I don't try my cases in the media," she said.

"He does." Steve motioned to the television, where the reporters could be seen surrounding Arthur Tyrell as he appeared on the steps.

There was no swagger in Tyrell's step, no smile on his face. His expression was one of barely controlled outrage, his cheeks red, his eyes narrowed, his jaw set tight, as he made his statement to the reporters.

"What has happened to Lacey McClure is reprehensible and unconscionable. She was brutalized by organized-crime figures who murdered her husband because she wouldn't let them use her movies to launder their blood money. And she was brutalized again by the LAPD homicide detective assigned to the case, who betrayed her and the public trust for personal and professional gain," Tyrell said. "Lacey McClure isn't a murderer. She's the victim of a blatant and inept police conspiracy. The fact that she is sitting in jail today is a travesty of justice that makes me physically ill."

"You aren't the only one feeling sick, buddy." Steve said to the TV.

A reporter shouted out a question to Tyrell. "What about the stuntwoman?"

Tyrell grimaced, as if he'd just tasted something sour.

"Moira Cole is an innocent victim of this far-reaching conspiracy, who is resisting relentless attempts by the police to coerce her into making false statements against Lacey McClure. What this poor young woman has endured at the hands of one corrupt detective is utterly despicable."

"He can't be serious," Steve said.

Karen picked up the remote and turned off the TV. "He's demanding a preliminary hearing as soon as possible."

"The evidence against her is overwhelming," Steve said. "You'd think he'd take all the time he could get to prepare a defense."

"You just heard his defense," Karen said, taking a seat behind her desk.

"He's going to attack me instead of the evidence."

"It's not that simple. He's trying to frame the parameters of public debate. Now every discussion about the case will start first with the notion of police corruption rather than with the evidence," Karen said. "Pretty soon that's how everybody will think of the case. Tyrell hopes by the time we get into the courtroom, we will be forced to concentrate our efforts on defending your integrity instead of the integrity of the evidence."

"Aren't they inextricably linked?" Steve asked.

"If the evidence is strong, it doesn't matter whether you're a lying, inept, corrupt scumbag," she said. "The evidence will speak for itself."

"If it's not drowned out by all the noise he's going to be making about me and the department," Steve said.

"I'm not going to give him the chance," she said. "If it's an immediate hearing he wants, that's what he's going to get. I won't take the full ten days allowed by law. I'll get him in the courtroom tomorrow if I can and kill the negative debate before it starts."

Steve tried to imagine the courtroom matchup between the frail looking half-Asian-half Caucasian woman and the stocky, aggressive lawyer. Would Tyrell steamroll right over her? Or was her frailty an asset that would lead Tyrell to underestimate her tenacity and strength?

"You must be feeling pretty confident about the evidence if you're willing to give up your prep time, too." Steve said.

"I'm calling his bluff," she said. "Once the judge rules that there's sufficient evidence to support our charges, Tyrell will have to scramble for a new defense in time for the trial."

"Tyrell is taking a big risk," he said.

"Not really."

"How do you figure that?"

"Simple," she said. "His clients can't be any worse off than they already are."

After the impromptu press conference, Arthur Tyrell stopped by Ruth's Chris Steak House in Beverly Hills for the biggest rib eye on the menu and two side orders of mashed potatoes swimming in butter.

From his seat in a dark booth in the corner, he could see the TV set in the bar, which was tuned to the news. He could see himself on-screen, and although he couldn't hear what was being said, he could see how his attack against Steve Sloan was playing with the crowd of businessmen. They were watching the TV in rapt attention, unconsciously nodding in agreement with Tyrell's words.

Lacey McClure wasn't some crack whore or sociopathic gang member. She was a beautiful movie star. A heroine who battled crime in black leather. Nobody wanted her to be guilty. Whether they knew it or not, they desperately wanted her life to play out like one of her movies. So the Mob had to be the killers and the police had to be wrong.

They wanted a happy ending.

So did Tyrell. He ordered a slice of carmelized banana cream pie and imagined what the beleaguered ADA's reaction was going to be to his comments on TV. She'd want to call his bluff, to go immediately to the preliminary hearing to keep him from dragging Steve Sloan and the LAPD through the mud for days.

He smiled to himself. She'd be so busy preparing for his assault on Steve Sloan that she wouldn't be thinking about his real target, about the biggest weakness in her case.

Tyrell finished up his dinner, left a generous tip, and walked back to his office. When he stepped out of the elevator, he saw two people in the wood-paneled lobby—the receptionist and a young man with a large briefcase on his lap.

The receptionist smiled at Tyrell and motioned him over with a nod of her head. "Good evening, Mr. Tyrell."

"Marcia," he said.

"That gentleman has been waiting for you for the last two hours," she said.

"What does he want?"

"He said he'd like to talk to you about some doctor named Sloan," she replied.

Intrigued, Tyrell glanced over at the man, who was obviously aware that he was being discussed. Even so, the man remained in his seat, showing neither eagerness or anxiety. He seemed completely relaxed.

"Thank you, Marcia," Tyrell said, then strode over to the man with the briefcase and offered his hand. "I'm Arthur Tyrell. What can I do for you?"

The man rose and shook the lawyer's hand. "It's what we can do for each other, Mr. Tyrell."

The man opened his briefcase and handed Tyrell a thick file, bound with rubber bands to hold all the papers in place. "There are a few facts I've compiled on Dr. Mark Sloan and his activities at Community General Hospital over the years. I thought you might find it interesting—particularly his relationship to the adjunct county medical examiner and his free access to her lab, her files, and the corpses she examines."

Tyrell took a seat beside the man, pulled off the rubber bands, and opened the file on the glass-topped coffee table. He browsed through it quickly. It was apparent to Tyrell after only seeing a few documents that he'd just been handed a treasure chest. There had to be a catch, which he imagined was in the high five figures, minimum.

"I take it you're expecting some kind of financial consideration in return for this information."

"Not at all, Mr. Tyrell," the man said. "Consider it a gift. No strings attached. Just don't ever say where you got it."

Arthur Tyrell stood and gave the man his biggest, warmest smile. "Please, call me Arthur. I'm afraid you have me at a disadvantage. I didn't get your name."

"Noah Dent, chief administrator of Community General Hospital. But you may call me Noah."

Tyrell studied his gift horse for a moment, wondering what his true motives were. "Do you like brandy, Noah?"

"I do, Arthur."

"Excellent." Tyrell picked up the large file and led Dent towards his office. "Then let's open a bottle and talk some more about Dr. Sloan, shall we?"

On his way back home, Steve stopped at BBQ Bob's to catch up on business and walked into a mini-crisis. One of the cooks had called in sick and they were short a waitress, who'd abruptly quit without any notice.

Steve was immediately pressed into service as a waiter. He tied on an apron and began taking orders and serving meals. There was a big crowd, all of them hungry and impatient. They kept him on his feet, running back and forth between the kitchen and the tables. As exhausting as it was, it was a welcome diversion. He didn't think about the case, or Lacey McClure, even once.

But the respite was broken as soon as the dinner crowd waned, and Steve took a moment behind the counter to get himself a Coke. There was a man in a suit, tie loosened at the collar, sitting on a bar stool with a ready smile.

"Must be a lot of work running this place," the man said to Steve.

"It's a lot of work running anything," Steve said.

"Bet it would be a lot easier if you had a million dollars," the man said.

"Everything would be easier with a million dollars," Steve replied.

The man reached into his jacket, took out a check, and set it on the counter.

"Life just got easier," the man said.

Steve glanced at the check. It was from Toffler & Templeton and it was made out to him for one million dollars. He'd heard of the venerable publisher, of course. Anyone who'd ever walked into a bookstore in the last sixty years knew their ubiquitous logo: two "T"s separated by an elegant quill as an ampersand.

"I'm Mitch Stein, senior editor of Toffler & Templeton's true-crime imprint," Stein said, offering his hand. "We'd like to hear your story."

"My life isn't really that interesting."

"It became interesting when you arrested Lacey McClure for murder," Stein said. "We'll pair you up with Pulitzer Prize-winning journalist Andy Andrews to create the definitive account of your investigation."

Steve set his Coke down on the check, using it as a coaster. "I'm not interested."

"You don't have to do a thing except talk." Stein looked down as the ring of moisture beneath the glass widened, the absorption heading for the red ink of the inscribed amount and signature.

"If I participate in the writing of this book, my career is over," Steve said.

"No offense, but your career is already over," Stein said quickly, racing the absorption, hoping to change Steve's mind before the ink smeared, voiding the check. "You're going to need this money to live on."

"I'll live," Steve said.

"Wouldn't you prefer to live well?" Stein asked.

"I've still got to live with myself," Steve said, walking away.

Stein glanced down at the check. It was wet. The moisture from the glass had smeared the red ink. What was once a million dollars now looked like drops of fresh blood.

# CHAPTER TWENTY-THREE

Superior Court Judge Aurelio Rojas stared down from the bench at his crowded courtroom with weariness and disapproval, as if the very presence of the people before him was a disappointment. The only thing that would have pleased him was greeting an empty courtroom, which would prove that at least one day had gone by without a lawless act being committed that demanded his judgment.

But that day was never going to come, and, rather than accept it, he wore a permanent expression of glum disdain and chronic displeasure. If his expression was an accurate reflection of his attitude, then it probably boded well for the prosecution. It was the only edge the prosecution appeared to have, since they were clearly outmatched in sheer star power by the expertly coiffed and outfitted group at the defense table.

Their backs were to the spectators' gallery where Mark and Steve sat. Even so, the defense table radiated beauty, poise, wealth, power, and supreme self-confidence with such intensity that Mark felt like he should be wearing sunscreen.

Lacey McClure was dressed in the same conservative suit she wore in her movie *Thrill Kill* when she played the housewife who takes on the Mob. She also wore the same look of moral outrage she displayed in the courtroom scenes when the killers of her cop husband were set free on a technicality. Her performance on this day wasn't so much for the benefit of the judge, who didn't seem to notice it, as for the cameras, which noticed everything.

Her codefendant Moira Cole didn't have her idol's, admittedly limited, acting ability or natural charisma, but she did have her natural beauty, though with a harder edge. An attempt had been made to soften that edge and to de-emphasize her resemblance to Lacey with a new haircut, makeup, and a sexier wardrobe that accentuated her femininity.

Arthur Tyrell managed to look both respectful and utterly at ease, leaning forward with his elbows on the table, his gold pen poised to take notes on his brand-new blank legal pad. There were no notes, files, or papers in front of him, which by itself conveyed his command of the facts, and projected strength.

ADA Karen Cross sat at the prosecution table with several files stacked beside her, using the last few seconds before the hearing to scribble a couple more notes to herself on a pad seemingly already filled with writing. She looked like a student cramming at the last minute before a final exam and wore an off-the-rack suit that accentuated her frailness. Mark wondered if she, too, was affecting a pose, to look like the vulnerable underdog up against the aggressive, high-powered attorney. Then again, it wasn't so much a pose as a clear statement of the truth, even if she was consciously taking advantage of it.

The truth was that Karen Cross already had a distinct advantage. The threshold of proof required to establish that there was enough evidence to go to trial was exceeding low. The defense rarely succeeded in getting the case dismissed.

The gallery where Mark sat was filled to capacity with witnesses and reporters, who represented only a small fraction of the journalists who were camped outside the building. But no one was being deprived of the experience of watching the preliminary hearing unfold. The hearing was being broadcast live on Court TV from a single camera mounted above the jury box.

Mark had no doubt the hearing would be covered with ridiculous significance and high drama by Court TV's team of legal pundits, despite the fact that there was little doubt what the outcome would be. The hearing would play like a dress rehearsal of the murder trial, a preview of the block-buster entertainment event to come.

Judge Rojas cleared his throat and looked directly at Tyrell, as if he were a child who might misbehave at any moment.

"This is a preliminary hearing to determine if there is enough evidence to merit a trial," Rojas said, more for the benefit of the public than of the experienced attorneys in front of him. "It is not a trial, so save your histrionics for the jury. Is that clear?"

Rojas didn't expect a verbal answer, but looked to the two attorneys to see the acknowledgement on their faces.

"Are the People ready?" the judge asked.

Karen Cross rose from her seat. "Yes, your honor."

"Is the defense ready?" the judge asked.

Arthur Tyrell glanced significantly at his clients, cleverly drawing everyone's attention to them, giving the two women a chance to shamelessly emote for the cameras, then he rose and faced the Judge. "Yes, Your Honor."

"Proceed," the judge said, tipping his head to Karen.

"Your Honor, the People call Officer Tony Blake to the stand."

The uniformed cop, the first to respond to the murder scene, rose from his seat in the gallery, was sworn in, and took his place on the witness stand.

Karen asked him some straightforward and perfunctory questions to establish that a crime had actually taken place, and where and when it had happened.

Officer Blake set up a couple of key points Mark knew that the prosecutor would come back to later: that the police responded to a "shots fired" 911 call at four thirty p.m., and arrived at the scene to find Cleve Kershaw and Amy Butler naked together in bed, shot to death.

Karen sat down. Tyrell rose and strode casually up to the witness stand.

"Officer Blake, were there any witnesses to the shooting?" Tyrell asked.

"No," the officer replied.

"Did anyone report seeing either of my clients at the scene?" Tyrell tipped his head towards the prosecution table to indicate Lacey McClure and Moira Cole, who both un-flinchingly met the officer's gaze.

"No," Officer Blake said.

"Did you see either of my clients at the scene?"

"No," Officer Blake said.

"Who called 911 and reported hearing gunshots?" Tyrell asked.

"According to my dispatcher, it was a neighbor who identified himself as Dr. Mark Sloan."

Tyrell nodded, then looked directly at Mark. And in that one, economical glance, Tyrell communicated a wealth of information, none of it good. The lawyer was saying he knew exactly who Mark was and where he was sitting. And Tyrell wouldn't have known that unless Mark mattered to him. And there was only one reason that Mark would matter.

In that instant, Mark knew what was going to happen to him and that he was powerless to stop it. The realization and the dread must have shown on Mark's face, because Tyrell allowed himself the tiniest of smiles before turning back to face Officer Blake.

Karen Cross didn't appreciate the significance of Tyrell's glance at Mark, but she noticed the smile and knew it meant misery for her.

"Were there any other calls to the police reporting the gunshot?" Tyrell asked the officer.

"Not to my knowledge," Officer Blake said.

"So the only evidence that you had that the shots were fired at four thirty that afternoon was the phone call from Dr. Sloan."

"Yes," the officer said.

Tyrell paused, as if mulling this new information for the first time. He wasn't, but Karen Cross was. She was trying to extrapolate from the question what Tyrell's line of defense was going to be and how it might affect her case. She didn't have to wait long to find out.

"When you arrived at the scene," Tyrell asked, "did you discover anyone in the house with the victims?"

"Yes."

"Who was it?"

"Dr. Sloan," The officer said.

"In fact, you caught him in the act of butchering Amy Butler with a knife."

Karen bolted up from her seat. "Objection! That isn't a question, it's a statement. He's putting words in the witness' mouth."

"Sustained," the judge said, then turned to Tyrell. "I remind you, Mr. Tyrell, that this is a courtroom and not a stage. You're making your case to me and not to the cameras. I won't tolerate any more dramatic performances."

Tyrell nodded. "I'll rephrase the question."

But the damage had already been done. The image of Mark Sloan, gutting a naked young woman in bed with bloodthirsty glee, was already planted in the minds of the viewers watching the hearing on television.

Steve glanced at his father, who was stone-faced. Mark was trying hard to keep his emotions from showing. He didn't want to look guilty, though he certainly felt it—well aware now how his actions could be misinterpreted and used to torpedo the prosecution. But there was no way to stop Tyrell now. The best Karen Cross could hope to do was to contain the damage.

Tyrell faced the officer again. "Was Dr. Sloan with the victims?"

"Yes," the Officer conceded.

"Was he holding a sharp implement in his hands and cutting into Amy Butler's naked body?"

"Yes."

"Did you draw your weapon?"

"Yes."

"Why?" Tyrell asked.

The officer was taken aback. This was not a question he could dodge with a simple yes or no answer. It took him two long seconds to think of how to respond in a way that would cause the least damage to the case.

"It's standard procedure when responding to a call of shots fired to be prepared to defend yourself against an armed assailant," the officer replied. "We were startled to encounter Dr. Sloan with the bodies."

"I don't blame you for being startled," Tyrell said.

"Objection," Karen said.

"Withdrawn," Tyrell replied. "You arrested Dr. Sloan, didn't you, Officer Blake?"

"Yes."

"Why?" Tyrell asked.

Once again, Officer Blake shifted uncomfortably in his seat, wrestling with another question he didn't want to answer.

"Although we were responding to a report of gunshots, we didn't know for certain how the victims had been killed," Officer Blake said. "We discovered him holding a scalpel to one of the victims."

"Was he performing a lifesaving medical procedure?"

Karen Cross objected. "Officer Blake isn't qualified to answer that question. He isn't a doctor, nor does he have medical training."

"Sustained," the judge said.

Tyrell sighed. "Would it be fair to say, Officer Blake, that at the moment you entered the room and saw Dr. Sloan slicing the victims, you weren't certain whether or not you'd caught the murderer in the act?"

"Yes," Officer Blake replied.

"In fact, the only information you had that shots had even been fired came from Dr. Sloan, the man you found hacking up the bodies. Isn't that true?"

"Objection," Karen said. "Argumentative."

"The witness has already testified that Dr. Sloan made the 911 call and that he discovered him cutting into one of the victims," Tyrell argued.

"There's a big difference between a small surgical incision and hacking," Karen argued.

"Is there?" Tyrell asked, enjoying the opportunity to underscore again the negative image of Mark Sloan he was creating.

Karen realized too late that she'd been expertly manipulated once again. She would have been better off not objecting. All she'd managed to do was multiply the damage.

"Objection sustained," the judge said, glaring at Tyrell. "Please try to present the facts without embellishment, Mr. Tyrell."

"Yes, Your Honor." Tyrell approached the witness stand. "Officer Blake, would it be accurate to say that Dr. Sloan initiated this investigation and controlled all the facts as you knew them?"

"Objection," Karen said, unable to disguise her irritation. "Officer Blake wasn't then, nor is he now, omniscient."

"Sustained," the judge said. "Please limit your questions to matters that mere mortals, and this witness, are qualified to address."

"Yes, Your Honor," Tyrell said, turning his attention to the witness again. "Was Dr. Sloan alone with the bodies before you arrived?"

"Yes."

"Do you have any idea how long he was alone in that house, or what other procedures he might have performed on the victims?"

"No," Officer Blake replied.

"You testified earlier that you arrested Dr. Sloan," Tyrell said. "Was he transported to the station and charged?"

"No," the officer said, his face beginning to redden from both anger and embarrassment.

"He wasn't?" Tyrell asked, feigning surprise. "Was he released without being charged?"

"Yes," Officer Blake said.

"But you caught him in the act of cutting up one of the victims," Tyrell said. "Isn't tampering with evidence a crime in this state?"

"Yes."

"Then why was Dr. Sloan released without being charged?"

"You'd have to ask Lt. Sloan," the officer said.

"You mean *Dr.* Sloan," Tyrell corrected him with a patient smile.

"I mean Lt. Steve Sloan, the homicide detective in charge of the investigation," Officer Blake said. "Dr. Sloan is his father."

"Let me make sure I understand." Tyrell leaned against the witness stand so that he faced the camera mounted above the jury box, beckoning the audience with a glance and slight arching of an eyebrow to pay attention to what was coming next. "You're saying that the detective investigating the homicides is the son of the guy who reported the crime and was caught cutting up one of the victims?"

"Yes," Officer Blake said.

Tyrell looked incredulously at Officer Blake, then at the camera, and finally at Judge Rojas, who was staring at the witness with much the same expression. It was a joy for Tyrell to see.

"No further questions," Tyrell said, and returned to his seat.

The defense attorney quit while he was well ahead. He'd effectively made his point, exacting as much damage to the prosecution's case as he possibly could with this witness. Now that he'd successfully laid the foundation for his attack, he knew it would be a lot easier to eviscerate the witnesses to come.

Mark and Steve and Karen knew it, too.

# Chapter Twenty-Four

Dr. Amanda Bentley seemed confident, professional, and entirely at ease on the witness stand as Karen Cross walked her through the formality of establishing her professional credentials as the adjunct county medical examiner.

There was no reason for Amanda to be nervous. The questions were perfunctory and she answered them by rote, as she had in hearings and trials a hundred times before. Soon Karen would lead her into recounting the facts of the case, but Amanda wasn't worried about that, either. It wasn't a complicated autopsy. The cause of death for both victims was obvious, as were her methods and conclusions.

She knew the defense attorney would have to take a swing or two at her just to earn his salary, but since the case was so straightforward, she wasn't worried.

But Mark Sloan was.

Amanda hadn't been in the courtroom for Officer Blake's testimony. She was prepared to defend her work and her scientific conclusions, not to handle an attack aimed at undermining the evidence by discrediting Mark and Steve.

Throughout the early stages of her testimony, Mark tried to make eye contact, to somehow convey to her the ordeal she'd soon be facing. But when their eyes met, all his gaze managed to create was a moment of confusion. She didn't get why he looked so grim, when the facts were so simple and clear.

Guided by Karen's questions, Amanda testified that she arrived at the crime scene at six p.m., an hour and a half after the bodies were discovered.

"In the absence of definitive indicators, like a car accident or a shooting that was witnessed by others, how do you determine the time of death?" Karen Cross asked.

"It's not an exact science. We can't definitively state the time of death, we can only provide a reasonably accurate estimate," Amanda said. "The first thing we consider are indicative acts which, in this case, would be the 911 call at four thirty reporting the gunshots. We also look at body temperature, lividity, rigor mortis, and degree of decomposition."

"Was the physical state of the victims consistent with deaths that occurred at four thirty p.m.?"

"Yes."

"All the factors considered, would you have determined four thirty p.m. as the time of death?"

"Yes."

Karen nodded, letting that sink in for the judge and, presumably, for the millions of people watching.

"But you would have been wrong, wouldn't you?" Karen said.

Amanda didn't hesitate to answer. "Yes."

"How do you know that?"

"Because before I arrived, Dr. Sloan made an important discovery." Amanda glanced at Mark and was again disturbed by his grim demeanor. Ordinarily, this was a moment he would have enjoyed, the moment when one of his deductions came into play in the undoing of the murderer. So she had to ask herself: *Why wasn't he enjoying it now?*

In attempting to answer the question for herself, Amanda began to get a general sense of what Mark was trying so hard to communicate to her with the expression on his face.

*You're in trouble. This isn't going to go the way you expect. Prepare yourself.*

Amanda still didn't know what kind of trouble, but suddenly she felt her heart racing. It was as if she'd just started walking down a dark corridor where she knew someone was waiting to jump out and scare her. Knowing the scare was coming didn't make it any easier to take.

"What was that discovery?" Karen prodded, snapping Amanda out of her thoughts.

"A gunshot victim will bleed out even after death has occurred," Amanda said. "Dr. Sloan arrived at the scene a few minutes after the gunshots, but the blood was already clotted."

"Objection," Tyrell said, without bothering to rise from his seat. "Dr. Bentley doesn't know when Dr. Sloan arrived or what he saw and heard. This is hearsay."

"And this is a preliminary hearing, not a murder trial," Judge Rojas said. "I'll allow it. Please continue, Dr. Bentley."

"If the victims were killed at four thirty, the blood couldn't have been clotted yet," Amanda continued. "It's impossible."

"But it would have been clotted by the time you arrived, is that correct?"

"Yes."

"So you would have missed that vital clue," Karen Cross said.

"Yes."

"But Dr. Sloan's contribution to the accurate determination of the time of death went beyond reporting to you what he saw, isn't that true?"

"One of the factors we consider in estimating the time of death is, as I said before, body temperature. Normal body temperature is 98.6 degrees. After death, the body loses about 1.5 degrees per hour," Amy explained. "Dr. Sloan made a postmortem incision into Amanda Butler's liver to get an accurate reading of her body temperature. It was 97 degrees."

"So if Dr. Sloan hadn't checked the liver temperature before your arrival, you would have miscalculated the time of death."

"Yes," Amanda said. "Based on Dr. Sloan's findings, and my subsequent autopsies, I estimated the time of death at between three and four p.m."

"Would it be fair to say that Dr. Sloan's actions aided your examination?"

"Absolutely," Amanda replied.

"What was the cause of death, in layman's terms?" Karen asked.

"Gunshot wounds to the head and the heart with a .45-caliber handgun," she replied.

"Did anything else come up in the autopsy?"

"I discovered rohypnol in both victims," Amanda said.

"What is rohypnol?"

"It's a sedative."

"What did that indicate to you?" the prosecutor asked.

"That both victims were unconscious at the time of their deaths," she replied.

"Did you determine how the drugs were administered?"

"Yes," Amanda said. "I saw champagne glasses in the living room at the scene. The crime lab discovered someone had injected the drug through the cork into the champagne bottle."

"Thank you, Dr. Bentley." Karen returned to her seat.

Tyrell whispered something to Lacey McClure, then rose from his seat and strolled up to the witness stand.

"What was your first reaction when you learned that Dr. Sloan had cut into one of the victims?"

"I don't recall," Amanda said.

But Mark remembered what she'd said and was certain Amanda probably did, too. She was committing perjury to protect him, herself, and the case against Lacey McClure.

Steve remembered, too, and he had to use all his self-control not to close his eyes and groan. He knew that Tyrell wouldn't be asking the question if there wasn't some way to prove the answer.

"Then let me help you remember," Tyrell said, as if reading Steve's thoughts.

The defense attorney went back to his desk, opened up his briefcase, removed a video cassette, and approached the judge's bench with it.

"This is a copy of a video shot by the LAPD Scientific Investigation Division to document the crime scene," Tyrell said. "I'd like to play a portion of it to help jog Dr. Bentley's memory."

"Proceed," Judge Rojas said, nodding his head toward a TV and VCR on a rolling stand in a corner of the courtroom.

While Tyrell wheeled the stand over, turned on the equipment, and inserted the video, Karen Cross glanced back at

Mark and Steve. Their faces gave away nothing. Since she didn't know what Amanda's reaction at the crime scene had been, the prosecutor was pondering a different question: *How did Tyrell get his hands on the SID tape?*

Tyrell hit PLAY. The photographer slowly moved the camera around the living room to methodically establish the geography of the home and what was in it.

The camera passed over Mark, his hands cuffed behind his back, having a conversation with Steve and Amanda. Although other people were talking in the room, Amanda's voice could clearly be heard as she angrily addressed Mark.

*"Tampering with the evidence at a murder scene is a crime,"* Amanda said. *"Especially when it's my evidence."*

Tyrell stopped the tape.

Amanda felt as if everyone on earth was staring at her. Glancing up at the camera mounted above the jury box, she realized the majority of them probably were.

"Tampering?" Tyrell said. "That wasn't how you described Dr. Sloan's actions in your testimony, was it?"

"I obviously made that comment before I was fully informed of what he had done," she said, trying to keep her voice steady and calm.

"Does that change the fact that what he did violated the law?"

"Objection," Karen Cross snapped angrily. "Dr. Bentley is a medical examiner, not a judge."

"She knows and understands the law in question," Tyrell argued. "She demonstrated that in the video."

"Overruled," Judge Rojas said to Karen, who sat down, simmering.

When this day from hell was finally over, Karen was going to tear Steve Sloan apart, assuming Arthur Tyrell left anything behind when he was done.

Tyrell looked at Amanda. "I'll repeat the question. Did Dr. Sloan's explanation change the fact that he broke the law by performing an invasive postmortem procedure on a murder victim?"

"No," Amanda said quietly.

"I'm sorry," Tyrell said. "I couldn't hear you."

"No," she said louder.

"So why wasn't he charged?" Tyrell asked.

"I don't know," Amanda said.

Tyrell gave her a skeptical look, but decided to let that pass.

"You assumed the murder occurred at four thirty because of the 911 call made by Dr. Sloan, correct?"

"Yes."

"And you also took Dr. Sloan's word for when he arrived at the scene and the amount of blood clotting that had occurred, correct?"

"Yes."

"But you hadn't actually examined the bodies yourself yet, had you?"

"No," Amanda said.

"In fact, isn't it true that you talked to Dr. Sloan as soon as you arrived at the scene, before even taking so much as a peek at the bodies?"

"Yes," Amanda said, knowing now what Mark had been trying to warn her about, and knowing that it was far too late. She'd fallen into the covered pit and was already impaled on the spikes. The only question now was how long she'd be made to suffer.

"So for all you know, the blood still hadn't clotted yet and he was distracting you until he was certain that it had?"

"Objection!" Karen said, practically yelling it out.

"Sustained," Judge Rojas said, not even waiting for her to make an argument. "Mr. Tyrell, save your theorizing for your inevitable press conference on the courthouse steps."

Tyrell acknowledged the comment with a curt nod, then confronted Amanda again.

"You testified that you found rohypnol in the bodies and learned that traces of the drug were found in the champagne bottle," Tyrell said. "Do you know when the drug was put in the champagne bottle?"

"I assume before Cleve Kershaw and Amy Butler opened it," she replied.

"You assume," he repeated. "But you don't know for certain, do you?"

"No."

"It could have been introduced into the bottle after they were dead, couldn't it?"

"Yes," she said reluctantly, knowing exactly what the lawyer was implying: that Mark might have tampered with the bottle while he was alone in the house. But she couldn't figure out what Tyrell was hoping to prove. Did he honestly think that anyone would believe that Mark had killed Kershaw and Butler? What possible motive could Mark have?

"You also can't say for certain how the rohypnol entered the bodies, can you?"

"I didn't find any needle marks on their bodies or—"

Tyrell interrupted before she could finish her reply. "Yes or no, Dr. Bentley?"

"No."

Tyrell nodded and paced in front of the witness stand for a moment. Amanda looked at the defendants, mostly because she couldn't bear to look at Mark—not with what she was doing to him. Lacey and Moira had thin smiles on their faces, clearly enjoying her discomfort.

"Where is the adjunct county medical examiner's office?" Tyrell asked.

"It's in the pathology lab at Community General Hospital."

"Isn't that the same hospital where you practice as a pathologist and where Dr. Sloan serves as chief of internal medicine?"

"Yes."

Tyrell looked at Mark, then back at Amanda. "Is that where you took the victims for autopsy?"

"Yes."

It was clear to her, of course, where Tyrell was going with this line of questioning and where it would end. There was nothing she could do to stop him. She was forced by the law to be an unwilling accomplice in the character assassination of Mark Sloan. If that wasn't painful enough, she was also committing professional suicide for the amusement of a live television audience.

"Dr. Sloan was instrumental in convincing the city to establish the adjunct county medical examiner's office in your hospital, wasn't he?" Tyrell asked pointedly.

"We worked together on it," Amanda said. "But it was my idea."

"So you would say the two of you are very close?"

"Yes."

Tyrell nodded. "As chief of internal medicine at Community General Hospital, and as your close personal friend, Dr. Sloan can come visit you in the lab any time he wants, can't he?"

"Yes," she said flatly, resigned to her fate now. It was inevitable.

"And if you're not there, he can still visit the lab whenever he wants, day or night, and even examine the bodies, isn't that true?"

"Yes."

"The fact is, he has examined the bodies of murder victims with and without you present on many occasions over the years, hasn't he?"

"Yes."

"Does Dr. Sloan have access at Community General to rohypnol?"

"Yes."

"So it's possible that Dr. Sloan could have introduced the rohypnol into the bodies, or into the blood and tissue samples at any stage of the testing without your knowledge, is it not?"

Karen Cross immediately objected and was just as quickly overruled by the judge. The prosecutor sat down, shoulders sagging with defeat.

"The witness will answer the question," the Judge said to Amanda. "Yes or no, Dr. Bentley?"

She looked out at Mark, her friend and mentor, and saw nothing but sympathy and understanding on his face.

"Yes," she said softly.

# CHAPTER TWENTY-FIVE

When the hearing recessed for lunch, Karen Cross went directly to the private meeting room she'd reserved in the courthouse. She wasn't surprised to find the chief Masters and the district attorney Burnside waiting for her. They acknowledged her with a nod but didn't say a word. She took a seat beside them and waited.

A few moments later Mark and Steve walked in, looking like two condemned men. As soon as the door was closed, Karen spoke, addressing herself to Steve.

"You never told me that Dr. Sloan was arrested," she said. "It never appeared in the police reports, either."

"I didn't think it was relevant," Steve said.

"Well obviously it was!" she shouted. "You should have recused yourself from the investigation the moment you saw him in handcuffs."

"He didn't commit a crime," Steve said. "We wouldn't have a case if it wasn't for him."

"That's exactly what Arthur Tyrell hopes to prove," Burnside said. "It's clear he's trying to establish a police conspiracy, mounted by you and your father, to frame Lacey McClure for murder."

"That's absurd," Steve said.

"Not to anyone who has heard the testimony so far," Burnside said. "What's absurd is that Dr. Sloan reported the shooting, Dr. Sloan discovered the bodies, Dr. Sloan performed an autopsy at the scene, and Dr. Sloan controlled the laboratory that analyzed the evidence."

"You're taking the facts out of context," Steve said.

"Tyrell established the context," Karen argued. "And he's reinforced it with every question."

"My father has investigated hundreds of homicides," Steve said. "His presence at a crime scene has never been questioned before. And his association with Amanda and the adjunct county medical examiner's office is old news."

"Not to the fifty million people watching television today it's not," Burnside said.

"It's what the judge thinks that matters," Steve said.

"Grow up, Lieutenant," Burnside said with disgust.

"My father isn't the one on trial here," Steve said. "It's Lacey McClure. She's the one who killed two people, remember?"

"Did she?" Burnside asked. "Or did you and your father manufacture this entire case?"

"Don't tell me you believe that," Steve said.

"It's not a question of what I believe, Lieutenant, it's a question of what the evidence proves," Burnside said. "And right now, thanks to your inept handling of the investigation, the evidence isn't quite as convincing."

During the exchange, Chief Masters sat quietly in his chair studying Mark, who seemed lost in thought.

"You've remained unusually quiet, Dr. Sloan," Masters said.

Mark looked up at him. "I've been thinking about the testimony I've heard and the testimony to come."

"Have you reached any conclusions?" the chief asked.

Mark nodded. "I think the district attorney is right: The case is in jeopardy and my actions are to blame."

Steve was shocked. "You have nothing to apologize for, Dad. You saw through Lacey McClure's tricks, took apart her alibi, and proved she was a murderer. She would have gotten away with double homicide if it wasn't for you."

"She still might, Steve," Mark sighed. "We've underestimated her again."

"This is only a preliminary hearing," Karen said. "It's the murder trial we need to worry about. Perhaps we should be thankful that Tyrell has shown us where we're vulnerable, even if he has poisoned the jury pool in the process."

"I'll be sure to send him a gift basket," Burnside said. "How did Tyrell get his hands on the SID video?"

"Tyrell clearly has sources within the department— someone with an agenda, debts they can't pay, or a weakness for celebrities," Chief Masters said. "I'll find the leak and seal it. My immediate concern is how to repair the damage that's already been caused in the courtroom and keep it from spreading."

"We can't," Karen said. "If I address his charges in my questioning, I add credibility to them and reinforce them. We have to present our case as originally planned, but be careful not to provide him with any new ammunition."

The chief rose from his seat and strode towards the door. Somehow, he looked even taller now to Steve, or perhaps Steve just felt smaller.

Masters paused at the door and turned to face the room.

"Considering Dr. Bentley's testimony today, I'm going to demand that she be immediately removed as a county medical examiner and that an investigation be launched into her questionable conduct," the chief said. "I'll also urge the board of supervisors to shut down the adjunct medical examiner's office at Community General Hospital."

"I think that's wise," Burnside said. "We'll look like we're proactive, rather than responding to the public uproar."

"There hasn't been any," Steve said.

"There will be," Karen said. "I'll lead it myself."

The chief glared at Steve. "Regardless of the outcome of this case, your career as a homicide detective is over. You can resign or be fired. I'll leave the choice up to you."

"He's not responsible for what has happened," Mark said, rising from his seat. "I am."

"You're right," the chief said and walked out.

There are people in this world who actually buy underarm deodorant by the gallon. This was a little-known fact that Dr. Jesse Travis learned by visiting the Buy Bulk Club Warehouse Superstore in Westlake Village, California, a suburb of Los Angeles.

He couldn't imagine buying a one-gallon jug of deodorant, no matter how much cheaper it might be in the long-run than buying those little roll-ons. Nor could he envision buying a five-hundred-yard roll of dental floss, a five-pound box of Cap'n Crunch, or a package of thirty-six pairs of underwear.

But now Jesse finally understood why there were so many SUVs on the road, and why all the new tract homes in the suburbs had four-car garages. It was so people could transport and store their gallons of Listerine, pounds of Cheetos, and pallets of brassieres.

The wide aisles of the vast warehouse were gridlocked with customers, their gigantic carts overflowing with bulk goods. The people appeared to be stocking up for some kind of looming disaster, like an earthquake, hurricane, or a prolonged siege by invading alien hordes. If any of those things were scheduled for the coming weeks, someone must have forgotten to copy Jesse on the memo.

But Jesse wasn't at the Buy Bulk Club to go shopping, but to talk with Horace Beckler, the owner of the store and a former graduate school roommate of Noah Dent.

They sat eating extra-long hot dogs and drinking extra-large Cokes at one of the indoor picnic tables under a patio umbrella that gave them shade from the massive fluorescent lights.

Horace was only in his early thirties, but had already resorted to the desperate art of the comb-over, attempting to use a few long strands of hair from one side of his head to hide the ever-expanding baldness on top. But the comb-over was the least of Horace's appearance challenges. He had the build of a man who not only sold in bulk, but consumed in bulk as well.

"A few months before I graduated from business school, I walked into a McDonald's on Wilshire Boulevard and had an epiphany," Horace said. "The woman behind the counter asked me if I wanted to super-size my meal for just a few cents more. Imagine that, Dr. Travis. Super-sizing."

"It boggles the mind," Jesse agreed.

Horace shook his head at the wonder of it all. "I foresaw in that instant the future of American consumer culture. The era of super-sizing, going large, and the Big Gulp. Not just in food, but all things, including homes, cars, electronics, clothes, and breasts. I shared this vision with Noah, but he couldn't see it."

"He was more interested in hospital management," Jesse said. "Which is why we love him."

"I tried to explain to him that he should think big like I was, but he was fixated on taking over a hospital someday," Horace said. "Now look around today and what do you see?"

Jesse saw an old woman wrestling a six-pound box of instant mashed potatoes out of her cart and onto the conveyer belt at the cash registers. He saw two children helping their mother drag an enormous sack of diapers. He saw a man clutching a jug of peanut butter under one arm, and a quart of hair gel under the other.

"Women with thirty-six-inch busts are driving Humvees into their McMansions, where they have 500 channels on their sixty-five-inch TVs," Horace said. "Big is a growth industry that's only going to get bigger. Noah could have been part of this."

"But he was driven by a passion for Community General instead," Jesse said. "If the tribute I'm organizing in his honor is going to succeed, we need to understand how that passion was born."

"So ask him," Horace said.

"We want this tribute to be a surprise," Jesse said. "That's why I'm quietly going to his friends to find out more about him."

"Well, when you find out, will you let me know? Because it never made any sense to me. Hospital administration is something you end up with, not something you strive for," Horace said. "But whatever the reason is, it's got to go way back. It was already on his mind when I met him."

"How do you know?"

"He was always cutting out articles about the hospital and the doctors, sticking them into this big file," Horace said.

"Any doctors in particular?"

"I wasn't paying that much attention," Horace said. "I was looking into the future. And it was big."

"What do you know about Noah's family?" Jesse asked.

"What does his family have to do with it?"

"Maybe one of them was born at Community General, or founded the hospital, or was a doctor there," Jesse said, though he'd already checked out those possibilities. He and Susan had spent the last few days exploring Mark's past as both an investigator and a doctor, looking for any point where his life might have intersected with Noah Dent's. They didn't find one.

"He's from Toronto, came here to go to graduate school. I think he mentioned once that his dad sold insurance and that his parents were divorced," Horace said. "Have you lined up a caterer for the event?"

"Not yet," Jesse said.

"Keep us in mind." Horace reached into his coat and handed Jesse a brochure. "We do party platters of all kinds. We'll give you a discount."

"Will you super-size our order for a few dollars more?" Jesse asked.

"Of course," Horace replied.

Jesse thanked Horace, swore him to secrecy about their meeting, and was on his way out of the store when he saw the crowd gathered around the big-screen TVs. He stopped to take a look, expecting to see a clip from the latest blockbuster action movie.

What he saw was a live broadcast of the preliminary hearing of Lacey McClure. He only had to listen for a few moments to the play-by-play from the commentators, which included a prosecutor from the O. J. Simpson trial, to realize he wasn't actually watching a dry legal proceeding.

It was an execution.

# CHAPTER TWENTY-SIX

Lacey McClure wasn't the only actress in the courtroom. Assistant District Attorney Karen Cross was doing a remarkable job of acting like a confident prosecutor in complete control of the evidence she was presenting. Nothing about her expression betrayed her belief that her case was disintegrating in front of her eyes, or her nearly uncontrollable desire to leap into the witness stand and strangle Steve Sloan to death.

Instead, she calmly led Steve through the facts of the case against Lacey McClure in chronological order, from his initial interview with the movie star and on through the key deductions that led to her arrest for murder.

Along the way, Karen introduced the major items of evidence: the results of Lacey's gunshot-residue test, the magazine interviews referring to her cancer surgery, the love scene from *Sting of the Scorpion,* private detective Nick Stryker's illicit video of Lacey's rendezvous with Titus Carville, the CD recording of gunshots recovered from Cleve Kershaw's beach house, and the infamous home video of Lacey and Cleve making love.

Karen stuck to the script she and Steve had agreed on days before the preliminary hearing began. She didn't change her strategy or her questions to counter points Arthur Tyrell raised in his aggressive cross-examinations. The last thing she wanted to do was add credence to Tyrell's implications of official misconduct by acknowledging them.

Steve concluded his testimony for the prosecution by summarizing the case: that Lacey staged the rendezvous at the Slumberland Motel to establish a false alibi for herself while she murdered Cleve Kershaw and Amy Butler, who'd already been rendered helpless by the rohypnol she'd injected into their champagne bottle. Lacey intended for the murder to be blamed on organized crime and for the revelations to give a massive publicity boost to her new movie, which revolved around a Mob theme.

Karen didn't want to give up her witness, to sit down and let Tyrell begin his attack, but there was no point in trying to delay the inevitable. She returned to her seat behind the prosecution table and braced herself for the bloodbath to come.

Steve did much the same thing, taking a sip of water and wishing it was something stronger. Although he knew exactly what Tyrell hoped to prove, and how the attorney would do it, it didn't lessen Steve's anxiety. For Steve, it was like visiting the dentist to have a few cavities filled.

So he focused his attention on Lacey McClure, reminding himself why he was here and what she had done, drawing strength from the certainty of her crimes and the necessity for justice. Something in the intensity of his gaze unsettled Lacey, who looked away, almost guiltily.

Tyrell saw this and walked to the front of the table, intentionally blocking Steve's view of his client. "Lt. Sloan, when the report of the shooting came in, were you the detective in line to respond to the next case that came in?"

"No, Lt. Sam Rykus was."

"So how was it that you were the one who responded to the call?" Tyrell asked.

"I asked Rykus if I could take it," Steve said.

"Because it involved a powerful producer who was the husband of an internationally famous movie star?"

"Because the shooting occurred a few doors down from my house," Steve said. "And I heard that it was my father who called it in."

"Since your father was involved, shouldn't you have recused yourself from the investigation?"

"I didn't think so," Steve said. "I still don't."

Tyrell looked perplexed. "Wasn't it an obvious conflict of interest?"

"My father didn't commit the murder," Steve said. "He only reported that he heard gunshots. Besides, my father and I have frequently worked together investigating homicides before."

"Is your father a police officer or a licensed private investigator?" Tyrell asked.

"He's a police consultant."

"Really?" Tyrell said. "Does he receive a salary?"

"No," Steve said.

"Does he consult with any other detectives besides you?"

"He was recently appointed to the chief's Blue Ribbon Task Force on Unsolved Homicides," Steve said, dodging the question. "I think that says something about the respect the law enforcement community has for him."

"Wasn't another member of that same task force unmasked as a serial killer?"

"By my father," Steve replied.

"Makes you wonder what the qualifications were to be appointed to the task force, doesn't it?"

"Objection," Karen said, standing up. "That's not a question, it's an opinion. And I fail to see the relevance that a disbanded task force has to this case."

"Neither do I," Judge Rojas said. "Your objection is sustained. Move on, Mr. Tyrell."

But Tyrell had delivered his blow with deadly precision. He'd been ready for Steve's defensive reply to his question and had a rehearsed line ready to counter it. With one clever retort, Tyrell managed to wound not only Steve's credibility, but Mark's as well.

Mark watched Steve's testimony unfold with increasing discomfort and fury. He wanted to protect his son, to stand up and challenge Tyrell to come after him instead. But he knew it wouldn't change anything. Tyrell would be coming after him anyway—right after he thoroughly shredded Steve's credibility.

All Mark could do was sit there, watching his son take the beating. But he didn't blame Tyrell for what was happening. The attorney was just doing his job, and doing it to the best of his abilities, as he would for any defendant.

Mark blamed himself.

"Lt. Sloan," Tyrell continued. "When you arrived at the scene, your father was in handcuffs, under arrest, but you let him go. Why?"

"Because I determined that his actions were misinterpreted by the officers and that he'd made an important contribution to the investigation."

"By altering the condition of the bodies before the police, crime scene investigators, or the medical examiner arrived," Tyrell said.

"I wouldn't put it that way," Steve said.

"Would you encourage other citizens to cut up homicide victims before authorities arrived?"

"No," Steve said.

"Would you encourage them to disturb the crime scene in any manner?"

"No."

"So it's against the law for everybody else but okay for Mark Sloan because he's your father?"

"I didn't say that," Steve said.

"You didn't?"

"Objection!" Karen Cross said.

"Sustained," the judge said, almost before the word was out of her mouth. "Move on, Counselor. You've made your point."

Indeed he had, Mark thought. The judge may have sustained the prosecutor's objection, but in doing so, he conceded that Tyrell had gotten through to him. This couldn't bode well for their case. Then again, nothing was boding well today.

"In previous testimony, Officer Blake, Dr. Bentley, and even you concede that the investigation began with Dr. Sloan's four thirty p.m. phone call reporting the shootings. There were no other calls, were there?"

"No," Steve said.

"So you only have Dr. Sloan's word that shots were fired at four thirty p.m., correct?"

"Yes."

"But if you exclude his report of the shootings, it calls into doubt the time of death and renders irrelevant his conclusions about the body temperature of the victims and the clotting of their blood, correct?"

"Yes," Steve reluctantly replied.

"Is it customary for you to be accompanied by a civilian when you conduct your investigation?"

"No."

"And yet you brought your father with you when you questioned Ms. McClure, Mr. Carville, and Elsie Feikema, Amy Butler's roommate, isn't that true?"

"Yes."

Tyrell gave Steve a quizzical look. "Why did you bring him with you?"

"Given the contributions he'd already made to the investigation, I thought he could provide insight that might help me solve the case," Steve said.

"By 'contribution,' you mean the tampering of evidence at the crime scene?"

"I mean discovering there was something that didn't fit about these murders," Steve said.

"You're a homicide detective with the LAPD, aren't you?"

"Yes."

"And you're paid to investigate and solve murders?"

"Yes."

"Are you incapable of doing the job on your own?"

"No."

"So why does your father help you?"

"This was a unique situation," Steve said.

"Didn't you just testify that your father has assisted you on numerous homicide investigations?" Tyrell countered.

"They were also unique cases," Steve said.

"Considering the number of cases your father has helped you with, a unique case would actually be one you solved on your own, wouldn't it?" Tyrell said.

"Objection." Karen nearly jumped out of her seat. "The counselor is badgering the witness."

"Sustained," the judge said. "If you have questions relevant to this case, I suggest you begin asking them."

"Of course, Your Honor." Tyrell said. "Lt. Sloan, while

you were questioning Ms. Feikema at her residence, what was your father doing?"

Steve shifted in his seat. He knew what Tyrell was getting at and how it was going to look, but there was no way to avoid it without lying. And even if he did, Steve knew Tyrell wouldn't raise the issue if he didn't already know the answer and have a deposition from Elsie to back it up.

"He was wandering around the apartment," Steve said.

"Out of your sight and Ms. Feikema's," Tyrell said.

"Yes."

"Was he gathering evidence?"

"No," Steve replied.

"Didn't he, in fact, take some magazines from the victim's night stand?"

"That wasn't evidence," Steve said.

"Then why did he take them?" Tyrell asked. "What was he doing taking anything?"

"The magazines had articles about Lacey McClure," Steve said. "He asked Ms. Feikema's permission to borrow them."

"And that makes it all right?"

Karen Cross objected, and Tyrell quickly withdrew the question. But once again, it was too late. He'd already succeeded in creating doubt by implying that evidence might have been planted, tainted, or destroyed by Mark Sloan. But Tyrell wasn't going to let it go at that—not without hammering it home even harder.

"The truth is, Lt. Sloan, you have no idea what Dr. Sloan was doing in Amy Butler's room, do you?"

"Just what he told me," Steve said.

"Just what he told you," Tyrell repeated, his words laced with disdain. "When you questioned Titus Carville, Ms. McClure's assistant, was Dr. Sloan allowed to wander through his home as well?"

"Yes."

"Was he alone in Titus Carville's office?"

"Yes."

"Do you know what he was doing in there?"

"He was looking around," Steve said.

"And you know this because that's what your father told you?"

"Yes."

"Was he in there long enough to burn a CD?"

"Objection," Karen said, unable to hide the desperation from her voice this time. Tyrell's accusation was striking at the very heart of their case and couldn't be allowed to stand unchallenged. "Lt. Sloan isn't an expert in computer technology. He doesn't know how long it takes to burn a CD. Mr. Tyrell might as well ask him if Dr. Sloan was in there long enough to bake a cake, build a rocket, or write a poem. It's irrelevant."

"Overruled," Judge Rojas said. "The witness will answer the question."

"He might have been," Steve said. "But that doesn't mean he did."

"It doesn't mean he didn't, does it?"

"No."

"In fact, your father later claimed to find a CD of recorded gunshots in Cleve Kershaw's stereo system, didn't he?"

"Yes."

"A disc you later traced back to the CD burner in Titus Carville's home computer?"

"Yes."

"The same disc introduced today as evidence to support the People's claim that my client fabricated an alibi for the time of the murder?"

"Yes."

"How was this disc recovered, Lt. Sloan?"

"My father found it in Cleve Kershaw's home," Steve said.

"When?"

"Several days after the murder," Steve said.

"And you know this because Dr. Sloan told you?"

"Yes."

"Like he told you he didn't do anything in Titus Carville's office?"

"Yes," Steve said weakly, feeling as if he'd taken a punch in the stomach.

Tyrell started back towards the defense table, as if he might actually be ready to let Steve go, when he stopped, let his gaze sweep over the gallery until it settled on Mark Sloan.

"One more thing, Lieutenant," Titus said, turning back to Steve. "How did your father find the disc?"

"He returned to the crime scene," Steve said, trying, and failing, not to sound as defeated as he felt.

"Alone?"

"Yes."

"So you don't actually know if the CD was ever in Kershaw's house, do you?"

"No."

"And without the CD, what evidence do you have that the murder didn't occur at four thirty, the time your father called 911 to report the gunshots?"

"The clotted blood and the body temperature of the victims," Steve said.

"Details which also came from your father?"

"Yes."

Tyrell studied Steve for a long moment. "Isn't it possible your father fabricated all the evidence he provided?"

"No," Steve said.

"No, it's not possible, or no, you don't want to admit that it's possible?"

"My father wouldn't do that," Steve said, his face flushing with anger.

"Not even if it gave you the chance to solve a high-profile murder case that would get you international attention?"

"I don't benefit in any way from this," Steve said with contempt.

"You don't call the offer of a million-dollar book contract a benefit?"

Steve stared at Tyrell, his jaw quivering with rage. The offer last night was a setup—a quick and dirty way to create evidence to support their otherwise empty accusation that Mark had a motive to fabricate evidence. Without the check, it was just a vague theory. There was nothing vague about a million dollars.

"I turned it down," Steve said.

"Were you ever offered a million dollars before you charged Lacey McClure with murder?"

"No."

"Thank you, Lt. Sloan," Tyrell smiled. "No further questions."

No more were necessary. From Mark's vantage point, he could see Lacey McClure give Moira Cole's hand a reassuring squeeze under the table. They had a lot to be happy about.

# CHAPTER TWENTY-SEVEN

The last person on Karen Cross' list of witnesses was Dr. Mark Sloan. But after Tyrell's cross-examination of Steve Sloan, she couldn't see what possible good could come from putting his father on the stand. It would be inviting a massacre. So she took the only option she felt was left.

She stood up and addressed the court. "The prosecution rests, Your Honor."

Mark was frustrated at being denied the opportunity to defend himself and his son but, at the same time, he understood Karen's reasoning. As much as he wanted his chance to refute each and every one of Tyrell's charges, the risks the prosecution faced in cross-examination were simply too great.

"Do the People have a closing statement?" the judge asked.

"Yes, Your Honor," Karen said, fully realizing this was her last chance to salvage her case. "Lacey McClure conspired with Moira Cole, her body double, in the premeditated murder of Cleve Kershaw and Amy Butler. We have established not one but three motives for Lacey McClure to have committed these murders. We have the surveillance video shot by private detective Nick Stryker of her staged rendezvous with Titus Carville. We have the footage from her movies and her statements in magazine interviews, which prove conclusively that it is not her, but Moira Cole, in the surveillance video, thus nullifying Ms. McClure's alibi. We have the gunshot residue on her hands, recovered immediately after the murders. Lacey McClure is a calculating killer who murdered two people while they slept, and Moira Cole helped her do it. The People have proven there is sufficient cause to believe these defendants are guilty of the crimes for which they have been charged."

Karen sat down. The judge turned to Tyrell.

"Does the defense have any affirmative defenses?" the judge said, referring to pleas the defense might offer, such as insanity.

"No, Your Honor. I move for the immediate dismissal of all the charges against my clients," Tyrell said. "The integrity of the physical evidence presented by the People to support their charges is hopelessly tainted by the involvement of a civilian at every stage of the investigation. What evidence remains is circumstantial at best, and open to broad interpretation. By any legal measure, the People have not met the burden of proof necessary to create a reasonable basis for their charges. Therefore, I ask the court to dismiss the charges against my clients on the grounds of insufficient evidence."

Judge Rojas made a notation on some documents in front of him. "The defendants will rise."

Lacey McClure and Moira Cole stood up alongside their attorney.

"It appears to me from the evidence presented that there is insufficient cause to support the charges against Lacey McClure and Moira Cole," the judge said, leveling a cold gaze at Karen Cross. "The defense motion is granted. All charges are hereby dismissed. Ms. McClure, Ms. Cole, you are both free to go."

The slam of his gavel ricocheted through the courtroom like a gunshot. Lacey and Moira hugged each other. Tyrell beamed, looking directly into the camera and into a future that undoubtedly included a lavish home theater, a book deal, a guest shot on Letterman, and probably a television movie.

Mark, Steve, and Karen were looking at no future at all, at least not in their present professions. Lacey glanced over her shoulder and gave Mark a smile that said she knew all that and more. She'd beaten Mark at a game in which he was a master, and she was reveling in it.

"I don't believe it," Steve said to his father. "She's getting away with a double homicide."

"I won't let that happen," Mark said.

"It just has."

"This is only a preliminary hearing," Mark said. "Double jeopardy doesn't apply. She can be tried again."

"Not with any of this evidence," Steve said. "None of the evidence we've presented here will ever be accepted by a judge or jury. It's contaminated with reasonable doubt now."

"Then I'll find something else."

"There *is* nothing else. We've been beaten," Steve said. "And we're in for a lot more beatings before this is behind us."

"As long as she is free and unpunished for her crimes," Mark said, "this will never be behind us."

BBQ Bob's was closed for business that night. It was the only place the media wasn't staking out yet. Mark and Steve sat at the counter in the empty restaurant, with Jesse and Susan, watching the early-evening news on the wall-mounted television.

Chief Masters and District Attorney Burnside held a press conference, jointly condemning the actions of Lt. Steve Sloan, a "rogue officer" who violated department policy in his investigation of the murders of Cleve Kershaw and Amy Butler. They criticized him for allowing his father, a civilian, to handle evidence and participate in the questioning of suspects. Lt. Sloan's conduct, they said, "imperiled" justice and did not reflect "the high investigative standards" of the LAPD.

The chief apologized to Lacey McClure and Moira Cole, and promised the public, and the families of the victims, that justice would be done. He revealed that the department was already vigorously pursuing "compelling evidence" that "key figures in organized crime" were actually responsible for the killings.

Jesse aimed his remote at the TV and muted the sound. "What does this mean for you, Steve?"

Steve shrugged. "Suspension, an internal-affairs investigation, and then my firing, assuming I don't quit first."

"Will you?" Susan asked.

"I didn't do anything wrong," Steve said.

"They are going to push you out anyway," Jesse said. "Why put yourself through the ordeal of a drawn-out investigation when you know how it's going to end? If you quit, you save yourself a lot of misery and the media will stop dogging you."

"You're right, but I can't help feeling that by quitting, I'm tacitly admitting guilt." Steve glanced at his father. "For both of us."

"I am guilty, Steve," Mark said. "Not of planting evidence, but of sloppiness. We've never been involved in such a high-profile case. I should have paid a lot more attention to how my actions could be twisted and used against us in court. If I'd been more careful, Lacey McClure and Moira Cole would still be in jail."

"You weren't alone, Dad," Steve said. "I made the same mistakes, too. I was the homicide detective on the case. I'm solely responsible for blowing it."

"Give yourselves a break," Susan said. "You aren't psychics—you had no way of knowing exactly how this would play out. You did the best job you could, the only way you knew how."

"And let a killer walk free," Mark said.

"Think of all the other killers you've put away," Susan said. "I know it's a cliché, but you can't win them all. And until today, you've been on a thirty-year winning streak."

"But no one is going to remember that now," Steve said.

"The families of all the murder victims you found justice for will remember," Susan said. "And so will all the murderers spending their lives in prison because you two caught them when no one else could."

"You could write a book," Jesse said. "I'm sure the million-dollar offer is still on the table. It might even be higher now."

"What good would that do?" Steve asked.

"It would make you rich, for one thing, and give you some financial security," Jesse said. "And it would get your side of the story out."

"But Lacey McClure will still be free," Mark said.

Amanda knocked at the front window. Steve got up, unlocked the door, and let her in. She lumbered up to the counter and sat wearily on the stool beside Mark.

"The press is all over the hospital," she said. "They're parked outside my house, too."

"You went back to the hospital?" Mark asked.

She nodded. "Right after I testified. I had work to do. When I got there, I found the lab sealed. Dent told me the county was firing me. And so was he."

"Dent fired you?" Jesse said. "He can't do that."

"But the board can, citing my unprofessional and unethical conduct," she replied, handing Mark an envelope. "They've fired you, too. Forgive me for peeking."

Mark set the envelope aside without opening it. "You're forgiven."

"Dent must be celebrating tonight," Susan said.

"Looks like you're the only one who's still got a job," Amanda said to Jesse. "You may have to start supporting us."

"Dent will find a way to force me out, too. It's only a matter of time." Jesse glanced at the clock on the wall. "Speaking of time, I've got to get going."

"Early shift in the ER?" Mark asked.

"Late flight at LAX," Jesse said, untying his apron. "I'm taking the red-eye to a friend's wedding. I'll be back in a day or so, unless you'd like me to stay."

"Isn't that a question you should be asking Noah Dent or Steve?" Mark said. "You don't work for me. As far as I'm concerned, you can go anywhere you like whenever you like."

"I was thinking you might need me to do some snooping for you on Lacey McClure or Moira Cole."

"I appreciate that, Jesse," Mark said, genuinely touched by the young doctor's offer. "But there's far too much attention focused on her, and on us, for me to resume my investigation. The last thing I want is for you to get caught up in this scandal, too. Enough of the people close to me have been hurt as it is. So go, have a good time. Try not to think about all this."

"Then I guess I might try to get in a little fishing while I'm there," Jesse said and shared a look with Susan, who knew exactly what he was referring to. What she didn't understand was why he wasn't telling Mark the true reason for his trip. She would have asked him, but Jesse gave her a quick kiss and hurried out the door without pausing to give her the chance.

Amanda stared at Mark. "You can't be serious about going after Lacey McClure again."

"She can't be allowed to go unpunished for her crimes, Amanda."

"But you can't be the one to go after her," she said. "No one even remotely connected to the case will talk to you and the press will crucify you the instant they learn you're asking questions again."

"She's right, Dad," Steve said.

"If I don't pursue it," Mark said. "Who will?"

"The press is all over Lacey McClure now; a few of the reporters are bound to be digging," Steve said. "Maybe one of them will turn up some new evidence someday."

"And maybe not," Mark said.

"It's not your responsibility," Steve said. "It never was."

"I don't have a choice," Mark said. "I can't let it go. You know it's just going to keep eating at me until I set things right."

"Making this your cause could ruin you," Amanda said. "You could lose everything."

"Not as much as Cleve Kershaw and Amy Butler lost," Mark said.

Amanda knew there was no point in arguing with Mark about it. His mind was made up, and his course of action was set in stone, the moment he discovered the bodies.

There would be no stopping Mark now until Lacey McClure was in prison, even if it was a goal he couldn't possibly achieve.

Out of the corner of her eye, she saw a picture of herself on TV. She snatched the remote and turned up the volume on the television, just in time to hear Arthur Tyrell refer to her as "one of Dr. Sloan's ethically corrupt myrmidons."

She flicked off the TV in disgust and turned to Mark.

"There are five hundred channels on TV," she said, "And there's still nothing good on."

# CHAPTER TWENTY-EIGHT

Toronto was a city Jesse had seen a hundred times, only never as Toronto. He'd seen it posing as Chicago, New York, Atlanta, Indianapolis, Washington, D.C., and Seattle in scores of TV shows and movies.

As long as cameras avoided capturing the CN Tower— the city's requisite Space Needle-inspired landmark—or the maple-leaf flags and banners in nearly every merchant's window, the place was virtually indistinguishable from any major American city.

What made Toronto so attractive to filmmakers wasn't its malleable sameness. It was the weakness of the Canadian dollar and tax benefits offered by the government to lure movies and TV shows over the border.

None of that meant anything to Jesse, of course, except that it explained the eerie feeling of familiarity he felt in the city, even though he'd never been there before. He was in a foreign country that didn't seem foreign at all.

The subliminal conditioning of cheap television shows and movies was far from the only reason Toronto felt familiar. As he made his way through the airport, rented his Camry, and drove into the city, he couldn't help but notice all the American cars. All the American stores. All the American restaurants. All the American-looking Canadians. And all the American news. The Lacey McClure case was as big a media event in Toronto as it was in LA.

Jesse headed east along the Gardener Expressway, a shoreline freeway that skirted the city center and took him to a residential neighborhood known as The Beaches. He found a parking spot on Queen Street, a strip of quirky store-front shops and cafes almost entirely free of franchises and chain stores, then walked down to the beachfront to find the house the Dents lived in.

Because Jesse had been living in California for the last few years, and was an avid viewer of *Baywatch,* the name of the neighborhood immediately conjured comforting images in his mind of long stretches of golden sand, crashing surf, and bronzed women in bikinis sunning themselves.

But Jesse was thousands of miles northeast, where there was more than one season, where the skies were gray and the temperature was chilly. The only resemblance The Beaches in Toronto had to those in California were the big signs erected in the sand warning people to stay out of the toxic water. There was neither ocean nor waves, just the frigid, calm, and apparently filthy waters of Lake Ontario. The sand had the consistency and the crunch underfoot of fine gravel. A wooden boardwalk ran the length of the broad beach, drawing a line of separation between the sand and the green, tree-lined park that ran parallel to it.

Behind the park was a neighborhood of virtually identical, two-story duplexes, with big front porches under enormous decks. According to the guidebook Jesse bought at the airport, this was supposed to be a very desirable, and quite expensive, area to live in. And yet most of the homes, much to Jesse's surprise, had backyard barbecues strapped securely to the wooden railings of their decks, the propane tank and rubber wheels dangling over the front steps like mistletoe.

They were called *backyard* barbecues for a reason. Jesse couldn't understand why anyone would want to mount one on the front of their home. The barbecues were hardly stylish or pleasant to look at. He wondered if maybe the size and brand of one's barbeque was a status symbol in Canada, the way the make and model of a car parked in someone's drive-way was in LA.

Jesse was still pondering the mystery of the hanging barbecues when a black squirrel darted across his path, startling him. It's not that he was afraid of squirrels, he'd just never seen a black one before. He knew that Mark had, but those poor creatures had been ablaze at the time, running out of the flames of the Malibu fire. Or were those bunnies? Jesse couldn't remember. Either way, it was a chilling image.

This squirrel wasn't on fire, and at first Jesse wasn't even sure if it was real. He thought maybe it was his imagination, which wasn't such a stretch. Jesse hadn't slept on the plane and it had left him feeling blurred. He was certain that if he saw his reflection, it would appear as an almost-double image, with his spirit-likeness floating just outside the boundaries of his physical body.

The blurred feeling didn't come simply from sleep deprivation and one too many glasses of cheap white wine during the five-hour flight. It was the unexpected and shockingly sudden destruction of Dr. Mark Sloan, a man he held in higher esteem than anybody else in his life.

No murderer, no lawyer, no *hospital administrator*, had ever outsmarted Mark before. Jesse never considered the possibility that such a thing could ever happen, and now that it had, his whole life felt unhinged. This was a big reason why he was in Toronto, desperate to restore order to his world by, at the very least, getting Mark his job back.

Noah Dent came from this street, where black squirrels roamed under the shadow of perilously perched barbecues. Jesse was convinced that the answer to Dent's hatred of Mark Sloan was here somewhere. He wasn't going back to Los Angeles without it.

Jesse found the house he was looking for, dashed under the barbeque, and rang the front doorbell. It was answered almost immediately by a jovial, potbellied man in a checked flannel shirt and corduroy pants.

"May I help you?" the man asked.

"Yes, I'm looking for Grayson Dent," Jesse said.

"That's me!" Grayson replied energetically. "Are you with the Prize Patrol?"

"The Prize Patrol?"

"From Publishers Clearing House," Grayson said, his eyes sparkling with good-natured mischief. "Have I won a million dollars?"

"No, I'm Dr. Jesse Travis and I work with your son Noah

at Community General Hospital in Los Angeles," he said. "And I'm the chairperson of his tribute."

"His tribute ?"

"And the gala ball," Jesse added. "It's a surprise. I'm here to get background for my speech and the video we're going to show."

"Come in, come in, I want to hear all about it." Grayson stepped aside and ushered Jesse into the house.

The home was, unlike Noah, very warm and inviting. All the couches and chairs were overstuffed, upholstered in dark fabrics, and adorned with hand-knitted afghans and fluffy pillows. Every inch of available wall space was covered with framed photographs of the Dents with their family and friends.

*How could someone as heartless as Noah Dent come from a home like this?*

"You didn't come all the way here from Los Angeles just to talk to me, did you?" Grayson said. "You could have called me on the phone."

"It's not the same as meeting the people who shaped his character," Jesse replied. "Noah has only been at Community General a short time, but already he's made a huge impression on all of us. We want this event to show him how we truly feel."

Grayson whistled, impressed. "Like father, like son. Noah's always been a people-person."

"He certainly is," Jesse said. "I can honestly say he's touched a lot of lives. We want to salute him and all his achievements. But we also want to get to know him, to reveal the man behind the consummate administrator."

"I'm so happy to hear that he's established himself in his field. I tried to steer him into being my successor in the family business—to carry on the proud Dent tradition," Grayson said. "I won't lie to you, it was a big disappointment to me when his life took a different path."

"What's the family business?" Jesse asked.

"If you lived in Canada, you wouldn't have to ask that question. You can't take a whiz without doing it on a Dent," Grayson said with a laugh, more at Jesse's bewilderment than at his joke. "Dent Fixtures and Flushometers. We make urinals, toilets, and flushers."

Grayson picked up a thick catalog from the coffee table, and handed it to Jesse, who flipped through it. The catalog was filled with glossy pictures of urinals and toilets with names like the Continental, the Fifth Avenue, the Renaissance and the Evergreen—as well as a variety of stainless steel piston flushometers.

"We patented our first Dent Piston Flushometer in 1928," Grayson said, "and we've been innovators in the field ever since, eventually expanding into restroom fixtures in 1957. Virtually every public and commercial toilet in Canada is a Dent."

"Why didn't Noah go into the family business?" Jesse asked, straying over to the nearest wall and letting his eyes wander over the countless pictures.

Grayson shrugged. "I wish I knew. He seemed destined for it until college, when suddenly he just changed his mind. All he was interested in was hospital administration."

In the pictures, Noah looked like any other kid. Exuberant, happy, friendly, with the same jovial air as his father. Jesse had a hard time reconciling the pictures with the Noah Dent he knew.

"Did he ever say why?"

"Not in so many words," Grayson said. "But he obviously had a passion for it that he didn't have for the toilet trade. And if you're going to succeed in this business and deliver a superior product, you need to be passionate about it."

"Did he ever mention Community General Hospital?" Jesse asked.

"Nope," Grayson said, then pointed to a picture of Noah and an attractive older woman. "That's Noah when he was a teenager, and that's his mother, Beatrice. She left me when Noah was in college for one of those artsy-fartsy urinal designers. You know the type."

"Oh yeah," Jesse said. "They're irresistible to women."

"Twenty-five years of marriage flushed down the drain," Grayson said with a chuckle. "Pun intended."

"Did Noah ever mention Dr. Mark Sloan to you?" Jesse

asked, glancing at a photo of Noah Dent in a rowboat, catching a gigantic trout.

"Not that I can recall," Grayson asked. "Why do you ask?"

"They've just come to mean a lot to one another," Jesse said. "Frankly, I'm just trying to figure out why Community General is so special to him."

"It's all about passion," Grayson said. "I have it for toilets and, lucky for you, Noah has it for hospitals."

Noah certainly treated the hospital like his toilet, Jesse thought. His gaze fell on a photo of a teenage Noah and his date that had apparently been taken in the living room before his high school prom. Noah wore an ill-fitting tuxedo and a proud smile on his face, his arm around his girlfriend, an unbearably cute teenager with radiant eyes.

"They look great together," Jesse said, understanding now why Noah wasn't the jovial, happy man his father was, and why he never would be. The hatred Jesse felt for Noah Dent abruptly evaporated, replaced by a profound sadness.

"They were high school sweethearts, madly in love. They went off to separate colleges and I suppose they drifted apart," Grayson said. "She was a cute girl. I wonder what ever happened to her."

Jesse could have told him.

Her radiant smile was gone. Her life was destroyed. And Dr. Mark Sloan was to blame.

The night after the preliminary hearing, Mark was unable to sleep. After leaving BBQ Bob's and braving his way through the throng of reporters outside his house, he planted himself in his recliner in front of the TV, where he remained all night, unable to tear himself away from the continuous coverage of his downfall.

There was some other news related to the case that Mark learned watching TV. Elsie Feikema had accepted an invitation to be one of the housemates in the next edition of *Big Brother*. The box-office take on Lacey's movie *Thrill Kill* had already reached $50 million and was projected to crack the $100 million mark domestically, fueled by the intense media coverage of her arrest and release. There were rumors that a bootleg copy of Nick Stryker's surveillance tape would be hitting the Internet as a "pay-per-stream" event that industry observers speculated could generate more revenue than Lacey's illicit sex tape did a few years earlier. And the WB was actively developing both a sitcom and a reality show centered on the Slumberland Motel.

Mark nodded off shortly before dawn, when Steve came up from downstairs, switched off the TV, and draped a blanket over his father before going out for a run.

The media vultures weren't dedicated enough to be up at that hour, so Steve had the beach to himself as he jogged through the morning fog. Steve wasn't quite sure what to do to occupy himself in the days ahead. His life was in limbo until he either quit the force or the LAPD decided to fire him.

But he wasn't ready to think about that now. He wasn't ready to think about anything.

When Mark awoke at around noon, Steve was long gone, hiding out from the world, and from his own thoughts, in the kitchen at BBQ Bob's. There was plenty Steve could do to busy himself there, especially with Jesse away.

Mark didn't have such a convenient distraction from his troubles. He was a virtual prisoner in his own home. If he left the house, he would be dogged by the press, eager for fresh footage to chronicle the destruction of his reputation.

So what was there to do? He couldn't engage in his two favorite pursuits—the practice of medicine and the investigation of homicides—and might never be allowed to again.

Perhaps it was time, he thought, to bring out the easel and try his hand at painting once more. The notion brought his thoughts back to the murders of Cleve Kershaw and Amy Butler—not that his mind had drifted far from the subject for more than a few seconds anyway.

The fact was, Mark Sloan was happiest when his mind was occupied with a challenging problem to solve. And there was no problem greater than the one at the source of all his troubles: proving Lacey McClure guilty of murder.

For the rest of the day, Mark reviewed the case and the material he had at hand. He looked over the crime scene photos, read the FBI transcript of their wiretap of Cleve's meeting with Daddy Crofoot, scanned Lacey's magazine interviews, fast-forwarded through her movies, rewatched Lacey and Cleve's infamous sex tape and scrutinized Nick Stryker's Slumberland Motel surveillance film.

Then Mark sat in his recliner and thought about the facts of the case, rejecting all the evidence they'd presented in court to see if there was anything left to work with as starting point for a new investigation.

There was only one thing.

It wasn't evidence, really, but a question raised and never answered.

On the FBI wiretap of Daddy Crofoot's limo, Cleve Kershaw claimed he had some leverage against his wife he'd use to force her to continue laundering Mob money through her movies.

The question it begged was simple, and now in light of everything else, tantalizingly compelling: *What did Cleve Kershaw have on his wife?*

Once he asked himself that, Mark reconsidered everything he'd seen and heard since those four gunshots dragged him into the case. And in doing so, he realized to his dismay that he'd seen the key piece of evidence the moment he discovered the bodies, but it was so glaringly obvious that it was rendered invisible.

To pursue the lead he'd have to leave the house, but he didn't think he'd be able to elude the reporters outside, who were sure to follow him.

Then again, he thought with a smile, that might not be such a bad thing after all.

# CHAPTER TWENTY-NINE

After the preliminary hearing, Lacey McClure spent her night at home in much the same way as Mark Sloan did, glued to the television.

Lacey was delighted to find herself on every channel she switched to. It was like watching a marathon of her movies, only this time it was all new to her and much more exciting. She was once again cast as a woman wronged who, through sheer courage and extraordinary physical prowess, conquered her evil adversaries. There were surprising plot twists, some steamy sex scenes, even some action. And when it was all over, she emerged as the undisputed heroine.

Her beauty, her innocence, and her inner strength came through in every scene. Best of all, she didn't have to learn any lines, listen to any directors, or deliver a single spinning kick.

Her enjoyment of the coverage was interrupted many times by congratulatory phone calls from agents, managers, studio execs, directors, actors, and publishers, all eager to profit in some way from her staggeringly positive worldwide publicity. So far, the only offer she'd agreed to was a three-hour CBS "docu-drama" based on her ordeal, which she'd star in and executive produce as soon as she finished making her current movie.

Filming on her movie, which had been shut down after her arrest, would resume in a few days, but with a new, A-list director and an infusion of money from the studio to amp up the action and accelerate the postproduction. Both she and the studio were anxious to finish the movie and get it into theaters as soon as possible, to capitalize on her newfound global popularity before it waned.

Not that she'd let the attention dim without a fight. The instant Lacey sensed that interest in her was flagging, she'd invite Barbara Walters over for a televised chat, and start sobbing over the tragedy. After all, her marriage had fallen apart, then her husband got killed, and then she was arrested for a crime she didn't commit. It was powerful stuff, sure to rocket Barbara to the top of the ratings, and spark countless follow-up articles, commentaries, and more TV interviews. When those started to dry up, she'd sneak out very publicly to visit her husband's grave and tearfully place flowers on his tombstone, making sure plenty of paparazzi saw her do it. And just when people finished dabbing the tears from their eyes over those heart-wrenching photos, she'd selflessly establish an acting scholarship in poor, young Amy Butler's memory.

By then, her new movie would be in theaters, the "docudrama" would be airing, and the second wave of Lacey McClure publicity would sweep the world. She'd be commanding $20 million a movie in no time. Maybe she'd even start directing.

Everything had worked out far better than Lacey ever dreamed it could, despite encountering the worst luck imaginable right at the get-go.

She'd planned every detail of the murders, considered a hundred different ways it could go wrong, but never once thought to check out who her Malibu neighbors were. It never occurred to her that one of them might be a homicide detective and his father, a deductive genius who loved to solve murders.

It was a cruel joke of epic proportions at her expense.

It was Lady Luck giving her the finger and running over her dog.

And yet, Lacey didn't panic. She swallowed her fear, took a deep breath, and rose to the occasion, confronting her adversaries head-on. She engaged in a dangerous game of cat-and-mouse with Mark Sloan as if she was merely improvising a scene at an audition.

And she *rocked*.

She never wanted the fight, but now that it was over, her victory over Dr. Sloan, and his complete ruination, was the sweetest part of all. It was funny how life worked—how something that at first seemed so horrible could turn out to be something so good. She discovered through adversity that she possessed skills she never knew she had.

Lacey spent the day after the hearing working out in her home gym with Moira, sweating the jailhouse stiffness from her limbs, loosening up for the strenuous week ahead of filming, press conferences, and high-level deal-making.

She'd never felt so good, so in control.

When Lacey and Moira returned to the main house, Lacey's private line was ringing. Lacey answered the phone and heard a voice from the dead.

*"I've got leverage against her she doesn't know I have. I can bring her into line without putting her in a hospital bed."*

It was Cleve. She recognized his voice immediately and it terrified her. It was a toss-up, though, what scared her more: his voice or what he was saying.

Cleve never got around to threatening her before she killed him, so this was the first she'd heard that he had any kind of "leverage" against her. But she knew what it must be. What it *had* to be.

Moira saw the fear on Lacey's face and, without hearing a word, knew what this call had to be about. There was only one thing that could frighten Lacey, and that would be the prospect of losing what she'd fought so hard for—what she'd killed to protect.

"Who is it?" Moira whispered.

Lacey shook her head, unable to answer the question, just as another voice spoke into her ear, this one only vaguely familiar.

"I've got his leverage now," the man said. "And it will cost you $600,000 to buy it from me."

Now Lacey recognized the caller. It was Nick Stryker, the inept PI that Cleve hired, the jerk she'd manipulated so masterfully to her benefit.

"You tried this once before," Lacey said. "And look what happened. I'd have thought you would have learned something from the experience."

"I have. That's why the price is double," Stryker said. "I don't appreciate getting screwed. You cost me my PI ticket, honey."

"Boo-hoo," she said.

"This is a one-time offer," he said. "Or I sell the video to the highest bidder."

"You don't have anything I want." She started to hang up, when she heard him say something she couldn't ignore.

"Just a little girl-on-girl action," he said.

She brought the receiver back to her ear and met Moira's gaze, telegraphing her fear.

"What did you say?" Lacey asked.

"It's a lesbo porn movie I secretly shot for Cleve in Topanga Canyon not so long ago," Stryker said. "The stars are you and Moira Cole, frolicking at her place. Cleve kept the tape as kind of an insurance policy, only now it looks like I'm gonna be the beneficiary."

"Nice try, but that never happened," she said. "You'll have to do better than that."

Stryker laughed. "Okay, fine with me. You're so hot right now, I'm sure I can find plenty of people willing to buy it from me, and for a lot more than $600,000. Look for it on the Internet real soon."

He hung up before she could say another word.

She stared at the phone for a long moment, glanced at Moira, then picked up the receiver and punched in a phone number.

Stryker answered on the fourth ring, making her sweat.

"Where and when do you want to meet?" she asked.


Jesse dozed only for a few moments on the flight back from Toronto, tortured by memories, by regrets, and by the ugliness of what he had to do. It couldn't wait, not even for a night's sleep, a shower, or a fresh set of clothes. He went directly from Los Angeles International Airport to Community General Hospital to get it over with.

Noah Dent was sitting at his desk, studying a spreadsheet, when Jesse barged in unannounced and set the prom photo down in front of him, still in its original silver frame. Dent couldn't have been more startled if the picture had materialized on his desk by magic.

Once the shock passed, Dent realized the lengths Jesse must have gone to discover his secret and retrieve the picture.

"I knew Tanya," Jesse said. "I used to look forward to her paramedic unit coming in, even if it was just to catch a glance at her rushing past, wheeling a patient down the hall to one of the trauma rooms. I had a crush on her."

Noah nodded, looking up from the photograph. "She was hard not to love."

"What happened to her was a horrible tragedy," Jesse said gently.

"Then how can you stand to be near Mark Sloan after what he did to her?" Noah asked.

"She forced him to make a choice nobody should have to make," Jesse said. "In the end, he had to do what was morally right."

"That's just it: he didn't," Noah said.

"She murdered a man," Jesse said.

"He wasn't a man. He wasn't even human. He was a monster," Noah said, and he could tell from the look on Jesse's face that the doctor knew it, too.

"That doesn't change what she did," Jesse said.

"Tanya was walking alone to the dorms after studying late at the library. He was waiting in the darkness. He raped her, beat her, and left her for dead. Just like he did to half a dozen other women. And he got away with it. He was never caught."

"Yes, he was," Jesse said. "Tanya caught him, years later, when she was a paramedic, when she responded to a bus accident and recognized him as one of the injured riders. But instead of treating him, instead of pointing him out to the police, she killed him and tried to make it look like he died in the accident."

"He deserved to die for what he did to her," Dent said. "No one would mourn for him. Mark Sloan had to know that."

"Mark knew it," Jesse said.

"So what if she killed that bastard? It was justice," Noah said. "Sloan could have kept it to himself. Instead, for the pleasure of the hunt, he turned her in. Sloan didn't care about her, about the horror the monster she killed put her and all those other women through."

"Tanya murdered a man and Mark knew it," Jesse said. "He made a moral decision. He decided that he couldn't abide murder, no matter what the circumstances."

Noah gently stroked the picture frame as if it were a woman's cheek. "I've visited her in prison. Her soul is dead, trapped inside her body. It's like looking at a terminally ill patient being kept alive by machines. Is that what she deserves for killing a serial rapist? Is that morally right?"

Jesse took a deep breath, hating himself for what he was about to do, what he *had* to do.

"You're going to reinstate Mark and Amanda to their positions, apologize for firing them, and recommend that the adjunct county medical examiner's office be reopened," Jesse said. "You'll also rehire all the nurses you let go and reimburse them for lost pay."

"The hell I will," Dent said.

"If you don't, I'll go to the board and tell them how you abused your position to seek revenge," Jesse said. "Your career will be destroyed."

"My career doesn't matter," Dent said. "It was all for Tanya."

"I'll also go to the press. All the lurid details of what happened to Tanya will come out," Jesse said. "Her deepest, most intimate secrets will become public. It will all be twisted to make the best headline, the most shocking sound bite. Her family's privacy, and your own, will be invaded. Think what this will do to her chances for parole, if she has any left at all."

Dent looked at Jesse with revulsion. "You'd do that to her—rape her again in the media—after everything else she's been through?"

"I'd do that for my family," Jesse said. "Mark Sloan, Amanda Bentley and Susan Hilliard *are* my family. That's the moral choice I'm making. Now it's your turn to make one."

Jesse walked out of Dent's office without waiting for a reply and without looking back. He knew Dent had no choice, really—not if he still cared about Tanya. That certainty, and the way he used it, sent Jesse rushing to the nearest men's room. He barely made it to the toilet before he started throwing up.

# CHAPTER THIRTY

Vasquez Rocks is a boulder-strewn landscape of jagged formations that look as if they exploded out of the earth's core, mainly because they did. But this dry corner of the high desert, sparsely covered with yucca and scrub oak, wasn't named for the fault line that created its stunning outcroppings, or the Indian tribes who lived there for centuries. It was named for Tiburcio Vasquez, a violent but charming sociopath who, in the mid-1800s, liked to hide out there with his gang between bloody robberies and senseless killings.

In daylight, Vasquez Rocks looks like the surface of Mars because, for as long as there have been movies, it has been Mars. It has also been prehistoric Earth, the Vulcan home world, and the *Planet of the Apes,* among others. But at night, it becomes 800 acres of pitch-black desolation and a fine place for a wide variety of criminal pursuits including, but not limited to, ransom drops, body dumping, drug transactions and, on this occasion, a blackmail payoff.

Moira Cole drove her rented Ford Explorer down a long, bumpy dirt road, deep into the desert. Lacey sat beside her in the passenger seat, calling out the directions that Stryker had given them. The meeting place, agreed upon after some tense negotiation on the phone, satisfied the needs of both Nick Stryker and Lacey McClure. He didn't want to be lured into another police ambush and she didn't want there to be any chance of them being seen together. The location also had the benefit of being familiar to Lacey. She'd shot two of her movies out there.

The ride would have been a lot smoother in Lacey's

Hummer, but the movie star didn't want anything tying her to the place. The Explorer was rented using a stolen credit card, just like the Taurus that Moira had driven to the Slumberland Motel the day of the murders.

They topped a rise and saw Stryker's Escalade parked below them in a bowl of rock, awash in an otherworldly blue glow from the TV screens imbedded in the rear of his headrests and on his dash. As Moira drove up closer, they could see he was watching an *Everybody Loves Raymond* rerun while waiting for them to show up.

Moira parked beside the Escalade and the two of them got out, Lacey carrying a bulging gym bag. Lacey got into the front passenger seat and sat down beside Stryker. Moira went around to the driver's side and slipped into the backseat, directly behind him, just in time to catch Ray Romano on the headrest TV, getting squirted with mustard by his wife.

Stryker switched off the TV and twisted in his seat to get a look over his shoulder at Moira.

"I see you brought the missus," he said. "I don't recall sending her an invitation to this party."

"This involves both of us," Lacey said.

"It certainly does," Stryker said with a leer. "So that sex tape of you and Cleve, that was all just a scam you came up with to make a buck and fool anybody who might think you're gay, right?"

"You're sharp, Nick," Lacey smiled.

"I've been playing this game for a while, Lacey," he said.

"As uncomfortable as this situation is, I appreciate that you came to me first with what you have rather than taking it to auction on the open market," Lacey said. "So, let's be honest with each other, okay?"

"Works for me," Stryker said.

"You're gonna give me a copy of the tape of Moira and me tonight and walk away with $600,000," Lacey said. "But the fact is, this is just the beginning of our relationship. You've got the original tape hidden away, and you're going to keep coming back to me for money as long as I live."

Stryker shrugged. "Here's how I look at it, Lacey. I know I'm taking advantage of you, but no more so than the managers, publicists, agents, trainers, stylists, and everybody the hell else you have on your payroll. I want to keep this friendly and professional. I'm never going to ask you for more than a couple hundred grand a year. You spend more than that annually on lunches. Think of me as just another business expense, part of your entourage. You can even call me for security advice, free of charge."

"Are you bugging this conversation, Nick?" Lacey asked.

"Nope."

"I thought we were going to be honest with each other and already you're lying to me," Lacey said. "With all the high-tech stuff you've got in this car, you've got to be recording this."

"What good would a tape of this conversation be to me?" Stryker said. "I'd only be implicating myself as a black-mailer."

"I can't take that chance, Nick," Lacey said. "I'm going to have to set this car on fire."

That's when Moira looped a piece of rope around his neck from behind and pulled him back against the headrest, strangling him. As he struggled, Lacey casually leaned down and unzipped her bag, to reveal a gasoline canister, some rags, and a box of matches.

"I'm going to take your advice and treat you as part of the cost of doing business," Lacey said, "just like I did with Titus. I can't afford to let anybody have anything on me."

Stryker gurgled and flailed desperately in his seat, his legs kicking, his eyes bulging in terror.

"You may have the tape, but I'm willing to bet you've hid it so well, it's going to stay hidden once you're dead," Lacey said. "But we'll firebomb your office too, just in case. It will look like the work of an angry client. You must have plenty of those."

Stryker's foot connected with the dash. Suddenly the headrest monitor flashed on in front of Moira's face and she saw a high-angle, fish-eye view of the interior of the Es-calade on one half the screen and Dr. Mark Sloan on the other, sitting on the set of the KCBS "Action news."

"Let him go, Moira," Mark said, "unless you want to go to prison for murder, too."

Mark's face was directly in front of her, creating the startling illusion that they were actually confronting each other directly, that he was looking right into her eyes from the intimate proximity of a lover. The angle on Mark widened to include KCBS anchorman Chet Whittaker, who was sitting beside him.

"I'm not sure she can hear you," Chet said in his deep, sonorous voice.

"She can hear me," Mark said. "I can see it on her face."

Lacey stared in shock at the dashboard TV screen and at the two words emblazoned under Mark Sloan's face: LIVE BROADCAST.

"Think about it, Moira," Mark said. "There's no point in killing him now—not with a few million witnesses watching. It's over."

Moira let go of the rope and fell back in her seat, closing her eyes in defeat. Stryker clutched his throat and sucked air in deep, wheezing gasps.

"Wise choice, Moira," Mark said.

Now they could hear a helicopter circling overhead and distant sirens drawing near. There was nowhere to run and nowhere to hide.

Lacey looked up at the interior light on the ceiling of the Escalade and remembered that it hadn't gone on when they got in the car. Because it wasn't an interior light, she realized now, but an infrared camera, sending a signal back to some satellite truck hidden in the rocks. She looked straight into the camera, ready for her close-up.

Chet looked into his camera, too. "This is probably a good time to remind our audience that we're coming to you live from the KCBS newsroom. We're watching a live feed from hidden cameras in a vehicle parked at Vasquez Rocks, where Lacey McClure and her body double, Moira Cole, have just attempted to kill private detective Nick Stryker."

"How are you feeling, Nick?" Mark asked. "Can you talk?"

"I can sing you a show tune if you like," Stryker said, his voice hoarse.

Mark smiled. "You better rest your voice until the medics can take a look at you."

"He's a brave man," Chet said.

"He certainly is," Mark said. "Nick took a huge risk helping us, but we couldn't have revealed Lacey and Moira as the murderers they truly are without his help."

It was a surreal experience for Lacey McClure. The enormity of her exposure was so difficult for her to accept, that she sat there in mute disbelief, watching the broadcast as if she wasn't right in the center of it. But Moira Cole fully comprehended her predicament and sat quietly crying in the backseat.

"Joining us in this live report is Dr. Mark Sloan, who enlisted the assistance of Action News in revealing this murder plot," Chet said, then turned to Mark. "While we wait for authorities to arrive at the scene, please tell us what made you suspect that Lacey and Moira were lovers."

"It was something I saw in the bedroom of the beach house where Cleve and Amy were killed," Mark said. "There was ChapStick and a bottle of Glacier Peaks water on the nightstand on the right-hand side of the bed. I saw the same items on the nightstand in the bedroom of Lacey's trailer and again later in the master bedroom of Moira Cole's house. That's because Lacey McClure was sleeping in all those places. Once I realized that, I knew Moira was her lover."

"Does an illicit tape of them together actually exist?" Chet asked.

"I don't know, Chet," Mark said. "But I was counting on Lacey believing that it was a real possibility, and it worked."

"So the thing that actually brought her down—that undid all her careful planning—was her innocent habit of having bottled water and lip balm beside her bed," Chet said.

"I suppose so," Mark replied.

Chet shook his head. "Isn't human nature a funny thing?"

"I don't think Lacey McClure is finding it very funny tonight," Mark said.

"Let's ask her." Chet looked into the camera. "How are you feeling at this moment, Lacey?"

Before she could answer, the Escalade was blasted with light by the LAPD chopper circling above them and from the high beams of the dozen police cars closing in. The blinding white light, combined with the bone-rattling rumble of the chopper hovering low, made it feel as if some massive starship was landing in front of them.

The door beside Lacey was suddenly yanked open, but it wasn't some alien being standing there, silhouetted against the light. It was Steve Sloan, dangling a pair of handcuffs from his fingers.

But Lacey stared at him with the same dazed, uncomprehending look that she would have given him if he had been a naked green man with a pointy head and a ray gun in his hand.

"You're under arrest," Steve said, and read Lacey her rights. "It's time to thank the Academy and get off the stage."

Over the following week, the same reporters who had turned so quickly against the Sloans just as rapidly embraced them, celebrating them as heroes and branding Lacey McClure a killer.

The LAPD immediately cleared Steve Sloan of misconduct, with Chief Masters publicly reinstating him and praising Mark Sloan for his efforts. The chief also quietly retracted his request to have Amanda Bentley relieved of her position as a medical examiner.

Moira Cole quickly cut a deal to testify against Lacey McClure in exchange for a lighter sentence. With the testimony in hand, and the damning footage from the news, there was little doubt that the district attorney would breeze through the preliminary hearing and win a conviction at trial, using much of the same evidence that had been dismissed before.

Arthur Tyrell declined to represent the two women this time, choosing instead to take an "extended sabbatical" from the practice of criminal law to write a book about his experiences, and to become a Court TV commentator at Lacey McClure's murder trial.

Nick Stryker not only got his private investigator's license back, but cut a lucrative deal with ABC for a TV series pilot loosely based on his exploits.

The only truly surprising development in the aftermath of the arrests went unnoticed by the media, but had the most significant impact on the lives of Mark Sloan and Amanda Bentley. It was the sudden resignation of Community General administrator Noah Dent, who left behind letters revoking the layoffs of the nurses, retracting his proposal to sever the contract with the county medical examiner's office, and reinstating Mark and Amanda to their previous positions. Where Dent went, or why he left, was a mystery.

Mark was still puzzling over that as he hosted a casual celebration dinner at his beach house for Steve, Amanda, Jesse, and Susan. They were all gathered in the living room, having coffee and dessert.

"I can't understand why Dent backed down," Mark said. "The arrests didn't change anything at the hospital. He still could have pushed his agenda through."

"Perhaps he had a crisis of conscience," Jesse said.

"He didn't have a conscience," Amanda said.

"That was the crisis," Steve said.

Mark shook his head in bewilderment. "Dent seemed hell-bent on getting us out, it doesn't make sense for him to suddenly reverse course and disappear."

"There's something about the murders I don't get," Jesse said, quickly changing the subject. "Was Lacey really having an affair with Titus Carville?"

"Only long enough to establish her alibi," Steve said. "Moira Cole says she and Lacey have been lovers since high school in New Jersey. Lacey married Cleve and came out here with him just to further her career. Moira Cole came along, too, and became her stunt double, so no one questioned all the time they spent together."

"Did Lacey and Cleve really have a secret separation?" Susan asked.

"No," Mark said. "That's why the water bottle and lip

balm were on the nightstand at the beach house. She was still sleeping there, presumably with him. But once she discovered the money-laundering scheme, and that he was grooming a replacement for her, she decided to kill him."

"And take advantage of all the publicity it would generate," Steve said. "She was a lot smarter than Cleve or anyone else—us included—gave her credit for."

"Which reminds me," Mark said to Steve, "I never would have gotten involved in these homicides if it wasn't for the paint set you got me."

Mark went over to the corner of the living room, where something on the floor was covered with a white sheet. "So I have a present for you."

He whipped the sheet off to reveal his finished seascape painting—the one he'd been working on the fateful day of the shootings.

"I've signed and dated it at the bottom," Mark said, smiling with fake pride at his hideous painting. "In case it becomes a collectors' item."

Amanda studied the painting. "Why did you paint a picture of giant moths?"

"Those aren't moths," Mark said, trying his best to sound genuinely exasperated. "They're seagulls."

"Why are they flying around a Jell-O mold?" Steve asked.

"It's the ocean," Mark said. "How can you not see that?"

While Mark indulged in his mischief, Jesse and Susan slipped out onto the deck to admire the real seascape.

"Why didn't you tell Mark what you did?" Susan asked, once the door was closed, and they couldn't be heard by the others.

"Because it would have brought back all the ugliness again," Jesse said. "Mark hated himself for what he had to do to Tanya. If he knew why Dent fired him, Mark might not have accepted his job back, just to punish himself and make amends. It's better if Mark never knows."

Susan hugged herself to Jesse's arm and rested her head on his shoulder. "I love you," she said.

Jesse kissed the top of her head. "I love you, too."

They stood quietly for a long moment, enjoying the nearness of one another and the beautiful view.

"You don't think Mark was really trying to paint this, do you?" Susan asked, motioning to the surf.

"No," Jesse said. "Those were obviously white blood cells battling an infection."

"Why would Mark want to paint *that?*"

"This might come as a shock to you," Jesse said, "but Mark Sloan is a very strange man."

Turn the page for a preview of Dr. Sloan's
next adventure

## *The Waking Nightmare*

Coming soon from Signet

The woman sitting in front of Dr. Mark Sloan was determined to die and there was nothing he could do about it. He'd brought her into this world over forty years ago and, more than likely, he'd see her out of it, too.

Although Mark was Chief of Internal Medicine at Community General Hospital, he still acted as Lenore Barber's family physician. Despite all his dire warnings, she'd taken up smoking as a teenager and never gave it up. Seven years ago, she was diagnosed with lung cancer. She smoked on the morning of her lung surgery and during the five months of chemotherapy that followed.

It made Mark furious, but he understood her flawed, fatalistic thinking. She was dead already. What difference would it make if she kept smoking now if it gave her some comfort through the ordeal?

But luck was on her side. After six chemotherapy sessions, and the weeks of crushing fatigue, complete hair loss, and constant nausea that followed, all signs of the cancer were eradicated.

She'd survived.

He was certain the harrowing, near-death experience would have a profound effect on Lenore's life. The mere thought of another cigarette would surely repulse her. But if it didn't, all she had to do was look at herself naked to be dissuaded from having a smoke.

Lenore spent a small fortune on breast implants, a nose job, and elaborate orthodonture to make herself more competitively attractive to casting directors, eligible bachelors, and people she was trying to sell real estate to. The surgical scars on her body would be a constant, undeniable reminder of the fate she'd narrowly escaped. Mark believed that would be enough to guarantee that she'd never smoke again.

He was wrong.

She shrugged off the experience as if it was just a bad bout with the flu and fell right back into her old life as an aspiring actress, real estate agent, single mother, and heavy smoker. If anything, she smoked even more than she had before, as if losing a chunk of her lung and being bombarded with radiation had given her some kind of immunity from disease.

Over the ensuing years, Mark reminded her of the hell she'd been through. Did she want to endure it all over again? He urged her to try the nicotine patch, to enroll in smoking cessation classes, to do whatever it took to kick her deadly addiction to cigarettes. But she blithely ignored his admonitions.

A few months ago, she came in to see Mark for a routine follow-up exam, which revealed a tiny growth on her liver. Mark ordered a biopsy and the results confirmed his worst fears. The cancer was back, only now it had migrated to her liver. Lenore immediately began a new, aggressive regimen of chemotherapy.

Now she sat in an exam room with Mark, who reviewed the latest P.E.T scan results and blood work analysis from the hospital's Chief of Oncology.

It was good news. The growth was gone and her hematology was all normal. No more treatment was necessary, no surgery would be required.

She'd cheated death again.

"Wow," she said, scratching under the wig she wore to cover her radiation-induced baldness. "Just like that? It's gone?"

"That's right," Mark said.

"I don't believe it," she said. "I thought you were going to tell me it was time to start looking for a good surgeon."

"You were very lucky. I can't recall seeing results this positive after only three chemotherapy treatments," Mark said. "But if you keep smoking, I can guarantee you that the cancer will return."

"Can't you give me even a minute to enjoy the good news before lecturing me?"

"I know you've kept smoking throughout the chemo," Mark said.

"And the cancer is gone, isn't it?" she said with a casual shrug. "Obviously, it didn't make a difference."

Mark looked her in the eye. "You can't keep smoking, Lenore."

"I'm not smoking nearly as much as I used to," she said. "Give me a break."

"You just got your break," he said. "You're still alive."

"I didn't smoke at all yesterday and I didn't have a single cigarette the whole week I was in the Bahamas," she said, flashing a smile that showed her unnaturally bright teeth. "Maybe I should move there. Prescribe that."

"You shouldn't be smoking at all, anywhere," he said. "Think about your kids."

"I never smoke around them."

"You know what I mean," Mark said. "Who is going to raise them when you're gone?"

"Don't be so dramatic, Mark." Lenore got up from her seat and grabbed her purse. "So I had an itsy bitsy smudge on the x ray. If it comes back, we'll just zap it again. In the meantime, I'm going to celebrate. With a drink and a cigarette!"

And with that, Lenore kissed Mark on the cheek and quickly left the exam room, closing the door behind her.

Mark stared at the door for a long time, angry and frustrated. It wasn't like him to be so heavy-handed. He knew it was counter-productive. But he couldn't help himself. There were so many cancer patients who never got the second chance that Lenore had been given and she didn't seem to care.

Why couldn't she see how lucky she was?

Her self-destructive behavior infuriated him, more so because he felt a special responsibility to her. He was the one who delivered her, cut her umbilical cord, and laid her in her mother's arms. Mark couldn't help feeling that her good health had been in his hands ever since. It was the way he felt about any of the children he de-livered who, as adults, still were his patients today.

Intellectually, Mark understood Lenore's addiction. She was unable to control her need for nicotine and would sacrifice any-thing to satisfy it. But emotionally, he just couldn't accept it. After what she'd suffered, how could she light another cigarette ever again? Didn't she want to live? Didn't she want to be there for her children?

It was a deplorable and unnecessary tragedy. But unless she ac-knowledged her addiction and was willing to do something about it, he was utterly powerless to save her.

His frustration with the situation was a cancer, too. Malignant and spreading with each encounter with her. He could feel it gnaw-ing at his bones, eating him alive from inside.

Mark had felt that frustration with patients before and knew there was only one cure for his affliction: To distract himself with another insurmountable problem.

He thought of the murders he'd solved over the years as a con-sultant to the Los Angeles Police Department and wondered if one reason he did it was to compensate for all the times he couldn't help the living.

Why was it that the problems of the dead were so much easier to solve?

Mark got up and wandered down the hall to the doctor's lounge, where Dr. Jesse Travis was sitting at one of the chipped Formica tables catching up on his paperwork, a stack of bulging medical files teetering in front of him.

"You ever have one of those days you wish you weren't a doctor?" the young doctor asked, peeking around the corner of the pile at Mark, who was helping himself to a cup of coffee .

"As a matter of fact," Mark replied, "this happens to be one of them."

"Where's the excitement in paperwork?" Jesse said. "Where's the intimacy? Where's the human drama?"

"Today I wouldn't mind a little less human drama and lot more paperwork." Mark took a seat at the table beside him and stirred some sugar into his coffee cup.

"You want to talk about it?" Jesse asked, not really expecting Mark to unburden himself. After all, what knowledge or experience could the young doctor possibly have to offer his mentor, a man he tried to emulate as a doctor and even as a detective?

"Thanks," Mark said. "I could use your advice."

"You *could*?" Jesse asked in disbelief. Mark Sloan was actually turning to him for counsel. Like they were equals.

But Jesse's excitement quickly morphed into fear. What if he didn't have the answers? What if his advice was wrong? What would Mark think of him then?

Jesse didn't get the chance to find out.

Just as Mark was about to speak, he happened to take a casual glance out the window at the office building across the street. At first, Mark didn't quite register what he was seeing.

There was a woman sitting outside on the sill of her fifth floor window, as calm and relaxed as if she were on the edge of a swimming pool, gently kicking her feet in the water.

She was pretty, in her mid-twenties, wearing a loosefitting white blouse and a navy blue jacket that befitted a professional woman. She had pale skin and bright, green eyes that met his gaze as she pushed herself into the air.

Mark bolted up from his seat, spilling his coffee onto the floor.

"No!" he yelled, horrified.

Her jacket flared behind her like wings as she plummeted silently to the ground below. She smacked into a tree limb, snapping it in half, then dropped onto the awning that stretched over the street-level coffeehouse. She bounced off the awning and landed on top of an old Buick Skylark parked at the curb. The roof crumpled and the car windows exploded under the impact, spraying glass onto the street.

Mark dashed for the stairs.

Jesse glanced out the window, saw the woman's body splayed on top of the car, and ran after Mark. They scrambled down the stairs together, taking them two at a time. There was no need to speak. They both knew what they had to do.

They burst out of the stairwell into the busy Emergency Room, the doors smacking into the walls with an explosive bang that caught everyone's attention.

Mark ran out the lobby doors into the street while Jesse started gathering supplies and yelling orders to the nurses.

"I need a crash cart, cervical collar, and a stretcher, stat!" he hollered.

Mark raced across the street, weaving through the traffic that had already stalled to gape at the bloodied body and the damaged car. Several people gathered on the street around the car, staring at the woman, uncertain of what to do. He pushed through them, jumped onto the hood and leaned over the woman, who was on her back, her head lolling on the shattered windshield. Blood seeped out of her nose and mouth and dripped from under her hair. One of her legs was twisted grotesquely underneath her.

He felt for her pulse and found one. She was still alive. He lifted her eyelids and checked her pupils, which were reactive and equal, indicating that there was no bleeding in the brain. Mark took out his stethoscope and pressed it to her chest, listening. Her breathing wasn't good. Hitting the tree and the awning on her way down had broken her fall and saved her life, at least for the moment.

Jesse barged through the crowd, carrying an emergency medical kit and leading two orderlies with a stretcher and three nurses wheeling a battery-powered crash cart.

"She's alive," Mark said. "We have to get her into the ER."

He took a cervical collar from one of the nurses, and secured the woman's neck and head, while Jesse leaped up on the trunk so he was positioned at her feet. Mark and Jesse helped the orderlies ease the stretcher under the woman, and then the four men carefully lifted her off the car. The orderlies rushed her across the street to hospital, Mark and Jesse running alongside.

Mark could hear sirens wailing in the distance, getting louder as they grew near. Somebody must have called. By the time the paramedics got there, all they'd find was the damage and the blood. The woman would already be receiving treatment in the E.R.

The orderlies carried the woman into the first vacant trauma room, where Jesse's girlfriend, Nurse Susan Hilliard, was already standing by with her team, ready to assist the doctors.

Mark started shouting orders, but stopped when he couldn't

catch his breath. He let Jesse take over and went outside into the hallway, where he leaned against a wall, breathing hard, his hand on his chest. His heart was pounding. Sweat ran down his cheeks. After running as fast as he could down five flights of stairs, across the street, and back again, he was lucky he wasn't on the table in the trauma room himself.

He wasn't a young man anymore. He should have stayed behind at the hospital and let Jesse, who was more than capable, handle the woman in the street.

*What was he thinking?*

Mark wasn't thinking. He was reacting, going on pure impulse. He closed his eyes for a moment and saw the woman sitting on the window sill, staring right at him. One instant she was there, the next she was falling. . . .

"Are you okay, Mark?"

"I'll be fine," he said, his eyes flashing open to see Jesse standing in front of him, looking concerned.

Mark motioned to the trauma room with a nod of his head. "More importantly, how is she?"

"Lucky she fell outside a hospital," Jesse said.

"She didn't fall," Mark said. "She jumped. I saw her do it. She looked right at me."

"Did you know her?"

"I never saw her face until today," Mark said.

"Well, you're never going to forget it now," Jesse said. "She's comatose. She's got a fractured humerus, fibula and tibia, but no broken bones that appear to require surgery. There are no cervical or skull fractures, but her chest x ray shows three broken ribs on her left side and a small pnemothorax."

"I'll have to watch that," Mark said.

"*I'll* watch that," Jesse said. "Your shift is over and after what you've just been through, you could use the rest."

"What about her lab work?"

"Everything's normal," Jesse said. "She wasn't on drugs when she jumped. I've ordered a CT scan and then I'll send her up to the ICU. There's nothing more you can do here. Go home."

"Something made her desperate enough to want to kill herself," Mark said.

"It's too late to do anything about that now," Jesse said and went back into the trauma room.

Mark wasn't so sure. Today he'd encountered two women who faced a choice between living and dying. Both of the women looked him in the eye and chose death. Perhaps he could still save one of them.